ONLY

PORTAL

AWAY

THE CODEX OF INDRESAL 1

AKIRA VARMA

I'd say I apologize for the cliff-hanger...
But honestly, I'm not really sorry.
Can I be sorry for *not* being sorry?
Anyway, enjoy!

Content Warning

Please read the following content warning before reading the book.

This book mentions violence against people at all ages (yes, I mean ALL ages). There are mentions of death of loved ones, parents sacrificing their lives to save their kids (off the page), massacre, and genocide - both on and off the pages. Please *do* skip the parts that you are uncomfortable reading.

Your mental health is important and my priority!

Contents

Also by   319

Prologue

NAREIN KASHAERA WALKED THROUGH the rubble that was once his palace. He tsked as he gazed solemnly at all the damage surrounding him.

What were once study stone pillars were now just an obliterated pile of rubble that were strewn across the palace grounds. There wasn't an inch around him that wasn't covered with ruins or shattered jagged rocks. Sandstone walls, that once stood high and proud holding the crest of House Kashaera, began to slowly crumble. Dust from the battle settled gently on the broken marble throne. Smoke from the long extinguished fires rose up like the ghosts of the souls that fought valiantly in the battle a few hours ago.

What once stood as a mighty building of power, sending a shiver down the spine of anyone who had the ill fortune to have seen it, was now only a disintegrated crumbling mess. If only the people could see it now...

...If anyone was left alive, that was.

Because none of the fallen buildings or broken ornate statues compared to the number of bodies lying motionless in the midst of the falling castle. Blood from the fallen soldiers covered the stone pillars - or rather, what were once stone pillars - and the marble floors. For a palace that was in the middle of what was once a serene forest, the scent of the burning flesh permeated the air.

The slow breeze, swaying trees, rustling leaves, and the serene evening air that surrounded the palace betrayed the carnage that laid within it. It was only the silent forest around them that gave anyone the indication of the battle that was fought only moments before.

A silence that no animals or birds dared to disturb.

"Did you really have to make me do this?" Narein asked, almost as if he was exasperated.

He scratched his forehead, wincing at the throbbing pain pounding in his head. His dark cloak swished with every step he took, making him look as if he was gliding across the cracked marble floor.

He stepped over the bodies strewn about in the midst of the rubble - not sparing them even a glance. If anyone had seen Narein shaking his head now, they'd probably mistake his action for sympathy for the lives lost in the battle. Unfortunately though, empathy was an emotion Narein couldn't identify with at the moment.

And why would he?

He was the reason they were all dead anyway.

Narein cracked his neck and rolled his shoulders trying to soothe his sore, aching muscles. He could feel himself slowly becoming lethargic. His feet faltered with every step he took. The battle was a long and arduous one. And Narein had just shown the world how powerful he truly was. He showed them what would happen to them if anyone dared come in his way.

But unfortunately, using all his power meant that he could barely stand, much less walk, at the moment.

His energy drained with every step he took towards the throne. His sluggishness was nothing compared to his unbridled glee as he gazed upon the throne. His body ached everywhere he'd been hit - enough that he knew he'd have bruises if he didn't treat them. Narein didn't mind the blood trickling from the wound on his arm down to his hands and down down onto the floor - leaving a bloody path to his destination.

Not that he cared at all for his other wounds.

Nor did he care for the pain pulsating from every stab or broken bone.

Narein walked to his best friend. The word 'enemy' would normally be used in this situation but the man currently struggling on the floor was someone Narein grew up with. Someone that Narein looked up to. The man truly was Narein's best friend, in every sense of the word - that was until he refused to move out of Narein's path.

Narein looked up to his best friend, Arvin, struggling in the distance from his injuries. Narein narrowed his eyes, giving his friend a once over.

Arvin's short black hair clung to his face as the blood flowed from his head down his face. Narein couldn't see where Arvin's injury actually was though. Arvin clutched the gash on his ribs, shaking as he struggled to breathe. He couldn't even seem to move his legs, however, making Narein purse his lips.

Narein really didn't want the battle to end like this, with him fighting his own best friend. And now, with his friend gravely injured, Narein had just realized...

This was how it was supposed to end after all.

This was where all the roads of their destiny were leading to.

With him and Arvin on the two different sides of the battle. Because for all that he planned, Narein hadn't considered that Arvin - of all

3

people - would be the one to stand in his way. Not after all that they'd been through.

Narein shook his head, lifting his hands at the damage around them. He walked over to one of the injured soldiers, barely alive as the soldier struggled to breathe. The soldier's eyes widened watching him like a hawk as Narein approached him. The sweet innocent smile that Narein gave the soldier did nothing to soothe the injured man apparently. The soldier's chest heaved the closer Narein got. Lifting his hands to the soldier's forehead, Narein let out a soft smile.

"Thank goodness. He still has enough strength." Narein said, loud enough.

A soft relieved chuckle escaped Narein's lips. He gave the injured man a small smile, one that slowly turned into a smirk. Narein closed the distance between them to touch the soldier's forehead, only to be interrupted by Arvin's shout.

"Leave him alone!"

"Hm?" Narein looked at Arvin lazily.

"Leave him alone." Arvin said through gritted teeth. Although, Narein didn't know if Arvin's strained voice was from the pain from Arvin's injuries or his barely concealed anger. "It's me that you want. You can have me. Let him go."

Narein gave his friend a tight smile. "Don't worry. I'm coming over to you. I just need a little…" Narein trailed off, pursing his lips and scrunching his eyebrows as if he was trying to find the right word. "Sustenance." He said, dismissing Arvin's protests before turning to the soldier in front of him. "I, honestly, don't know if this will hurt you or not. Either way, it'll be good for me. So, I do not care."

That was all he said, before Narein placed his hand on the soldier's forehead. He could see the soldier's eyes widen as he struggled against Narein's grasp. But there was no use. Narein had already felt the soldier's life force brimming in the injured man's chest. A life force from another person that Narein alone could access. It didn't take Narein long to access it either. Months of practice had assured him of that.

Months of practice perfecting using another living being's life force to sustain his own.

The soldier's struggled against Narein's grip; his punches, getting weaker as time ticked by. Seconds turned into minutes as the soldier's eyes slowly glazed over with each attempt to escape.

All that struggle was in vain, however. It didn't matter that the soldier in front of him was dying and slowly turning gray. Every breath that the soldier took was a struggle; every attempt at getting Narein to stop, getting weaker. Narein could feel the life source from the soldier slowly seep out and into Narein.

Filling him up.

Rejuvenating him.

Narein, on the other hand, had never felt more alive.

He could feel the wound on his shoulder stitching itself up, the life force from the soldier slowly healed his other wounds. He could still feel the soldier struggling against his grasp - barely, that was. But all that struggle was futile. As the seconds passed, Narein could see the cloud form over the soldier's eyes. The man's weak protests subsided as his hands lay limp beside him.

With a final breath, Narein sapped the last remaining life force from the soldier, leaving the once injured man to fall to the ground unscrupulously. Narein didn't care for the soldier any longer.

But that was ok. The soldier served his purpose.

Sapping up a person's life force... that was getting easier for him. Narein could still remember the time when that was probably one of the hardest things that he'd accomplished. He's started small, of course. Taking the life of ants, first. Then, the bigger animals like rabbits and squirrels. The lynx was an accident, of course. He only had to take the life of the lynx when it attacked him one day. But his first human...

That wasn't a mistake.

No, that was intentional.

He reveled when he saw the life deplete from his first human, smiling giddily as he felt the man's life fill Narein up. It gave him a high like no other. No amount of Icthum root could give him the euphoric feeling. But for all the euphoric feeling taking another person's life force provided, it had been hard. Taking from a human was far more difficult than Narein had imagined. It was even harder when they were struggling and he couldn't get to them.

But now?

Narein looked at his handiwork. The soldier laying on the ground, motionless, turned completely gray and devoid of life.

"Thank you." Narein tried to tell the soldier as sincerely as he could. Although, that emotion was betrayed by the smirk Narein gave. Narein kicked the soldier's leg to make way for him to walk to his friend.

Narein tilted his head as he looked at Arvin, stalking towards him, as he scrutinized his friend. Arvin's glares did nothing to stop his slow gait, however.

"I have to give you credit." Narein said. "You're the only one not afraid of me."

"I'm not afraid of cowards." Arvin spit out, hatred laced with every word.

Narein clutched his ribs tighter as if every word sent jabs of pain through his chest. That wasn't completely an act, of course. Hearing those words coming from his best friend certainly hurt.

But he scoffed it off. Narein lifted his hands as he turned around. "Me? A coward? You came to my kingdom with an army. I was able to do..." Narein looked around at his castle again. "This. And you think that *I* am the coward?"

Narein stopped only a couple feet away from his friend. Although Narein still considered Arvin to be his friend, it was sad for him to think that Arvin didn't think of him as such.

"This could have all been avoidable." Narein said just loud enough for Arvin to hear. Not that there was any other soul in the palace that could hear him. "How many times, Arvin? How many times did I have to tell you to leave me alone? I made you a deal. I told you I'd leave you and your kingdom alone if you let me be."

"Leave my kingdom alone at the expense of all the other kingdoms. How many people have already suffered under you?" Arvin struggled to even talk. But that didn't stop him from snarling at Narein. When Narein didn't answer, Arvin's expression turned softer. "You still have the chance to change this." The desperation in Arvin's voice was undeniable. "You don't have to do all this. I'll be there for yo-"

"No!" Narein roared at the man. "No, you won't! You never were!"

"I know! I made a mistake. I shouldn't have. I'm sorry. But you can change this now. And I'll be there every step of the way." Arvin pleaded. He lifted his hand clutching his ribs towards his friend.

Narein scoffed again. "Try to change me? No, it's too late for that, my friend. I'd say I'll show you exactly how much worse I can be. But I'm sorry, you'll not be alive to see it. You're already a pain now. I can't have you thwarting my plans for the future."

Narein closed the distance between him and his friend. He crouched down to his friend and raised the dagger. "At least I'm giving you the grace of dying. Don't make me take your life source."

And with that Narein brought the dagger down onto his friend, not realizing that with that one act, he'd started a war that would last almost 700 years.

700 years of tears and bloodshed.

Earning himself the name of the Dark One.

All of which led to this point where the story starts...

1

"Present Day, Earth" - Aliya

"**A**NOTHER BODY HAS BEEN discovered with the same gruesome maulings of who the authorities are calling 'The Slasher'. As of now, the authorities cannot explain as to who the Slasher might be..."

The reporter's high pitched voice rang loud from the radio in the silent car, bringing Aliya out of her reverie. Aliya stared at the red traffic light, willing it to turn green. She paid no attention to the reporter on the radio shouting out the emergency broadcast. Her voice only seemed to raise as the commotion behind her increased.

But Aliya only sighed in response.

Aliya was finally at the end of her day, driving back home from her second job. And the only thing that was on her mind was her bed, a soft fluffy blanket, and sleep. She didn't even have the energy to make herself something to eat from all the groceries she'd just bought.

Aliya let out a small smile as she thought of her bed.

Finally realizing that the light turned green, Aliya shook her head. She began to drive again, with her attention back on the reporter on the radio.

"There has been no footage of him anywhere. The police have been quiet about any DNA that has been obtained in the crime scenes. With this being the third death of the night, authorities are urging the residents of Atlanta to practice caution when they are outside. Always stick to groups and unless it is absolutely necessary, do not go outside tonight. Especially since the perpetrator seems to not be selective in who he targets - old, young..."

The slasher? Aliya's face scrunched as she thought of the name they gave the serial killer. *They already gave him a name? That's quick.*

This was the first time she'd been hearing of these murders. She hadn't heard of them in the morning when she drove to her classes. So, this had to be relatively new... and the media already had a name for the killer. She didn't know whether to be impressed or annoyed by that fact.

With the number of serial killer documentaries she'd seen on Netflix, Aliya wasn't really surprised though.

So, Aliya just shrugged.

Aliya sighed again as the reporter droned on, paying very little attention to the details of the incident. The killings were in Atlanta and she lived almost an hour and a half outside the city in Athens. She didn't have to worry about it. So, Aliya just filed the information in the back of her mind.

But what if he escaped the city? Her mind added unhelpfully. But she was too tired to explore her thoughts any further. Aliya simply shook her head trying to clear that thought out of her mind.

She already had a very long day.

After running around to get to her classes, working at her second job, and then shopping for her groceries for the next week, Aliya was exhausted. The last thing she wanted to think about was a serial killer on the loose. That was not her problem now. She just wanted to head home, cuddle with her blanket and fall asleep with some show playing in the background.

Aliya sighed again, lazily turning the steering wheel of her 2010 Honda Civic. She'd been very happy when she got a secondhand car in the color of her choosing - midnight blue. It'd been driving smoothly then, and it continued to drive smoothly even now.

Or rather... relatively smoothly.

There were random noises every time she put her car in reverse. Her car doors still had scratches from when someone scraped it. Aliya painted over it herself, of course. It definitely did not look good, but it got the job done. There was no scratch anymore - one that she could see, that was.

Tired of listening to the gloomy news report, Aliya changed the station before turning into her college campus. A small smile graced her lips as she bobbed her head when she heard Billie Eilish singing "Bad Guy".

That's fitting for 'The Slasher'. Aliya thought, chuckling. She drove into her neighborhood, trying to avoid any potholes on the way to her house.

Rows of rickety single-story homes lined along the street. The trees amidst the houses swayed in the cool autumn breeze. Everything was wet from the rain that poured down just a few hours ago. Normally, Aliya would have been able to see people walking about at all times of the night. But tonight, it was different. There wasn't a single person walking around - not drunk or sober. Aliya checked to see the time. It couldn't have been that late into the night.

10:30pm. The clock on her dash showed her.

Huh... people must have been really spooked by the serial killer. She wondered. Aliya began to question if she was the one being nonchalant about the serial killer or if the people were overreacting.

She truly didn't understand why, considering Atlanta was almost 60 miles away from where she lived. Her nonchalance could also have been her tired brain not wanting to think of the danger that might be looming.

She just wanted to lay down on her bed. Was that too much to ask?

Aliya drove to the last house on the street - her house. Or rather, the house she was renting. She'd always been happy with the privacy of her house being the last one on the block. With neighbors only on one side of her house, and the woods covering all the other three sides, Aliya had all the seclusion she needed as an introvert. And given that someone had died in the house five years ago, she was able to afford the cheap rent.

It was perfect!

Aliya parked her car in front of her house. She got out and opened her trunk to look at the six plastic bags filled with her groceries. Aliya pursed her lips as she placed her hands on her hips.

I can do that in two trips. She thought, before her face turned sour.

No... She whined to herself. *I don't wanna do two trips.*

Aliya took in a deep breath and grunted as she grabbed all six bags - three on each arm. Her grunts only grew louder with every step she took to walk up to her house. She hissed when the plastic bags dug into her hands pinching the skin.

But Aliya was still adamant to carry the bags in one trip.

Once she entered her house, Aliya kicked her front door close, letting the bags drop to the ground in front of the door. She rubbed her palms, hissing as she soothed the pain. As the pain began to subside, Aliya clutched her waist and arched her back, panting at the mini workout it took to get the groceries into her house. Aliya blinked to adjust her eyes to the dark as she walked around, feeling the wall for the light switch.

Just as she was about to turn it on, however, Aluya felt the hair on the back of her neck stand up. She could feel her breath hitch. Her chest heaved. Her mind had yet to catch up to the one change in her house that her body seemed to instantly recognize.

A simple change that hadn't been there when Aliya left her house that morning.

A faint purple glow emanated from her living room - a purple glow in the shape of a person that Aliya was sure she never had in her house before. There was nothing in her house that would even give off a purple glow.

Aliya looked up slowly in the dark, careful not to make any sudden movements. Maybe whatever or whoever it was hadn't seen her yet. And if she was slow enough, they wouldn't notice her. She hadn't turned on her lights yet, leaving her house drenched in darkness. She cursed herself for buying thick curtains. They usually helped her block the light from the outside when she had to sleep.

But now?

Now, there was scarcely any light entering her house that she had a hard time seeing anything else.

Maybe it's just your imagination. She tried to soothe herself. Her hand hovered over the light switch.

Turn it on! She almost chastised herself.

No matter how much she tried to gather her courage to turn on the light, her hand simply didn't comply.

With bated breath, Aliya lifted her head, her eyes searching her very dim living room. Everything seemed to be in its place... from what she could see in the dark, that was. So, what was the problem? Why hadn't she turned on the light yet?

Then came her answer.

A slight movement from the corner of her living room. The faint sound of cloth rustling as if someone shifted their position. If Aliya hadn't been looking for something amiss in her room, she'd have definitely missed it. Surely, her eyes couldn't have been playing tricks in the dark, couldn't they? Aliya peered in the dark corner again.

Another movement.

It was small, very easy to miss. But Aliya could see the faint purple glow coming from the figure in the corner. A thin yellow thread seemed to be attached to the figure's back... or was it front?

Is that really important right now?

Aliya could feel her chest heave. A slight shudder ran through her spine. Her hands trembled as beads of sweat began to form on her temples. She thought of all the ways she could leave the house. Maybe she could act as if she forgot something in the car.

The grocery bags! Aliya cursed herself for placing the bags in front of the door. Who in their right mind would do that?

Either way, Aliya took a tentative step backwards. Only, this time, she was stopped by the voice in her living room.

"Don't move." The deep voice chimed out. Just as the voice said, Aliya froze midstep. "Not a step."

The voice was almost warm and inviting. Nothing like she would have assumed a killer - was he a killer? Was he *the* killer? - would have sounded like.

Shit! I'm dead. I'm dead, I'm dead. That was all she could think of. *No! I can't die. I have a test on Tuesday.*

That gave Aliya a pause.

Screw the test! She scolded herself. If she could get out of this situation, she'd take a hundred tests if needed. Aliya went over all the ways she could get out of this predicament. *The door? No, there's groceries in front of it. Idiot! Maybe run to the window in the kitchen? No, that's locked.* Aliya felt for the phone in her back pocket. *Ok, run to the bathroom and then call the police.*

Even in the dark, Aliya could feel the figure walk closer. Almost as if he was stalking his prey. His faint footsteps on the wooden floor echoed in the stony silence. The faint purple glow engulfed him like a halo. She could see his silhouette in the purple glow as he stalked towards her. Tall and lean, he was holding onto his chest as he limped his way towards her. Even when he was hurt, Aliya would have to admire the grace as he glided across the floor towards her.

That was what brought her out of her reverie.

You need to get out now! She reminded herself.

With every step she saw him come closer to her, Aliya took a shaky step back.

"Light the lamps if it makes you feel better. But I'm not here to hurt you." The man said. It was only when she was closer that she realized that his deep voice was actually strained.

Light the lamps? What era - Aliya shook her head, clearing her thoughts. *Yeah, sure, like I'm going to believe that, you absolute nutjob.* Aliya scoffed. She didn't say it out loud though, fearing what he might do. Another look at the man walking and she thought. *Ok, he's hurt. I can still escape.*

Taking one deep breath to steel herself, Aliya quickly turned around. Her hand hit the switch turning on the light, but Aliya didn't dare turn around to see the man. She scrammed from her position knocking off the small dining table in front of her.

Aliya didn't care though.

She needed to get out of here as fast as possible. Aliya could feel her heart beating. Time seemed to slow as she waded past the fallen dining table and the broken glass dishes that were once neatly placed on the table. She didn't turn around to see where the man was.

She had to get out of here. That was her first priority.

Aliya wanted to live.

In her hurry though, Aliya didn't see the flash of purple light streaming towards her. The glow engulfed her. She couldn't move even if she wanted to. It was only when she couldn't feel the floor beneath her feet that she realized the man had somehow lifted her off the ground.

She didn't understand how though - especially since his voice still sounded distant.

Aliya screamed. Or rather, she thought she screamed but could hear no sound come out. Just as quickly as the purple glow surrounded her, it went away. Leaving her suspended in the air for just a second longer. Aliya heard her scream tear out as she fell towards the ground. She scrambled to gain some sort of control as she saw the ground approach closer.

But to no avail.

Aliya felt the hard ground hit her chest knocking the breath out of her. Clutching onto her chest, Aliya struggled to breath. She tried to crawl backwards, trying to put as much distance between the two of them as possible. She could see the black spots surrounding her vision.

No, no, no... now's not the time! She tried to scream at herself. She can't fall unconscious now. Not when she could get away.

Aliya wheezed. She saw the man saunter towards her from the corner of her eye. The closer he came, the more Aliya tried to move away from him but again… no matter what she did, she couldn't seem to move. It was almost as if he was pinning her in place.

But that couldn't be, could it?

He wasn't even touching her.

It was only when the man bent down closer that she saw him… truly saw him.

His dark strands of hair fell from his sides as he looked down at her. Although what confused her were his stormy gray eyes, looking down at her in concern – almost as if he was assessing the damage he'd done to her.

A little late for your concern. She wanted to shout at him. But with the terror gripping her chest, she couldn't even speak.

The man came closer. The purple glow now highlighted more of his features. With his high cheekbones, olive skin, angular face and shoulder length long dark hair, Aliya could swear he could be a dead ringer for her favorite character Crown Prince Enzo.

Except, your Crown Prince Enzo would not hurt you. Her mind chimed in unhelpfully. She was barely holding on to her consciousness. *Also, Enzo has pointed ears.*

The man tsked as if telling off a young child. "I did tell you to stay put. Now look at what happened."

The last thing that Aliya remembered before falling unconscious was the man bending over her. He pushed his long dark hair behind his ear.

And with one last thought, Aliya fell unconscious.

He has pointy ears.

17

2

"Who did he say he was?" - Aliya

ALIYA GROANED AS SHE rubbed her forehead, trying to shake off the weird dream she just woke up from. She tossed around, rubbing her eyes and winced when the pounding in her head only intensified.

Aliya refused to open her eyes just yet. It was a Saturday. It was her first weekend that she'd actually gotten to herself. The only way she would wake up was if a tornado barged through her house. She was that adamant about sleeping in and there was no way she or anyone else would ruin her sleep now.

But the dream continued to plague her mind.

Meeting her favorite fictional character...

Aliya chuckled lazily as she rolled around in her sleep. Only her tired mind would come with a scenario such as that. With how stressed out she was about her Statics exam and her two jobs, Aliya, honestly, wasn't surprised she had a dream like that.

Her smile turned into a chuckle. That was a really nice thought though. Her thoughts wandered to all the adventures she dreamed of having if Crown Prince Enzo was to be a real person - some savory thought while the others, not so much.

Either way, she knew for a fact she'd have fun.

Aliya turned around to find another comfortable position. She moaned, imagining herself cuddling the Crown Prince Enzo, waking up to him in the morning. His deep, warm voice would greet her in the morning as he cuddled her closer to him. A soft smile graced her lips only for that smile to turn into a frown as she winced at the light coming into her bedroom that early in the morning. Her frown only deepened when the light refused to go away.

Aliya wanted her room to be dark when she slept for a reason.

Hold on. Aliya stopped mid-rubbing her eyes and mid-stretch. *Light?*

There's no way there was light coming into her room this early in the morning. Not if she had any say in it. And this was her house and she *did* have a say in it. Aliya always made sure that her dark curtains were closed the night before just to make sure she didn't have to wake up to the light in her room.

Always.

So, who opened the curtains?

Her hand slowly moved up from rubbing her eyes to her forehead. She could still feel the bump from where she hit her forehead the night before. She winced as she touched and poked the wound. Aliya's hands began to shake as she slowly opened her eyes.

That was not a dream. She shuddered as she looked around the room.

"Well, you're finally awake." She heard the same deep voice say from beside her, making Aliya freeze. She slowly opened her eyes to see that she was still in her living room, sleeping on her sofa.

It's real. Everything's real. It's really real. Aliya could feel heart speed up again as her chest heaved. She wanted to move. She really did. But Aliya was frozen to the spot on the sofa. Her hands gripped the cushion so tightly that she was sure there was no more circulation to her hands anymore.

"I told you I wasn't going to hurt you." The voice said again. The man must have noticed Aliya still holding on to the bump on her forehead. "Sorry about that though. It couldn't be helped."

He didn't sound sorry at all though. In fact, the little mirth in his voice only made Aliya want to punch him.

If she was brave enough to look at him again first, that was.

Aliya dared to look back at the man sitting on the other chair, staring down at her. Although, what caught her attention was the man was holding her favorite book series. It was open on his lap, his fingers positioned as if he was turning the page. A smirk played along his lips as if he knew something she didn't.

Was he just sitting there reading the book? She thought. Aliya slowly moved to the other side of the sofa, trying to put as much distance between them as possible.

The man tilted his head as if trying to understand who she was. The silence between them stretched to uncomfortable lengths. Aliya bit her lip waiting for the man to say something, anything. He'd left her alive. There had to be a reason. And none of the reasons her mind came up with, soothed her. She had to find out why. Maybe for now, she could just play his game.

You can escape when he lets his guard down. She told herself, almost encouraging herself to stay brave.

The man looked around her living room before turning to her. Aliya took a moment to look over at the man in front of her. Sure, he looked just like the character in her favorite book. But there was no way that the pointed ears she'd seen before falling unconscious the night before had been real. Could it? Aliya wanted to bend her head to see if she'd just imagined his pointed ears. Though, she was afraid of what would happen if she were to move.

"Who are you?" The man asked.

That question threw Aliya off guard. *He came into my house and now he wants to know who I am.*

Before she could answer, however, the man turned serious. The playful smirk that graced his lips till now was no longer there. Aliya leaned back as the man leaned forward, analyzing her. Without moving, Aliya tried to look around her surroundings, searching for something she could use to defend herself.

Just play his game. She thought. But the way he was looking at her, Aliya couldn't find the words to reply.

She remembered using a retractable knife she'd used for a project just the week before. Well, she called it a knife, but it was a retractable dagger she bought from comic con just that year. Without moving, Aliya glanced at the table in front of her. She only let out the breath she was holding when she noticed the dagger still tucked beneath a couple books on the table.

Aliya slowly removed the blanket covering he-

Blanket? He had time to put a blanket on me last night? Who is he? She thought. That unexpected caring act confused her more about the man in front of her.

Making sure that he wasn't focusing on her, Aliya slowly removed the soft blanket that was covering her. Before the man could react, in one swoop, Aliya reached for the retractable knife. Pulling it out, she pointed the dagger towards him.

"Get out of my house." She fumed, waving the knife in front of the man as she stepped back.

Although her bravery slightly wavered when she saw the man just make himself comfortable in the chair. He leaned back, chuckling to himself. He crossed his arms and let out a sigh, as if he was the one that was disappointed in this scenario.

"A dagger?" He said, pointing to her. "I ask you a simple question and you point a dagger at me. Is that how you treat your guests?" His gaze shifted down to her hand holding the dagger. With an eyebrow raised, the man tilted his head, as if thinking of something. "Do you even know how to use that thing? Your stance is wrong."

"And you barged into my house!" Aliya scoffed. She ignored his assessment of her fighting skills.

To her, this was a dagger and any dagger would hurt if you poke it hard enough. But Aliya honestly, didn't know if she should have been more offended about him questioning her in her own house or judging her for trying to protect herself.

"What sort of dagger even is that? It looks so flimsy. Also, I just asked you who you were." The man asked, as if Aliya hadn't spoken at all.

Aliya looked at the dagger, insulted. It wasn't exactly a real dagger. It was a retractable one. More like a prop. Aliya had gotten it at comic con one year. But the man didn't need to know that. But it didn't seem to matter to the man that the dagger - whether real or not - was pointed towards him.

Shaking her head, she said. "Who am I? I should be asking you that question. Who are you? What are you doing in my house?" Her voice rose with every question.

"Lady, I asked the question first."

"And I'm the one with the weapon. So, my question comes first."

Was it smart to argue with an intruder? No.

Not that Aliya cared now.

The man rubbed his eyes exasperatedly. "You're holding it wrong." He rolled his eyes. "Really? You don't know who I am? You have a map of Indresal." He waved to the map from her favorite book she'd hung on the wall of her living room. "Apparently, someone was writing a book about the Great War." He waved the book he was holding in front of her. "You even have hearts every time my name comes up in the book. And you don't know who I am."

Aliya looked at him incredulously. She only had hearts around the name Enzo.

The Crown Prince of Ravendore - Enzo Asir al'Deron.

She loved him. She'd wished that he was real a million times. He was her favorite character from The Hollow Hearts Series.

But that couldn't be...

He couldn't be Enzo. There was no way a fictional character could come to life.

When she didn't answer, the man let out a sigh. "I'm Enzo. Enzo Asir al'Deran. Crown Prince of Ravendore. Now, who are you?"

Aliya looked at him exasperatedly.

Enzo? Enzo Asir al'Deran. Aliya scoffed. There was no way. She looked around her house. The map of the world of Indresal hanging behind her sofa as a decoration. *There was No freaking way.*

"You're Enzo?" Aliya deadpanned, only for him to look at her confused.

Enzo nodded slowly, like he was wondering what part of his introduction made her question his claim.

Mustering the fakest smile she could, Aliya said, "If you're Crown Prince Enzo, then I'm Queen Victoria."

"Queen?" Enzo's eyes widened. Aliya had never seen anyone straighten his posture as quickly as the man in front of her did. He stood up and bent down low in a bow. "Why do you live... here?"

"I'm sorry!" Aliya scoffed, incredulous. He did not just insult the house she was renting in.

"No, please do not apologize." Enzo was still sincere, not noticing that he'd just insulted Aliya. "We've been going through some tough times. The war has been tough on everyone an-"

"Stop!" Aliya interrupted him. "Just stop! You cannot be serious. Just because I'm playing along doesn't mean that you can look down on me. I know you're not Prince Enzo. Now, who are you? Why are you in my house? Choose your next words very carefully. Because I am very close to calling the cops."

"What's 'cops'?" The man mumbled to himself before asking out loud. "What makes you think I am not Crown Prince Enzo?"

"What makes you think that I'd believe you're a fictional character?"

"Fictional character?!" It was Enzo's turn to look at her incredulously. He stepped back, placing a hand on his chest as if the question itself knocked him over. He gave Aliya once over. "What part of me looks fictional to you?"

"And what part of me makes you think I'm a fool for believing that?"

Enzo took in a deep breath, trying to calm himself down. "If I'm not Enzo, how do you think I know of him?"

Aliya waved at the Map of Indresal hanging behind her sofa. The cloth map covered in intricate designs around the edges was detailed enough that Aliya could see the crests of each house that ruled the different kingdoms in Indresal. That was what drew Aliya to the map in the first place.

"I have a map right there!" She shrieked. "You were just reading the series that has Enzo as a fictional character. It'd be very easy for someone to make up that lie."

"Yes, sure, that could be a lie." Enzo stepped forward, his gaze not wavering once from hers.

Aliya stepped back, her eyes widening. Her grip on the dagger tightened as she pointed it higher at him. But the man didn't seem to care. His focus shifted.

Aliya saw a purple glow surround his hand, growing brighter by the second. She almost scoffed when he lifted his hand in a straight line. But her shock only increased when she saw a straight purple line form in the middle of the room - sputtering and crackling.

It seemed to take all of Enzo's strength to make the thin purple line open - as if he was ripping the fabric of space and time itself. It only opened a little. But that little opening was enough for Aliya.

Aliya didn't know where Enzo opened the portal to, but she could feel the heat emanating from the other side through the portal. Even through the small opening, she could hear the snarls of the horde of beasts as they seemed to scramble over each other to reach the portal. Aliya could feel her heart thud in her chest. She stepped back, trying to get herself as far away from the portal as possible.

It was only a small hole. She was sure that nothing from the other side would cross over. But with the snarls that she was hearing, Aliya wanted to put as much distance between her and the portal as possible.

For once, Aliya was happy that her curiosity had a limit. She did *not* want to see the beasts. Especially with how terrifying they sounded.

Aliya gaped at the sight before her. Her grip on the dagger, loosening.

Just as quickly as the portal opened, it seemed to sputter out. The crackling noises faded along with the portal, leaving Enzo and Aliya to sit in the silent room. Her eyes, wide in shock. With the crackling noise of the portal and the snarling beasts gone, Aliya could hear her heartbeat loudly in her ears. She didn't realize how shallow her breath was. She held onto the sofa as tightly as she could. Aliya stared at the spot that held the portal only a moment ago.

Yes, it was different from how it was described in the books but seeing the makings of a portal - however small it was - in the middle of her living room only made Aliya stare at Enzo in shock. She didn't know what to say.

There was no way.

But the portal...

No!

There was not a single chance that he was Enzo.

The Crown Prince of Ravendore. A person who she thought was fictional. He was there. In the middle of her living room. Living and breathing. He'd just created a portal in the middle of her living room.

Enzo looked at his hands in confusion - no, more like incredulity - as if they'd offended him somehow. He lifted them again, waving them in the air, trying to open another portal.

Although Aliya was weary about where the portal was going to open up to next. *Stop!* She wanted to shout at him but no words came out.

She could see Enzo's frustration build up. It seemed that no matter what or how hard he tried to create another portal, one wouldn't form again. Beads of sweat started to form on his forehead, dripping down his temple. Aliya could see him panting with every effort to get the portal open.

"What's happening?" He strained. His hand shook from the exertion. But Enzo didn't stop.

Sweat trickled down his brow. As the seconds ticked by, Aliya could see Enzo getting paler. He didn't want to stop though. When he suddenly let go of the portal, Enzo looked down at his hands, shocked.

"I can't do it." He gasped out, looking completely dejected. "I can't create a portal anymore."

But Aliya couldn't care less. She saw all she needed to and yet, she didn't know how to respond. The portal forming in front of her only confirmed that the man in front of her was Enzo.

She opened her mouth as if to say something only to close it a moment later. *He's real. He's actually real. How can he be real? There's no way that he's real.*

Aliya dropped her hand holding the dagger. She took a step towards Enzo, who himself looked shockingly at his hands. He continued to say, "I can't make portals anymore." As if that was his mantra.

Aliya ignored his mumbled. Instead, she gingerly stepped closer to him. Just as slowly, she brought her hand up and poked him, as if touching him any further would only make him disappear like the portal did just a moment ago. With how close she was to him, Aliya had to tilt her head to look at him. In her shock, there was only one thing that she could even say.

And she all but screamed that to him...

"You're real!"

3

"Hide all the books and fanfics. He doesn't need to know." – Aliya

I T'D BEEN ABOUT FIVE hours since Aliya had the revelation that Enzo - the man sitting in front of her, the man who hadn't stopped looking at his hands since the last few hours - was in fact *not* a fictional person.

She had been poking him at random times just to make sure that he was real. Not that Enzo seemed to respond or even notice.

He was busy wondering why he couldn't create any more portals. He had tried multiple times in the past few hours - none of his efforts were fruitful though. That only seemed to make his frustration grow.

Aliya bit her lip. She hung her head low, allowing her long dark, curly hair to cascade down her face - a pathetic attempt to hide her embarrassment. Because with the realization that the man beside her was her favorite fictional character came another daunting revelation.

Her entire living room - no, her entire house - was filled with trinkets from The Hollow Hearts series. And with that revelation, came the additional embarrassment that Enzo was actually reading the book before she'd woken up.

Aliya would have been fine with that. She truly would have been. But the fact that he'd seen the hearts she placed around his name every single time that it was mentioned in the series...

Aliya felt like digging her grave and burying herself in it.

No fictional character should know the extent you love them. Aliya pursed her lips. Her eyes widened at the thought of all the fanfiction that she had read of Enzo. Aliya bit her lip as her breath hitched. Trying to control her emotions was futile at the moment. Her mind raced with all the images from the times she'd imagined Enzo...

He wasn't supposed to know that!

No one was supposed to know that!

That was supposed to be between her and her grave!

He already teased her about the hearts around his name in the book series. What would he even think of her if he saw her browser history? That thought itself was daunting. No hole would be deep enough for Aliya to dive into to escape that embarrassment. He didn't need to know that.

And if she had any say in it, he wouldn't have known any of this.

But she didn't. And here she was, desperately hoping that the hearts around his name were the only thing that Enzo saw.

For now, Aliya was just happy that Enzo had just been looking at his hands the entire time. The veins on the back of his hand, the gold signet with the crest of House Deran on his left ring finger, and a platinum ring on his right thumb...

Aliya's mind wandered to all the things she read those hands did in the fanfictions she read. All the things she dreamed of him doing to her. Aliya peaked at Enzo through her lashes, trying to catch another glimpse of him. For all her surprise, he looked exactly like how he'd been described in the book series.

No, in fact, he was even more handsome than she'd imagined him.

Aliya bit her lip, clearing her throat a couple times to collect her thoughts. *No, stop! He's real! Stop thinking that!* She chastised herself.

Every time she looked at him, all she could think of was what he thought of her being his fan. Aliya's face scrunched as she cringed at the thought itself. She wasn't just his fan though. She adored him. No, she *loved* him.

The funko-pops of him and his horse on her bookshelf, the family crest of House Deran that was her bookmark, the map of Indresal covering the wall behind her sofa - they attested as much. Aliya's eyes widened in barely contained embarrassment. She was now acutely aware of how many trinkets she had of the series.

She wanted to hide them all. Throw them as far away as possible.

The Hollow Hearts series? What's that? Is that another new book series? I don't know what book he's holding. Aliya looked sheepishly at her small bookshelf, guiltily. *The hearts? My friend drew those! Yeah, she completely loves you. Not me though. I am fine. I don't even know who you are.*

It didn't matter to her that she wrote down 'Aliya x Enzo' in some of the pages, swooning every time she read about him being mysterious or saving some villager in a battle. It didn't matter that she'd drawn the sigil of House Deron in all her notebooks. None of those mattered.

Aliya's eyes widened as she realized something else.

Not only did she have the original first editions of the books, she even bought the special editions that were released only a year ago.

Did she have to forgo a couple lunches and a couple dinners to afford them? Yes. Was it worth it? Also, yes.

She had so many copies of this book series alone that seeing one in Enzo's hand made her want to vomit. All the reasons she'd thought of for having the books in her house and the hearts around his name only seemed comical in retrospect.

She just wanted to hide in embarrassment. Hide in a hole and scream and never come out. Ever. Aliya would never wish this on her worst enemy.

For the past couple hours, Aliya had been waiting for Enzo to say something. Anything to break the uncomfortable silence surrounding them. But all he'd been doing was looking at his hands incredulously as he mumbled to himself.

He hadn't spoken a word to her. Much less acknowledge her existence.

Not knowing what to do, Aliya gazed at him... this time, really taking in his features.

His stormy gray eyes were wide and his mouth slightly agape in shock. His face was exactly as the author had described it. Angular with sharp cheekbones -although now, it was also covered in cuts and bruises. Aliya's brows furrowed. Come to think of it, Enzo's entire body was covered in bruises. She began to wonder what he'd gotten himself into before coming into her world.

Tendrils of his long hair fell out of his half-bun as he looked down at his hands. His armor showing the crest of House Deran was battered as well, making Aliya wonder how many more injuries the armor was covering underneath.

Aliya could see the red stain on his shirt sleeve slowly increasing. Her brows further knitted together with her ever growing concern. "You're bleeding." She said.

Enzo looked up at her, although his gaze was distant. Clouded, as if he was haunted by whatever thoughts were rummaging in his mind.

"You're bleeding." She said again. But she doubted Enzo could hear her. He'd been deep in thought ever since he tried to open a portal.

Aliya shook her head and got up from her seat. Grabbing her first aid kit in the bathroom, she walked over to Enzo, sitting beside him.

He even smells of sandalwood! She thought, almost mesmerized. Aliya slowly took a whiff of his scent. His faint sandalwood scent mixed with the smell of his blood slowly trickling out from the gash on his arm. *Hm, he doesn't smell that good.*

No, focus. Concentrate! Shaking her head lightly, Aliya chastised herself before focusing on the injuries. *You're being a creep!*

Aliya slowly lifted her arm and winced when she looked at the gash. They definitely had to go to the hospital.

I don't know how to treat an elf! She almost screamed out loud.

Neither does the hospital! Her mind added, unhelpfully. *Is it even safe for him to go to the hospital?* Images of Enzo being taken in by officials raced through her mind. All the events from the dystopian novels she'd read previously ran in her mind. *No, let's just try to treat him here.*

Shaking her head, Aliya steeled herself before gingerly cleaning his gash. She winced every time the cotton ball touched the wound, bracing herself as if she was the one being treated. But Enzo didn't respond the entire time. He barely noticed her moving him from position to the other as Aliya tried to gain access to the injury.

Oh, thank goodness. It's not deep. Aliya let out a sigh once she finished cleaning his wound.

Wrapping a bandage around his arm, Aliya looked up at him. Even sitting, Enzo towered over her.

ONLY A PORTAL AWAY

Oh, dear...he's really real.

"So..." Aliya interrupted his mumbling. Although, Enzo didn't seem to hear her. Aliya continued though. "You're actually Enzo? Like the Crown Prince Enzo?"

"What?" It seemed to take a moment for Enzo to catch up to what Aliya was saying. But it didn't take him long to fire off questions. "Uh, yes, I am. Are you really sure that I'm fictional? What world is this? What even made you think I'm fictional? Who wrote this book? How do they know so much about my world? Do you know where the writer is?" Enzo turned the book over to see the name of the author. "Take me to her."

Aliya's eyes widened at the barrage of questions that Enzo poured out. So much that she wished she'd just let him stew for a little bit more.

"I-I... uh..." Aliya sputtered.

"What made you think I was fictional?" Enzo asked again, sensing her confusion. This time one question at a time.

"Until this morning I only thought you were a character in a book. Of course, I'd just assume you're fictional. No one ever thinks that the characters they read would just barge into their life and be... real!"

Enzo looked at the book he was holding. "A character in a book..." He muttered to himself. "Who in this god forsaken world would write a book about the Great War. Where even am I?" Enzo asked, incredulously.

"The Great War?" Aliya looked at him confused. "The book isn't about your Great War. It's about a young girl who escaped her war wrecked kingdom. It's about her struggle to get to safety. The story goes on about how she moves across the continent to get to safety and finds out that she's a witch. So, she goes around like a mercenary, protecting

33

people who commission for her and then she finds love along the way. You were just a side character."

Aliya would have waved Enzo off, except the insulted look on his face made her stop. She would have laughed if it wasn't for how offended Enzo looked.

"I'm a side character. I am not a side character. How could I be the side character? I am the Crown Prince." His sour expression only made Aliya chuckle silently. She was struggling to hold it back though.

"Even Crown Princes can be side characters in someone else's story." Aliya said between her giggling fits.

"Who wrote this book?" He held the book, looking at Aliya, his eyes narrowing, silently accusing her of the crime of making him the side character. Throwing the book on the small coffee table, Enzo leaned back exasperatedly. "Where even am I?"

All the giggles Aliya was struggling through vanished the minute Enzo threw her favorite book on the coffee table. Her giggles turned into a glare as she pursed her lips.

No one handles her favorite book like that. Much less disrespect it like Enzo did just now.

"The author writes under the pen name Kiana Roberts. She's been very secretive about her real name though." Aliya's brows furrowed. She tilted her head as she tried to think of a way to answer his second question. "And, um, you're on... Earth?"

Enzo nodded. "Earth?" He said, as if testing out the name.

"Yeah, Earth."

Shaking his head, he clarified. "What Kingdom am I in?" He looked her up and down, scrutinizing her. "I don't recognize your clothing..." His voice trailed off in the end.

"The kingdom of... America?"Aliya narrowed her eyes as she tried to connect her answers with all the questions he was asking.

"America?" There's no America in our world." Enzo muttered to himself, but in the quiet house, it was loud enough that Aliya could hear him.

"Yeah, well, you're not in your world anymore." Aliya muttered.

"What?" Enzo shrieked.

And with that shriek another couple hours passed with Aliya trying to explain to Enzo about the world he entered into. And in their entire conversation, one thing was certain... Neither of them knew how Enzo came from Indresal to Earth.

But the more she told Enzo of Earth, the more incredulous his expression became. She didn't know if he believed her but his dubious look only turned more comical the more she explained. That should be a good sign, right? Earth was, in fact, a bit confusing.

"If you're in a different world from mine, how does this author know so much of my world?" Enzo finally asked, exasperated. He lifted his arms as he paced around the small living room. Aliya sat on her sofa, her eyes trailing him.

"I don't know." She mumbled.

"Well, figure it out!" Enzo demanded.

"Pardon me." Aliya blinked. She bit the inside of her cheek, stopping herself from using some choice words. "Figure it out?" Aliya asked. *He did not just say that.*

Enzo's eyes widened. "I-I-I'm sorry, your highness." He sputtered out, truly looking sorry. He started pacing again with his hands in his hair. "This is bad. This is very bad. I need to go back. They need me now."

Aliya looked perplexed at Enzo calling her "your highness".

It was only then that she remembered telling him that she was Queen Victoria. She winced, letting out a sheepish smile. "I..." She trailed off, licking her lips. "I am not Queen Victoria." When Enzo didn't say anything, she continued. "My name is Aliya."

"Well, that explains the house." Was all he said before shrugging and turning around.

Oh, you insufferable little... Aliya pursed her lips, seething. *Maybe it was better when you were just fictional.*

Enzo swirled on his heel, turning to face Aliya. Pointing to her, he asked. "Is there a way we can talk to the author? If she knows of my world, she might know how to get back to Indresal."

Aliya was baffled. "You cannot expect me to barge into Kiana's house and expect her to give us some answers!"

"I know! I know that we can't do that. But just get me to her place and I will find a way to make her answer."

Aliya's eyes widened. "You are not torturing her!"

"No, I'm not going to torture her! I just need to talk to her. I need some answers. She has to know something for her to write a story this deep about my world." Enzo said, pleading with Aliya. "Please... I need to go back to save my people."

Aliya looked down at her hands clasped on her lap. She bit her lip, wondering if she should actually help him.

Are you seriously considering it? She chastised herself.

When Aliya was taking too long to answer, Enzo pleaded again. "Please..."

And with that one word from Enzo, and with the large pleading eyes he was giving her, Aliya knew she would help him get back to his world.

4

"Earth is very confusing." – Enzo

"**I** STILL DON'T UNDERSTAND how your world works." Enzo massaged his head.

Understanding Earth has only brought on a headache he hadn't been able to cure. Enzo craned his neck, trying to crack it, only for him to groan out loud when it didn't. Enzo massaged the back of his neck trying to relieve his sore muscles. He tossed and turned in his seat, trying to find a comfortable position that didn't aggravate his sore body.

With all the pain he was going through, he barely listened to whatever Aliya explained. She'd just told him about some machine called 'cars'. She'd even taken him out of her house to her car. Although to Enzo, it simply looked rickety and only confused him further when Aliya tried to explain how they worked. And the more questions he seemed to ask, the more Aliya pursed her lips. Her smiles became more forced every time making him wonder if he'd said something bad.

Her expression said that he did. But for the life of him Enzo didn't know what he could have said to make her react like that.

Now, Aliya was sitting on the sofa in front of him with what she called a laptop. She kept tapping on the keys, making Enzo wonder what she was doing. He squinted, trying to get a better look.

When she didn't respond, Enzo continued. "Yes, I understand it's impressive. But why..."

Aliya looked at him as if to say, "Choose your next words carefully."

Apparently, he'd already insulted her house and her car with his questions. He didn't want to insult her any further. She was the one that was helping him. Any wrong word from him and he would probably never go back to Indresal. The thought itself scared him. He needed to be with his people.

"Why would you have that contraption?!"

Aliya gaped as if Enzo had just insulted her entire family. With how different this world was, maybe he actually did.

No! Enzo shook his head slightly.

He'd only called her - what was it? Car? - car, a contraption. Wasn't that what it was?

"Do people of your world not have magic of any kind?" He continued, holding onto his injured arm. He craned his neck again trying to relieve his neck muscles but all he could think of was how different this world was to his. "No magic at all! What kind of world has no magic? How do you go about your life witho-"

He knew he should stop talking. With all the huffs and eye rolls Aliya had been giving him, he really should stop. Enzo didn't want to antagonize the only person in this world that would help him. But he couldn't stop.

Her reactions were just too cute.

And also the fact that he was in a new world... Enzo was a little curious how it operated. After the first half of the day of Enzo not speaking a word, all his questions came pouring out now. He hadn't stopped asking questions since Aliya agreed to help him find the author. Everything from electricity to Aliya's car, to her computer - everything seemed to fascinate Enzo.

"Will you let me concentrate?" Aliya piped up. She breathed heavily as if trying to remain calm. Enzo looked up to see her pursing her lips as she gave him a tight smile. "I'm trying to get you the author's information."

"In that thing." Enzo said, although his statement came out more like a question. He pointed to the instrument that she'd previously called a laptop.

"Yes, this thing. This thing is a laptop. It has all the information I could ever need. And if you let me work on it, I'll finally be able to find the information you need."

"Right..." Enzo said, skeptically. "I won't disturb you." He lifted his hands in mock surrender; although his tone made it certain that he didn't believe her.

How could one small instrument give you all the information you could need? In Indresal, they had libraries and magic that could help them. But this world? No, it seemed that all this world needed was a 'laptop'.

Maybe this world did have magic. They just call it something different. He wondered. Ignoring the hundreds of questions still swirling in his mind, Enzo simply nodded at Aliya.

His silence seemed to appease Aliya. She turned back to her laptop, sighing.

Leaning back against his chair, Enzo took in the moment to study the girl in front of him.

The way she was intently looking at her laptop, biting her lip occasionally as she mouthed the words on the screen. The light from the screen illuminated her smooth brown skin. Her dark brown eyes behind her glasses glided along with the words on the screen as her tongue glazed across her bitten lip. Soft, dark brown curls fell from her bun framing her face and making her look younger than before. Enzo had been itching to place them back in the bun. But given how frustrated she was, he wondered if she'd actually appreciate him doing that.

Chuckling to himself softly, he remembered the hearts she drew around his name. He wondered if she was worried if he'd seen them.

Maybe just tease her a little? Enzo though. He looked at Aliya wearing her glasses as she squinted at her screen again.

His gaze didn't waver from her. The more he looked at her, the more he saw her little quirks. The way she tapped against the laptop mumbling, the way she pursed her lips when she was frustrated, the way she placed the pencil back behind her ear after writing something in her notebook, the way she craned her neck to get a closer look at her laptop.

A soft smile made its way to his lips... that was until he shook his head breaking himself off his reverie. No. He was definitely not going to fall for the human girl in front of him. She seemed young. Much younger than his elven age, surely. She was a human, after all.

And most importantly, she was helping him.

She doesn't have to help you, you know. His mind chimed in, unhelpfully.

He didn't want to tell her that. All he cared about right now was getting back to his world. His people would be waiting for him. He needed to go back.

Yeah, and you're using an innocent person to go back and maybe putting her in danger in the process. His mind chimed in again. But before he could feel guilty, another thought occurred to him.

She thought he was a fictional character. She loved him when he was a fictional character. And he was using that love for him to get back to his world.

Guilt was slowly creeping along his spine forming a knot in his throat. He could feel himself become sick. Yes, he'd seen all the atrocities in the war - some even worse because of the berserkers he had to battle. But he'd never used an innocent person for his gain before. He'd never willingly put an innocent person in harm's way before. Especially one that seemed to like him.

And now, he began to wonder, if he could come into this world, what other things might have followed him here.

And if that was the case, how much danger was Aliya truly in for helping him?

It's ok, when you go back, it'll be all back to normal for her. It'll be as if she never existed.

Enzo's stomach knotted tightly. He didn't like that thought. Going back meant going back to a war ridden world. Back to the carnage and his responsibilities. Just the thought of it made his shoulders sag from the burden weighing heavily on him. The guilt of leaving his people and ihs army had already been eating him up ever since Aliya informed him of his arrival on Earth.

But more importantly... going back meant, he'd have to let her go. Let Aliya go.

And he didn't want to let her go just yet.

She was his escape. Even if it was just for a few hours... or days... or mont-

No, not months. That thought itself made him shudder. *I need to go back quickly.*

But Enzo would relish the few moments of levity that Aliya brought him. Her smile would be his solace for the moment. It's just been a day since he'd been on Earth. But this was the most he'd smiled in a long time. And the way Aliya helped him, bandaging his wounds, searching for the author, helping him find a way back to Indresal...

No.

If there was something or someone dangerous that followed him to Earth, he was going to do his best to protect Aliya. He had to. At least then, he wouldn't have the blood of at least one innocent person on his conscience.

But for now, Aliya was his hope, whether he wanted her to be or not. Enzo looked up at her again.

He could spend a lifetime watching her. There was nothing he could compare to the peace she'd brought him in just a few hours.

Aliya might have sensed his gaze on her as she turned to look at him. Enzo's gaze didn't waver though. He just gave her a soft smile, making her eyes flutter in embarrassment. Her head snapped back to the laptop. He could see her trying to look at him from the corner of her eyes, although she seemed to refuse to turn her head. Enzo took this as his opportunity. He leaned further back into his chair, making himself comfortable knowing full well that his slightly open shirt strained against his chest. He almost chuckled out loud as she pursed her lips and gulped.

"Go to sleep." Aliya said, finally, after a few minutes. Her voice was smaller than it was before. She still refused to look at him though. "You're tired. I'll have the information for you before you wake up."

Enzo pursed his lips, trying not to smile at her reactions. He wanted to protest. He wanted to see her work. She was fascinating. Her world was fascinating. But she was right. He had no energy to stay awake. Instead, he nodded, trying to make himself comfortable in his chair.

Grunting, Enzo stood up. He could still feel the soreness of his muscles, the stab wounds, the slashes.. Everything. He could feel everything. He'd lost his ability to heal himself. That'd gone along with his ability to create portals.

As peaceful as he'd been since he'd come to this world, as incensed as he'd been learning that this world had no magic, nothing infuriated him more than knowing that the lack of magic in this world meant that his magic was gone too.

He almost cursed out loud when he felt a piercing pain in his chest

These human medicines that Aliya helped him with didn't work. They wouldn't work on an Elf like him. He needed a witch's brew. But with how Aliya mentioned there was no magic in this world, he doubted if there were any witches here.

A world without magic. He almost scoffed out loud.

For the life of him, he couldn't remember how he got to this world. To a world without magic. A world where he couldn't heal himself. A world where he couldn't create his portals. He couldn't even remember the last moments in Indresal that brought him to this world.

"You can use the bedroom. It's straight and to the right." Aliya said without lifting her head from the laptop.

Nodding his head mutely, Enzo scratched his head as he limped to the bedroom. Although the moment he entered her bedroom, he paused, pursing his lips as he looked at the small mattress with a headboard.

I'm supposed to fit on that?

Enzo scratched his head again. He turned on his heel to look around the room. Opposite her small bed was a desk and a chair. Books, folders, and papers were strewn about on the desk. Enzo raised his eyebrow. He'd never seen such a mess before. Even his desk back home was immaculate. He made sure that his servants kept his desk and his room immaculately clean. But it seemed that Aliya didn't have any help.

Taking in a deep breath, Enzo looked at the small bookshelf that stood beside her desk. He smiled as he looked at all the books on the shelf. Although, that smile froze when he got a closer look at the figurines decorating the bookshelf.

Is... Is that me?

A small figurine of Enzo in full battle gear atop his horse in the middle of the bookshelf. Enzo clutched his stomach as he burst out laughing. He didn't care for the pain from his wounds or the soreness of his muscles. Looking at a small figurine of himself seemed to be enough. Someone loved him enough to have a figurine of himself in their bedroom.

That's it. I don't care if I die now. This is my achievement. He laughed again, louder this time. He didn't care that he was the Crown Prince of a kingdom. No, this was the highest point in his life.

"Please don't say anything!" Aliya's alarmed voice came from the other room.

Oh, but this is so easy for me to tease you about. He thought. But Enzo said nothing. There was still time to tease her. For now, the bed was calling him. *Maybe tease her another time.* He sighed.

Enzo groaned as he felt his tired muscles relax as he laid on the bed. Although, another chuckle erupted from him when he saw another poster of him directly above the bed, on the ceiling. His chuckle only increased when he heard Aliya's loud groan from the other room.

And with a small smile gracing his lips, Enzo fell into a deep slumber...

Enzo blinked hard, jolting in his saddle as if waking from a dream...

Saddle? His brows furrowed as he wondered where he was. His grip on the horse reins only tightened as he straightened himself. *Where am I?* He wondered again. He looked around again, trying to blink his tiredness away.

Large crowds of adoring people gathered along the sides of the cobblestone streets chanting Enzo's name. That brought him out of his daze. His eyes widened as Enzo shook his head as if waking up from his stupor. He looked around for a moment, confused as to how he got here. He just remembered laying down on Aliya's bed only a few moments ago - in a different world, no less - and now to see his own people, the people of Ravendore, showering him with praise only confused him.

His brows furrowed. Did he just imagine an entire world without magic? A whole new world where he met the one person who loved him. A sharp pang in his chest almost made him buckle and lose his balance on his saddle. His horse neighed in discontent as he jostled on the saddle as he tried to maintain his posture. Enzo didn't like the idea that he'd imagined it.

It felt so real.

The love he felt from Aliya was palpable. The map of Indresal adorning the wall of her living room, the hearts around his name in her book...

All of it could not just be an imagination.

Enzo looked around again.

No, he couldn't have imagined it.

In fact, the scene around him... the people of Ravendore chanting his name, it almost seemed like a memory. Like this had happened before.

AKIRA VARMA

Was he just remembering what happened before he came to Earth? That was the only explanation Enzo could think of as he watched the crowds lining the streets.

People of all ages cheered on the side of the cobblestone streets, welcoming Enzo and his army - or rather, what was left of his army - back to the Capital. He'd gone into battle with a thousand soldiers. But only about seven hundred of them returned back home with him. The battle was successful. They'd won. They were able to resist the Dark One's Disciples making sure another village didn't fall into the Dark One's hold.

But the cost was dire.

With the weight of the fallen soldiers on his shoulders, Enzo couldn't feel it in him to celebrate the victory. Unlike his people, it seemed.

He couldn't fault his people either.

With the way the resistance against the Dark One was going, any victory - no matter how small or big - needs to be celebrated. Because no one knew what kind of news the next battle could bring.

Enzo blinked as the woodsy smell of his Kingdom's Capital filled his nostrils. The cool autumn air flowed through his hair, prickling his skin with goosebumps. Enzo plastered a small smile and settled back into his saddle as he waved to the people cheering him on.

Oh, how they screamed his name over and over. He'd join in their jubilation... if only he didn't lose all those people in his army.

So, instead, Enzo gave them a strained smile and kicked his horse lightly, urging it to trot faster. With a neigh and a shake of its head, the horse obliged.

It was only when he was at the entrance of the castle that his grip on his reins loosened. The sandstone arches welcomed him, giving Enzo a sense of comfort that he hadn't realized he'd missed.

Once Enzo and his army were in the palace grounds, Enzo dismounted from his horse and handed the reins off to the groundskeeper. He turned around to see his army wincing as they got off their own horses. Enzo pursed his lips as the flashes of the battle played in his mind. He was proud of how his soldiers stood brave in the middle of all that terror.

When his army was finally on the ground and facing him, Enzo gave his people a once over before bowing down deeply to them - his way of thanking them for following him into battle. And with a small sad smile, Enzo made his way into the palace.

He wound through the corridors, making his way to the courtroom where he knew his parents would be speaking with their Generals. Enzo didn't bother about going to the infirmary to get his wounds healed. He didn't even bother to go back to his room to freshen up before meeting his family. No. Instead his legs took him directly to the Palace Courtroom.

Enzo only gave the staff and the guards a small, polite smile as he passed them. He would normally greet them cheerfully, but this was all he could muster at the moment. He tried not to wince as his sore muscles ached with every step he took, trying to put on a brave face in front of the palace staff.

It wasn't until Enzo was outside the closed Courtroom doors that he stopped. He stared at the giant door ornately carved with a leafless tree with its branches winding in the shape of a trident – the sigil of House al'Deran. Beneath the sigil were engraved in gold the slogan of House Deran - words that every al'Deran lived by.

Honor. Justice. Family.

Enzo nodded to the soldiers standing guard. As they opened the heavy doors, Enzo could see every head inside the Courtroom turn towards him.

In the middle of the Courtroom stood a large, ornately carved oval table. Enzo's father, King Rheon al'Deron, sat at the head of the table, while Enzo's mother, Anita Bashyr al'Deron, sat to the right. The other four chairs were occupied by his father's Generals and advisors.

As Enzo entered the courtroom, a smirk playing on his lips, Enzo saw his father get up from his seat. He only gave his father's Generals and advisors a small bow in acknowledgement.

"There he is!" King Rheon shouted, waving his Generals off as he stood.

His father hadn't changed much since the last time Enzo had seen him three months ago. King Rheon's graying hair was still combed back neatly without a hair out of place. His full graying beard was trimmed neatly. He was only an inch shorter than Enzo but Enzo had loved to point that out when he was younger. Not that he stopped now.

The closer Enzo got to his father, the more he could see how the stress of this war had aged him. The wrinkles around his eyes were more prominent. Even though King Rheon was smiling at his son, Enzo could see the dark circles lining his eyes and the frown lines marring his forehead.

King Rheon hugged Enzo before turning to his Generals standing by the table. "My son is finally back!" He shouted. "I'm throwing another feast! A celebration for my son's third successful battle!"

King Rheon didn't wait to see his Generals bowing to him as they left. Instead, he turned to look at his son again. His smile slowly fading as he gave his son a once over. Enzo saw his father's lips purse as he glanced at Enzo's wounds. His brow furrowing when he saw the blood on his son's shirt. King Rheon's hand moved down to Enzo's wounds, gently hovering over them as if he was afraid to hurt his son anymore than Enzo already was.

If Enzo was right, his father had already noticed him limp as he came into the Courtroom.

That cheer that his father had at his arrival seemed to pass when his father looked up at him again. Instead, it was replaced by a sad smile that quickly turned into a somber expression. "You need to be in the meeting tomorrow." He said, patting Enzo's cheek.

He let his hand rest on Enzo's cheek for a moment longer. His father's relieved expression was unmistakable. Relief that his son had come back safe. Injured... but safe.

Enzo recognized that look. He had the same look too. Happy to be back home but sad for the cost of his latest battle.

Queen Anita joined beside the two of them, seeming almost hesitant to hug Enzo. If Enzo had to guess, she was probably wondering if hugging him would hurt him further. He hadn't showered or even cleaned his wounds. And with mud possibly covering his face and body, Enzo was sure he looked like hell at the moment.

Instead Queen Anita searched Enzo's face – for what, Enzo didn't know. She might have gotten her answer because Queen Anita grasped onto his cheeks. She brought him down and placed a kiss on his forehead.

"Welcome back." She whispered, not letting him go.

"I always come back." Enzo said, cockily. His attitude only seemed to concern his mother further. Her brows furrowed as she pursed her lips. She placed her hands on her hips ready to chastise him. But before

Queen Anita could say anything else, Enzo changed the topic. "A feast, father? In my honor? I'm truly touched. Except something tells me that it's mostly an occasion for you to drink." Enzo joked. He didn't know if he could talk about this battle anytime soon.

"Ha!" King Rheon waved Enzo off. "I'm the King, you imbecile. I wouldn't need an occasion for me to drink."

"No, you're right. You just need mother's approval." Enzo smirked. The sheepish look his father gave his mother only made him chuckle.

It wasn't long before Enzo left the Courtroom. Ushered out by his parents as they urged him to get some rest before the feast. Enzo didn't want to go though. He didn't want to be alone. He was more afraid of the images that his mind conjured to remind him of the battle he'd just fought.

No, being with people was safe. Safe for him to forget the scenes of the massacres he'd witnessed in the battle. But with his parents urging him to get some rest, he couldn't deny them.

The entire way back to his chambers almost seemed like a daze. He didn't even remember walkin back. But that was where he was now.

Sitting at the end of his bed in his silent room, Enzo stared off into the distance. Although faint, Enzo could still hear the festivities and cheers from the crowd outside. Oh, what he'd give to have the noise of the cheers and crowds in his room right now. They would be just the distraction he needed.

But no...

Instead, the only thing he could hear in the quiet room was his heart-beat to a rhythm that only seemed to fasten as the seconds ticked by. He'd give anything to not have his mind go back to the last battle he'd just come from.

But that's where his mind went.

To the battle. To the screams of the villagers as they ran from the berserkers. One scream standing out above all else. The scream of a mother as she saw her child in the hands of the berserker. The berserkers' distorted screeches and snarls as they ripped bodies apart as they rampaged through the village.

Enzo had seen what the berserkers do to the ripped bodies. He knew of their bloodlust, but no one prepared him for his encounter with them. And how terrifying they'd truly be in person. Enzo felt a shudder crawl up his spine. He'd lost too many people from his army in this last battle.

Enzo knew his father and mother had been doing this for far longer. Although, he didn't know how they managed to stay sane. He'd finally understood the tiredness in his parent's eyes. After watching what the war could do...

He shook his head, trying to get the pictures and the screams out of his mind, but in the silence, they only seemed to intensify.

Closing his ears, Enzo shut his eyes, trying his best to calm himself. It didn't work though.

Focus on something, anything! He told himself.

But it was rarely ever that simple, was it?

Enzo slipped down from his bed, slinking into a dark corner as if trying to physically get away from the images in his head.

Desperation weighed heavily on his chest. Enzo's hands turned to fists as he tried to look around frantically to find something to calm himself. He shouted out in frustration. It didn't matter how much he tried to silence them, he could still hear the screams of the soldiers and villagers...

By the time the guards came to get him, Enzo was crouched down in the darkest part of his bedroom. His curtains were drawn and no lamps were lit. And in the silent darkness, Enzo sat, crouched down, with his hands covering his ears, as a lone tear ran down his cheek.

"It's time for the feast, your highness." The guard's voice came from the outside.

When Enzo didn't answer, his bedroom door slowly opened. Enzo didn't have the energy to tell the guard to leave him alone for another few minutes. He couldn't even breathe properly, much less form any words. Instead, he stayed quiet, hoping the darkness and the silence would send the guard away.

It was only when he felt a soft hand on his arm that he looked up to see his mother's concerned eyes looking down at him. The concern only reminded of the screams from the mother who cried for her child.

Enzo couldn't take it anymore.

He shut his eyes, not caring about the tears pouring down his cheeks.

He felt his mother bringing him closer to her in a hug. Rubbing soothing circles onto his back as she cradled his head, his mother said, "I'm not going to lie to you and say that it's going to be ok. And that you will be alright." She took in a deep breath before continuing. "But you will learn to cope. You will learn eventually, that even if it doesn't seem like it, you are actually helping."

This war had been going on their entire lives. It was being fought before they were born; it was being fought now; and it will continue to be fought after they die. There was no use in lying to him, telling him that what he would see wouldn't affect him anymore after sometime. There was no use in lying to him that he wouldn't see what he saw again.

Instead, like Anita said, he'd learn to cope. Because that was what she did. To escape from the atrocities she saw when she fought.

Anita learned to cope.

And so, Enzo would too.

Anita held his face in her hands, making him look up to her. That was the moment that Enzo recognized the heaviness in the gaze his mother carried.

Because it was the same one he'd be carrying from now on.

The heaviness brought on by the toll of war.

He wondered what his mother had seen that made her the way she was. Would he ever be able to be like her? But for now, Enzo just nodded.

The two of them stayed in the same position for a couple more minutes as Anita cradled Enzo. She brushed his hair gently, shushing him as he calmed down. When Eno finally felt like he could breathe again, he moved away from his mother. Stealing himself, he said with a smile, "The feast must have already started."

Anita waved him off. "Your father knows how to entertain. It's time for you to let yourself go. Forget the battle for one night. Just one night. That was the main reason your father set up this feast."

And so, that was what Enzo did.

The entire night, he gave no thought to the battle he'd just won. He didn't think of the people he'd lost. He didn't think of the berserker rampaging across the village. He acted as if the screams of the villagers didn't still puncture his eardrums even with the music blaring loudly in his ears and wine coursing through him.

Enzo walked around the banquet hall, laughing and talking. He was sure he didn't know half the people he was talking to. But they distracted him and they all laughed at anything he said. And their laugh was a noise he could replace from his memories of the battle. At least for now. At least until he fell asleep.

So, Enzo drank. He feasted. He flirted. He laughed. He ignored his parent's concerned looks. And he boasted. Throughout the night, he never let his glass go empty of the sweet wine in the banquet hall. By the time the feast ended, Enzo was more delirious than ever. All thoughts of the battle were in the back of his mind. Even in his daze, he knew those memories would come back in full force when he'd be sober the next day.

But that would be a worry for when he woke up.

For now, Enoz had no sense of time or direction. He honestly didn't know how he made it back to his bedroom.

But the moment his head hit his pillow, there was only one thing on his mind.

Deep, deep sleep.

And for once his body and mind complied.

5

"Why is he here?" – Enzo

ENZO GROANED AS HE woke up. He clutched onto his ribs, wincing as he lifted himself off his bed. Heaving a deep sigh, he looked around his room. Everything was just as it was before he left for the battle.

There was barely any sunlight entering his room thanks to the thick red and gold curtains covering the windows to his bedroom. Although Enzo could still hear the bustle of the town outside. The clanking of the carriage wheels against the cobblestone, the horses neighing, the people shouting as they went about their day, the shouts of the soldiers training on the palace grounds... all the sounds Enzo was thankful to have replaced the ones in his nightmares.

His wounds had mostly healed themselves in the night. But he could still feel how sore his muscles were.

Well, this is going to be interesting. Enzo thought. Letting out a loud audible breath, Enzo sighed as his soreness slowly subsided. Shaking his head, Enzo tried to focus on what he had to do for the rest of the day.

He was supposed to be in a meeting with his parents and their Generals that morning. But Enzo was starting to question if he wanted to go to the meeting.

That thought gave him pause for a moment. He could ditch it. Spend the time outside, in the gardens, and maybe even escape the palace for the day. His mind conjured up images of a quiet countryside, where he could imagine a life much more simpler. A life without the darkness that was threatening to swallow the land. It was very tempting. So very tempting.

But his father's words about meeting him in the Courtroom echoed in his mind, making Enzo sigh loudly in the quiet room.

Honor. Justice. Family.

Unfortunately, two of those things called to him to do the right thing. Enzo shook his head and bit his lip.

No, he had to do this. But he cherished the thought of the countryside for a moment longer. It didn't hurt to dream though.

Enzo took a deep breath. He let the memory of the battle wash over him as he went about his daily morning routine in solitude. He could see the weight of the last battle staring back at him in the mirror. So much that Enzo couldn't even recognize himself. Although that could also be because of the cuts and bruises that were evident on his face.

When he finally deemed himself ready to face the day. Enzo squared his shoulders as he left his chambers.

He didn't care for his breakfast as he hurried straight for the Court-room, only greeting the staff and other ministers with a simple nod. He nodded his greeting to the soldiers guarding the doors to the palace courtroom. Enzo didn't even bother to wait for the guards to open the door to the Courtroom.

Instead, Enzo simply walked in, not wanting to draw any attention to himself as he took his seat opposite his mother at the table. His father sat - or rather stood as he was doing now - at the head of the table, looking down at the map laid out.

The map of Indresal and all its kingdoms was stretched out, spanning the entire table. Little figurines of varying colors representing different kingdoms were placed on the map at different landscapes to show the areas with ongoing battle.

Although one color was more prominent in all of Indresal than any others.

Black.

Figurines which represented the influence of the dark one. Kingdoms that fell under the Dark Ones' rule were covered in a black cloth. A symbol of the silent mourning of the people and the kingdom that were lost.

And unfortunately for the remaining kingdoms of Indresal, the area the black cloth covered only seemed to increase.

Enzo's lips pursed at the sight. The black cloth cloth covered a lot more than when he saw it three months ago before going into battle. His one small victory seemed abysmal when compared to the amount the Dark One's disciples covered.

Enzo leaned forward, his eyes squinting as he listened to General Dhira.

General Dhira was one of the longest serving members under King Rheon. He'd watched Enzo grow from a mere baby to taking charge on the battlefield. In fact, he was the one that taught Enzo everything he knew. He sometimes made Enzo wonder how old the General truly was.

General Dhira's white hair was combed back into a slick bun just like King Rheon's. Although, unlike King Rheon, there were no stray strands of hair that fell from General Dhira's bun. His brown skin glistened against the rays of sunshine that came through the high windows in the Courtroom. His dark brown eyes scanned the map once again as he rubbed his chin.

"We've been hearing of random berserker attacks on the Illadoran pass here." Dhira pointed to the passageway between two mountains connecting Illadora and Qadia.

"Random?" Enzo asked, frowning. "Aren't berserkers supposed to be controlled by one of the Dark One's Disciples? Why would they be attacking randomly then?"

"They are. But our reports suggest that there was no one from the Inner Circle on the battlefield controlling them." Dhira said, shaking his head.

"They can't be rogue." Queen Anita shook her head, mumbling to herself.

Couldn't they? Enzo wondered. The Disciples controlled their berserkers with an iron grip. Literally. The bracelet that all Disciples wore golden bracelets infused with their magic. And each berserker created had a shackle placed around the berserker's neck infused with the same magic of the Disciple whose orders the berserker was supposed to follow.

In all the stories that Enzo heard throughout his life, he hadn't heard of a berserker being released from its shackles - voluntarily or not. Unless...

Unless, the berserkers weren't supposed to be released at all. *Could it have been a mistake?* Enzo's brows furrowed. Would it be possible for a berserker that had accidentally been released? Would that mean that the Disciples are losing their control? Possibly losing their power as well.

Hope bubbled with Enzo's chest. But Enzo quickly shook his head, squashing it. He looked at the map again. He looked at all the black cloth covering the areas of the Dark One's reigned over. With how much power they wielded, why would his Disciples lose their power now? It was more likely that the berserker's shackles were broken during a battle nearby.

Could the berserkers even break the shackles around their neck? Even by accident? Enzo wondered. He was taught that the metal used for the shackles was unbreakable.

Maybe the shackles weren't broken. That thought brought Enzo to a pause. If the shackles were not broken, that'd mean that the berserkers were not there by chance.

"The region has been our stronghold for the past ten years." Enzo mumbled just loud enough that everyone at the table could listen. "The Disciples have been trying to get through the pass for so long. But they couldn't. If the berserkers are from the previous battles, the Disciples could have left some of the beasts before they retreated."

"The battle you're talking about happened almost a year ago." General Dhira refuted. He clasped his hands behind his back as he stood straight as a pole. "If that's the case then, we'd have gotten reports of the berserker attacks sooner. No berserker can go that long without..." Dhira cleared his throat. "...food."

Enzo felt a shudder crawl down his spine at that word. He knew what that 'food' entailed and tried his best not to think about it.

"Besides," Rheon started. "all berserkers are linked to the Disciples. None of them are truly out of their hold. If they're attacking now and this randomly, it's because their dark one commanded the Disciples to do it."

"How is the Illadoran front holding up?" Anita asked, her brow furrowing.

To anyone, she might have looked like a concerned Queen plotting the next move. Their next strategy. But Enzo could tell just from the tension in her jaw that she was worried. After all, the Illadoran King was her own brother.

"Crown Prince Aryan Bashyr and his troops are on the front lines. Our reports say that they are able to thwart several attacks. We haven't received any communication in the past few weeks, however. None of our messages have been reaching them either and we haven't received any requests for assistance. The entire kingdom seems to be a black spot for us. We don't know of anything that's happening there."

Enzo didn't look up to see which of the General's was speaking. He was too focused on his mother and her reaction. To anyone else, she didn't seem to react at all. But Anita's slow deep exhale was the only sign that Enzo could see about how the news was affecting her. There was no news of her brother or his wife. Her nephew, Enzo's cousin, was on the front lines with his army.

With no news coming from Illadora, Enzo began to wonder just how dire the situation was. Were they being swarmed by the berserkers that much that Aryan couldn't send out a message? Enzo's heart sped as worry gripped his chest making it hard for him to breathe.

"Our soldiers have just returned. I know we just won ours." Anita turned to give Enzo a small smile. "But our soldiers need rest too." She turned to King Rheon. "Let's wait for a couple more weeks. Illadora should have everything under control. If not, we can send our soldiers there. By that time, our army should have enough time to recuperate."

That was a sound plan. A solid plan, in fact. A plan that was best for everyone involved.

But Enzo didn't like it.

"What if they need help right now?" Enzo chimed in.

"What do you mean, son?" Rheon asked.

"We're trying to send them battle reports and strategies. But none of them seem to reach them. What if they're trying to ask for help? But none of their messages are reaching us? Messages should go both ways, usually"

Rheon rubbed his lip as he thought for a moment. Finally, nodding, he asked. "What do you suggest then?"

Enzo's brows raised in surprise. He hadn't realized his father would agree so quickly.

"I can teleport i-" Enzo didn't have the chance to complete his sentence before his mother and General Dhira interrupted him.

"No!" They all but screamed. Anita looked at her husband sitting at the head of the table with his fingers rubbing his lips, as if he was entertaining the thought. "Don't tell me you're actually considering this!"

"That's a fool's plan, Prince Enzo." General Dhira tried to speak some sense into him. But Enzo's mind had been made up.

"But it's a plan that'll get us the information we need. And all of us know that I'm the only one that can do this." Enzo said with a finality. Hoping that the confidence he was feigning would make them agree. Enzo turned to his mother, pursing his lips, trying to get her to understand. "So, unless you know anyone else that can create portals and transport themselves to Illadora..."

"And just like our messages, what if you can't enter Illadora?" Anita asked.

"We won't know until we try." Enzo shrugged.

Although, Anita's expression made it clear she didn't appreciate his sass at that moment.

Enzo leaned towards his mother. "You know this is the only way." He urged. "If they need help right now, and we wait for a couple weeks before even sending them an army, we'd have lost Illadora."

When his mother didn't respond, Enzo shifted in his seat again. He saw her looking at Rheon and Dhira - a silent communication that Enzo wasn't privy to. The three of them had known each other for so long that they didn't need any words to communicate. He could see his mother stiffen in her seat. She took in a deep breath before turning to look at Enzo. Her posture had changed. She pursed her lips and sat straighter, her shoulders arched back as she leaned against her chair.

That was no longer his mother he was looking at.

That was Anita Bashyr al'Deron. Queen of Ravendore.

"In that case," She said. Her voice did not betray any emotion. Rather, it held a finality that even Enzo wouldn't date to cross. "You can go ahead for a one day mission. This is just to report what's going on in the front lines. You will not partake in the battle. If there's any sign of danger, you will return immediately." Her pointed look was fixated on Enzo as she stressed out the word 'immediately'. "And lastly, you will take ten of our best soldiers."

The smile on Enzo's face grew but was cut short when he noticed the scowl on his mother's face.

One day.

That was all it took for Enzo to prepare for the mission. Not many people knew about it either. And with how few soldiers were actually going on this mission, it wasn't hard to get them ready.

All night, he'd hoped that the mission would just be a bust. He hoped that nothing actually happened on the front lines of Illadora. That everything was under control. But the pit that formed in his stomach at the very thought of Illadora told him a different story.

The pit didn't go away even after he woke up to get ready for the mission. Rather, it only seemed to deepen.

It didn't take him long to understand what that pit was though.

Because the moment Enzo and his band of soldiers stepped out of the portal and into the Illadoran forests, they were bombarded with screams of soldiers running away. Ash filled the air as trees around them stood ablaze. What were once tents were now only pieces of charred cloth on the forest ground. Everywhere he turned, Enzo could only see wounded soldiers and the healers trying to heal them as they escaped the inferno.

But what caught his attention were the horde of berserkers stampeding in their direction like a dark wave blocking all light. It didn't matter how many times Enzo encountered the berserkers during battle. Seeing them in battle always made his heart race in fear.

Enzo turned back to his troop. "Get as many soldiers out as you can." He shouted at them. "I'll keep the portal open!"

He ignored all the bruises that were still ailing him. Not caring for how tired he still felt. He could feel the energy draining him with every second he left the portal open. But Enzo couldn't care about himself. Not now. Not this moment. Instead, Enzo mustered all the strength that he had, pictured the courtyard to his palace before lifting his hands to open the portal.

Enzo struggled to keep the portal open as more soldiers dashed into him. Enzo shouted in frustration as his portal fizzled out.

He tried his best to create another portal but with the berserkers closing in, Enzo turned to his troops. "Retreat! We'll portal somewhere else!" He shouted at them.

Enzo turned around to see the horde of berserkers rampaging through the forest. In the midst of all the berserkers running about stood a black horse charging at them. But it wasn't the horse that caught Enzo's attention.

No.

It was the man sitting on the horse, hands spread in the air around him as the dark magic swirled between them that caught Enzo's attention. His long silky graying hair flying with the wind, his black eyes staring with glee as the berserkers tore through the army ranks, his magic tearing through the blockades the Illadorans had set up like they were paper... No, there was no mistaking that man.

Damon al' Kara... Enzo's eyes widened. One of the disciples was here. *What's he doing here?*

He felt his heart racing as sweat began to drip from his temple. In all the battles he'd fought, he hadn't encountered any of the disciples.

And now, he was faced with one of the oldest and most feared ones.

For a moment, Enzo stood rooted to the spot. Screams from the soldiers seemed to fade into the distance as he could only focus on Damon's cackles. None of the soldiers dashing him as they ran away from the berserkers made Enzo tear his gaze away from the Disciple. He could see Damon raise his hands, dark black flames covering his hands. Stories didn't do the Disciple any justice. They only spoke of the fear he evoked whenever he brought out the dark flames. A power given to him by the Dark One himself.

It was only when one of Damon's fire hit the tree near Enzo, sending it hurtling down on some unsuspecting soldiers that Enzo snapped himself out of his reverie.

"Out!" He shouted at the soldiers again. "Retreat! Back here!"

He'd hoped his voice would help guide the panicking soldiers a direction to follow. Although in the back of his mind, he knew that drawing their attention would also draw the attention of the berserkers and Damon. Enzo didn't care though.

If he could distract Damon and his berserkers long enough, maybe he can save a few of the Illadoran soldiers.

Enzo could feel his heart thud in his chest. Every shout, every step, every noise he made...

That was until he saw Damon's attention turn towards him, his dark magic still swirling as wisps around his hands. Enzo's eyes widened as he involuntarily took a step back. He shut his eyes preparing for the blow.

But the blow never came.

And the more he waited, the more he felt like something was shaking him. Or rather someone.

It wasn't a violent shake. The gentle touch contrasted with everything he was feeling at the moment. He could hear a voice in the distance.

Enzo jolted awake. His hands turned into fists as he wailed around. He gazed around the room wildly as his confusion slowly set in.

He was not on the battlefield any longer. Nor was he in his own chambers at his castle.

No, was this...

It couldn't be.

6

"She said this world had no Magic." –Enzo

NZO BLINKED IN CONFUSION as he studied the room around him. He looked at the study desk and the bookshelf beside it. His figurine on the bookshelf was nowhere to be seen though. All the pictures of him that were once there were gone as well.

He was back at Aliya's place.

Enzo tried to take in deep breaths to calm himself down. But no matter how many deep breaths he took, his heart only seemed to race. He could feel his breaths coming in short. His lungs burned from the lack of air. He gripped the bed sheets tightly, trying to hold onto something, anything that could give him a semblance of reality.

He could still remember the fear when he first saw Damon on the battlefield. He could still hear the screams of the soldiers as they ran for their lives. He could still remember the heat from the burning forest that had surrounded him just moments before.

A chill ran up his spine as the memories of that night came rushing in.

Enzo almost swatted away the hand that reached out to him. It was only when he saw that the hand belonged to Aliya that he'd stopped.

He looked up to see Aliya staring down at him apprehensively.

Don't go. He wanted to say. *Please stay.*

But even though he opened his lips, no words seemed to come out. He knew he looked like a gaping fish trying to get the words out. So, he finally just stopped.

Aliya seemed to understand though, because the next thing she did was sit down beside him on the bed. She reached out, placing her hand gently on his arm as she rubbed soothing circles on it. He tried focusing on her smooth hands gliding along his skin, grounding him to the world around him.

He was here now.

He was no longer in Indresal. Damon was no longer chasing him. He was safe...

...At least for now.

It took Enzo a moment to realize that Aliya was speaking to him. "It's going to be ok. You're safe now. You're going to be ok." She continued to whisper, not stopping the small circles she rubbed on his arm.

Enzo focused on the feeling of her hand. Her touch brought with it a sense of comfort that he'd missed. It reminded him of his mother's embrace when he came back from his last battle.

"Breathe with me." Aliya said, as she turned to face him.

Slowly taking in a deep breath and letting it out. Once. Then a second time. Eventually enough times that Enzo could feel himself calming down. Although, he was more exhausted than before he went to bed.

Taking a deep breath, he looked down at the hand that was still holding onto his hand. He followed up the arm to gaze up into Aliya's concerned eyes staring down at him.

Enzo didn't know what she might have seen in his expression but her concern only seemed to grow.

"You were moaning." Aliya said, her lips pouting in concern.

When he raised his eyebrow, she continued, flustered. "Not like that. Like you were in pain. Do you need your dressings changed?" Aliya rushed out, stumbling over her words. She blinked furiously as a blush slowly crept its way tinging her cheeks pink.

Her audible gulp just made Enzo's smirk widen. He couldn't help it. Teasing her was almost becoming too addicting. She was making it too easy to tease.

Aliya looked around his bare chest, trying to avoid his eyes as she checked the bandages. Enzo's eyes never left her face though. He couldn't even if he wanted to. Enzo gave her a small smile before tapping her hand still on his arm.

It was only then that he realized how close they were sitting. He could feel her breath fan over his face as he looked at her.

Aliya pursed her lips and gulped again, shifting Enzo's gaze from her eyes to her lips. He could see a faint blush creep up her ears and smirked. He looked up into her eyes once more before leaning closer.

Enzo just wanted to see if she would blush again. "I'm sorry I scared you. It's ok. It's just a bad dream." He said. He was definitely not going to tell her what the dream was about. Enzo didn't want to worry her any more than she already was. "Thank you."

Aliya, however, could only seem to blink in response. Finally, as if shaking herself from a dream, she cleared her throat and removed her hand from his arm, much to Enzo's dismay. She stood up, stepping as far away from the bed as her small bedroom allowed, making Enzo chuckle.

"You, um..." Aliya took a step back, licking and biting her bottom lip, a habit Enzo realized she did when she was nervous. "I mean, I found the author's address." Was all she said before rushing out of the bedroom.

Enzo could only chuckle as he saw Aliya shuffle out of the bedroom. But the moment Aliya left the room, his sobering thoughts came back with a force that made him slump back.

Heaving a heavy sigh, Enzo grunted as he got out of his bed. He clutched his sides and let out a low groan as he limped out of the bedroom.

Is this how humans without powers coped? Enzo huffed, walking into the living room.

Aliya returned back to her spot on the sofa. She pushed her glasses up as she leaned closer to look at her computer.

Since when did she wear glasses? Enzo wondered. He was about to sit beside her when Aliya chimed in.

"There's food on the dining table for you. I made some rice and dal. I think you'll like it." Aliya muttered, not lifting her head once from her computer.

Enzo didn't know what the food she named was but he was grateful either way. His smile only widened when he spotted the food she'd plated for him. Not that Aliya saw the smile with how her head was stuck in the laptop. Grabbing the plate, Enzo took his place beside Aliya as she continued to write the address to the author's house.

"So, you found her?" Enzo said, humming as he took a bite out of the rice and dal.

Aliya yelped, not expecting him to sit so close to her. Enzo knew he probably shouldn't startle her too badly. But it was getting impossible not to. It was almost like a temptation. Her little yelps, the way her skin turned pink, and goosebumps rose on her arms, made him want to tease her more.

Shifting her eyes back to the computer and blinking furiously, Aliya nodded. "She has a couple houses. One here and another on the west coast. I've already sent her an email about our situation but I'm pretty sure she'd think we're crazy when she reads it." Aliya rolled her eyes, shaking her head. "But her house here is a little over a hundred miles away. So, we can check that one first."

"A hundred miles..." Enzo was starting to feel defeated. Without his ability to create portals, how long was it going to take them to reach the writer.

It'd take days!

His fear of being trapped in a new world without being of any assistance to his family or army in the battle was starting to weigh on him. If only he had his powers, they'd be there already. But he didn't. And now, they were going to have to travel for days just to reach the author.

Enzo didn't realize how consumed he was with his thoughts. The spoon he almost brought to his lips hung in mid-air as he dazed off into the distance. With a defeated sigh, he asked. "How long is that going to take us to reach her?"

"Oh, a couple hours." Aliya waved him off.

Enzo placed the spoon back on the plate. Was this a sick joke that she was playing? How could someone travel hundreds of miles in a few hours? Enzo's brows furrowed. He didn't know if she was joking. A way to get back at him for the teasing he'd been doing ever since Enzo had found a figurine of him. Surely, she couldn't be that cruel. But the expression on her face told him that she was serious.

"A couple hours? Are you sure?" Enzo was expecting the answer to be somewhere around a couple days. Not a couple hours. Questions swirled in his mind if that was even possible.

"Oh, I forgot. It's football season. There's going to be a ton of traffic. So maybe add in another couple hours. It's Saturday today. So, maybe if we leave before the game starts, we should be able to get out of town. But there's also the tailgating..."

Aliya continued to mumble to herself as she looked at the time and date. None of what she said made any sense to Enzo, however.

"It'll only take us a few hours to cover the hundred miles?" He asked skeptically, again.

"A Hundred and twenty miles approximately. But yes. Without traffic." Aliya smiled at him. She tilted her head as if she did not understand his predicament.

"Just a few hours."

Aliya simply laughed. "Yes, we're taking my car. It's not like we're walking the entire way to Kiana's house. That's her name by the way. Kiana Roberts."

Honestly, he'd expected them to be walking the entire way to the writer's - Kiana's - house. Maybe a horse ride. He wasn't expecting them to be taking that contraption - the car, as Aliya put it.

Is that car even safe?

No, he wasn't going to voice that. She was already sensitive about that death trap she called a car. If she was going to take him to the writer, he was going to make sure to stay on her good side.

Enzo simply nodded, continuing to eat his food. "And what if she isn't there? You said she had two houses."

"Yeah, her other house is on the west coast. In LA. If she's not at her house here, then we could probably check there next. And I could use a vacation."

"How far away is that?" Enzo asked, taking another bite of his food.

"About two thousand miles away." Aliya shrugged.

"Let me guess. It'll take us only a couple hours to get there as well." He chuckled, still not completely believing Aliya. A couple hours to travel that distance was not possible without a portal... or at least that was what Enzo thought.

"No, It'll take about four hours by flight."

"WHAT?" He choked out. Enzo coughed as the food got stuck in his throat.

Four hours?! There was no way. She had to be joking!

"Oh no! That's right! You don't have a driver's license. You don't have any identification." Aliya mumbled to herself. "We can't go by flight. We have to drive across the country. So, that'll take us three days?" She pursed her lips thinking. Aliya didn't look at him. She was much more absorbed in her own world, calculating the distance and all the things they needed to get there. She tapped the pen on her bottom lip as she counted. "Yup, three days. Especially if we have to take short breaks for food and sleep."

Enzo didn't know how to respond to that.

Three days? Three days?! That was all his mind could repeat.

Enzo didn't even notice Aliya placing the computer on the coffee table and getting up. He didn't even notice her going into her bedroom.

It was only when a piece of cloth hit him square in his face that he snapped back.

"That's my ex's clothes. I don't know why I still have them. So, don't ask." Aliya said, offhandedly. "But you guys look about the same size. You can change into them after you finish eating. We can go when you're done."

7

"This has to be the Twilight Zone, I'm Sure."
– Aliya

"THREE HOURS, SHE SAID." Aliya heard Enzo mutter. "It'll only take three hours with traffic at most, she said. Now, I'm stuck in this contraption." Enzo huffed.

Contraption?! Aliya thought, incredulously. Her eyes almost bugged out at how he described her car. Her baby.

Favorite character or not, she was not going to let anyone insult her car. This was her car. And her car was doing its job perfectly fine, thank you very much.

They'd been stuck in traffic for the past hour and a half.

Aliya had been right about the football season. She'd told him to hurry up with getting ready. But no, Enzo took his own sweet time wearing the gray sweatpants and hoodie. Although it didn't help that he pulled the sleeves to expose his forearm, making Aliya gulp every time she looked at him.

But unfortunately for her, they started their journey late... and now they were stuck in traffic.

Thank you, Enzo.

However, with the number of people tailgating and driving in for the game, Aliya and Enzo were barely out of town even after a couple hours. There was no place to move as cars lined bumper to bumper. Tents were lined on the grassy knoll beside the road.

Cheers erupted from the tailgaters as they prepared for the evening of fun. Music blared from all around them as people danced, waiting for the games to begin. With the clear skies and the gentle breeze blowing, it would have been the perfect day for the game. Perfect atmosphere to spend time with loved ones.

But that wasn't the atmosphere in the car. Enzo complained about the music she was playing

"It was too loud!" Enzo said when she played Imagine Dragons.

He outright rejected Harry Styles. Aliya was happy when he nodded along as Bruno Mars crooned '24K Magic'. He bobbed his head along with the sweet notes of a couple BTS songs one of Aliya's friends had suggested a few days ago.

"It's too..." Enzo pulled a sour expression when Taylor Swift began to sing. "Slow." Aliya almost threw him out of the car right then and there. 'Wildest Dreams' was her favorite song. And his opinion was *not* needed. It took everything in her to not do just that.

Calm down. Calm down. Calm down. She chanted. *God, give me patience so I don't kill him.*

Instead of listening to him, Aliya increased the volume as Taylor sang 'Wildest Dreams'. She'd gotten tired of his complaints with every song though. Finally with a huff, she'd turned off the spotify, choosing the silence over his complaining.

74

Aliya tried to be accommodating. She really did. He'd essentially moved to a different world where the rules of his world didn't apply. But now, she was at her wit's end with his complaining.

"When will this traffic move?" He whined again. "This is getting ridiculous. At this rate it'd be faster if we just walked."

Aliya was starting to think that might be true as the sun started to dip below the horizon.

"How are we getting to Kiana in a few hours if we don't even move?"

"If you're so bored with sitting, why don't you conjure up your portals?" Aliya finally snapped.

Enzo's eyes widened in shock. He sulked, frowning as he faced forward. Enzo folded his hands, looking more like a sulking child than the Crown Prince of a Kingdom. Aliya hadn't raised her voice the entire time she was with him. But now, he was looking at her as if he'd discovered a new side to her.

When Enzo didn't answer, Aliya simply nodded.

"Yeah, that's what I thought." Aliya said. "Now, shut up, and listen to the music." This time Aliya turned on the radio. She held up a finger. "And I don't want to hear any commentary about the music. We'll get there when we get there."

He didn't respond back.

There was peace.

Finally.

There were no complaints about the music. There shouldn't have been any complaints in the first place. Aliya knew she had excellent taste in music. There weren't any complaints about the traffic either. Just peace and quiet with the soft sounds of the radio playing in the background. Aliya turned around to look at Enzo, only to find him sulking in the same position.

Good. She thought, looking back at the road. *Stay that way.*

Biting her lip, Aliya elected to ignore him until they reached Kiana's house.

Which didn't take as long once the traffic started to move. Aliya giggled every time she turned to look at Enzo. He admired the way the other cars whizzed past them. He admired the lights from the cars and the buildings surrounding them. As the sun set, letting the city lights shine, Enzo became more enthralled with all that surrounded him. To Aliya, his wide eyed amazement just looked like a kid on their first day at Disneyland.

It took everything in her not to chuckle at his reactions. They were unnecessarily cute for a 70-year old elf.

Although he did complain occasionally that he couldn't see the stars, and eventually, just fell asleep with his head leaning on the window. Smiling, Aliya reduced the volume of the radio and drove the rest of the way silently.

It was only when Aliya parked her car in the alley beside Kiana's house a couple hours later that she turned to look at Enzo again. He was fast asleep, his mouth hanging open. He craned his neck, shifting in his seat trying to get into a more comfortable position.

"You look much better when you're silent." She muttered to herself before gently shaking Enzo awake.

Enzo's eyes fluttered open. Turning around to look at Aliya, he asked. "Are we there yet?"

Aliya nodded. She chuckled as he yawned and stretched. His back cracked in several places making her grimace.

Oh, that must have felt good. She thought.

"Not bad." Enzo mumbled as he got out of the car to look at Kiana's house. Aliya had to admit he was right. "It's much bigger than your house." He said, earning himself a side eye from Aliya.

She had to admit though. Kiana's house was not only bigger but looked more beautiful from the outside. She could only imagine how Kiana's house would look on the inside.

The house was a two-storey building that looked like it was straight out of a magazine. The floodlights around the house accentuated the carvings on the house. Aliya and Enzo walked the path leading from the driveway to the stairs. They stepped past the two giant pillars on either side of the entrance to the front door.

Aliya smiled into the camera before ringing the bell once... and then a second time. And then a third.

But no matter how long she waited, Kiana didn't answer the door.

"I don't think she's home." Aliya mumbled.

"What? That's it?" Enzo asked, incredulously.

"What else do you want me to do? She could be here. She could be at a party or one of her other houses. She may not even be in this country." Aliya answered back as she stepped down the stairs.

"How do you know that she's not inside?"

"In case you hadn't noticed, she didn't answer." Aliya pointed to the unopened front door. That should have been obvious.

"Fine. Maybe she has the information in one of her books that's inside."

Aliya looked at him skeptically. Her eyes narrowed at what he was implying. "Yes, she possibly could have. Which was why I brought you here so we could talk to her."

Aliya could see a glint in Enzo's eyes. It was only for a brief second before Enzo bolted from the front porch. Aliya's gaze snapped at him as she watched him run to the side of Kiana's house. She scratched her head, not knowing what to do as she looked around. Finally, she decided it'd be best if she just followed Enzo.

She ran behind him coming to a sudden stop when she saw what he was doing.

"Are you crazy?" She whispered loudly at him.

Enzo walked up to the open window on the first floor. He winced, holding his chest, as he stepped over the shrubs that lined the outside of the window. Crouching down, Enzo parted the curtains slightly to peak inside. But in the dark house, there wasn't much he could see.

"I don't think there's anyone inside." He whispered back.

"Yes, we kind of figured that when she didn't answer the door! Now, let's go!" Aliya gestured wildly to her car. She turned around, hoping he'd follow her. But when he didn't, she groaned, stomping at the ground like a child.

But Enzo didn't listen. Instead he stood up, not caring who might see him and placed one leg on the windowsill.

"No, no, no, no." Aliya muttered to herself.

She tried to rush towards him, trying her best to stop him from doing anything drastic. But before she could say anything, Enzo ducked and jumped inside the house.

Aliya could do nothing but stare dumbfounded at the empty spot where Enzo once stood.

"What the-" She blinked, still looking at the spot. "No. No. No." She could just leave. Just let Enzo do whatever crazy plan he had conjured up.

She didn't have to get involved. Everything would be fine. No one knew she was here anyway.

But he'd be alone. Her mind added unhelpfully. *And he doesn't know about our world.*

"No, Aliya, you can't do that." She told herself as she started to walk back to her car. Although every step she took made her feel like she was missing out on the opportunity of a lifetime. Her hands turned into a fist as her resolve began to weaken. "No, you will go to jail if you do this!" She told herself again.

But the urge to solve this mystery that was Enzo was eating at her. She walked back and forth, rubbing her hands, trying to ease her tension.

Finally with a dry sob for herself, Aliya turned around. "I'm going to jail. And then I'm going to get thrown out of college. And then I'll have to live my life somehow. And all for what, a stupid mystery because my favorite character came to visit me."

She continued to mutter to herself as she climbed and stepped over the windowsill and into Kiana's house.

"Enzo?" She called out quietly in the dark house.

There was barely any light anywhere. Aliya held out her hand, hoping they could feel what she couldn't see. She winced a few times bumping into Kiana's furniture. She palmed her surroundings, holding onto a hard table... no, not table. Was that a counter?

Is this the kitchen? Aliya wondered. She got her answer when she felt a large block with a knife set. *Yup, the kitchen.* She thought. *Who leaves the kitchen window open?*

Aliya really wanted to turn on the lights. She couldn't see anything. And the lack of light pouring in from the outside wasn't helping either. Aliya yelped when she felt another hand clasp hers.

"Calm down, it's only me." Enzo said, still holding onto her hand.

"This is breaking and entering." Aliya whispered back.

Enzo looked at her confused. "Yes, we're breaking into the house. What part of this is confusing to you?"

"We could go to jail for this." She muttered back but it seemed that Enzo didn't care. He didn't answer. Instead, he was more focused on searching for the book. Or the author's notes. Or something that'd allude to Indresal. Whatever he was looking for, Aliya was definitely not getting through to him.

Might as well get out of here with as little damage as possible. She gave up trying to convince him.

"What are you looking for?" Aliya asked, finally giving up on convincing him.

"Her library or really, any book that looks like it could contain her notes on my world."

"That's a really broad search, don't you think?" Aliya asked, confused. This could take hours and who knows? Maybe Kiana would be back home by then.

"Do you have any other ideas?" Enzo asked. Although Aliya's silence was answer enough. "Yeah, I thought not."

Aliya nodded, finally conceding, before realizing that he probably couldn't see her in the dark. "Fine."

She tried to walk away from him but his grip on her hand only hardened.

"We're searching together." Was all he said before walking in the dark.

The two of them walk about the house making as little noise as possible. The only sounds that were heard were one of them bumped into the furniture or into each other. Neither of them wanted to turn on the lights or bring any attention to the fact that there were people in the house.

"You know, I thought there was going to be more security for her house. Don't you think we got in very easily?"

Enzo just grunted in response.

"Does she have a library? I don't see any books anywhere?" Enzo mumbled.

"How am I supposed to know? It's not like I've been here before." Aliya whispered back before turning a corner. "This looks like an office."

Aliya pulled Enzo towards her as she opened the door to the office. Neither of them could see anything in the office in the dark.

The curtained windows barely let any moonlight into the room.

As Aliya felt around the room, she stumbled across the shelves in the office. "How does she have so many books?" She whispered.

"The information has to be here somewhere. Let's just check everything." Enzo whispered back.

"Or it could be somewhere in her house in LA." Aliya muttered to herself.

"Let's focus on one house at a time, yeah?" Enzo said.

Aliya stumbled as she felt the books across the shelves. She brought her phone up to light the books as she walked past the shelves. She could feel Enzo close behind her, his breath tickling her shoulder.

"How about you check the desk? Maybe it'll have the information you need?" A voice spoke up in the darkness.

Aliya was about to answer back when she realized that the voice was not Enzo's. Holding onto her phone, Aliya spun around to the voice. She gasped in shock when she noticed that they weren't alone in the room.

The light from her phone illuminated the other woman in the room. Sitting in the chair behind the desk was a middle-aged woman. No, not just any middle-aged woman. There sitting in the chair in the darkness was Kiana, staring back at them.

Aliya would have assumed that the woman would be furious to see her and Enzo walking about in her house. But instead, Kiana just smirked. Her smile only spread when she turned on the light to her study.

Aliya blinked in pain when the lights of the room turned on. She brought her phone back down, turning off the flashlight. Aliya wanted to apologize. She wanted to say something, anything, that would get them out of this predicament. But no words came out as Aliya could feel her throat go dry.

Aliya was so shocked and dumbfounded by the woman sitting in front of her that Aliya couldn't look anywhere else.

Kiana sat leaning on her leather chair, leg on her knee, and head held high as if a Queen sitting on her throne. Kiana played with the signet on her ring finger as she looked over Aliya, analyzing her. Kiana's expressionless face only made the situation that much more intimidating for Aliya.

Aliya gulped, trying to think of something to break the awkwardness of the situation. But her mind was completely devoid of any thoughts at the moment. She couldn't even think of a lie to get her and Enzo out of this.

Her unwavering gaze was trained on Kiana as she admired her favorite author. So much so that she didn't have a chance to get a good look at Kiana's office.

Kiana's office was everything Aliya had dreamt of.

Ornately carved wooden bookshelves lined one entire wall adorned with books of all genres and trinkets that Aliya could only dream of buying. The painting on the other wall seemed to depict a happy family of four laughing in the meadow. A man bounced a toddler on the grass as a woman and a young boy laughed, gazing lovingly at the baby girl.

Standing towards the window was Kiana's desk and chair which she was sitting in at the moment. A large window with a carved windowsill stood behind her. In the daylight, Aliya would have been able to see green woods that covered the back of the house.

But alas...

Aliya saw none of it.

Her gaze was completely trained on the woman sitting in front of her. Aliya could see the headlines right now.

Crazed fan breaks into her favorite author's house. Says her favorite character made her do it.

Oh, she was not going to jail.

They're going to throw her in the asylum.

No, she had to salvage this somehow. This was not the impression she wanted to leave on her favorite author.

When she looked back up at Kiana, Aliya's eyes were scrunched in confusion. Kiana was looking past her, training her unwavering gaze on Enzo. Aliya could see Kiana's eyes widen almost comically.

Aliya wondered if that was how she looked like when she saw Enzo. But what Kiana said next surprised even Aliya.

Kiana rushed to get up from her leather chair, not caring that it rolled back and hit the window behind with a force that made Aliya jump. Kiana walked around her desk. Holding her hands in front of her, Kiana tilted her head as a bow. Her eyes stayed trained to the floor.

"My prince. You're here."

8

"I am definitely in the Twilight Zone." – Aliya

ALIYA CONTINUED TO STARE in shock at Kiana. She'd heard what Kiana said. She just couldn't understand the situation in front of her right now.

Kiana hadn't moved from her position since she greeted Enzo. Not knowing what else to do, Aliya turned to Enzo, who seemed to look just as shocked as she was at the moment.

"Do you know her?" She whispered to him.

The shake of his head was not the answer that she wanted. She peaked at Kiana, who still hadn't moved from her bowing position. Kiana's eyes were glued to the floor as if she was waiting for a command. Her hands were crossed in front of her. Kiana barely moved from her position, looking almost like a statue.

"How does she know you?" Aliya whispered again.

Another shake of his head. "What did you say her name was?" He whispered back.

"Kiana. Kiana Roberts."

"No, my prince." Kiana finally answered. Her head, still bowing. She also didn't dare to move from her position either. "Kiana is my identity that I've created in this world. I was born in Indresal as Sienna." Aliya could hear the pride in Sienna's voice as she introduced herself. "I am Sienna el'Manaeryn of Pheandra."

Aliya's eyes widened. She couldn't help but gape at the revelation.

Pheandra? PHEANDRA?! As in the kingdom from the book series? Aliya looked between Kiana - no, her name was Sienna, apparently - and Enzo.

Sienna hadn't moved from her position. Her expression hadn't changed either. There was no sign from Sienna that she'd just dropped an earth-shattering revelation. Aliya didn't stop shifting her gaze from Sienna to Enzo. All Enzo could do was shrug in response. Apparently, he didn't know.

But he could have at least had a bigger reaction than just a simple shrug. Aliya felt like ripping her hair out. All of this felt like a prank that life was playing on her. Maybe she'd gotten into an accident on her way home from getting the groceries and was in the hospital, hallucinating. Or her friends were playing a prank on her. Or she hadn't realized how truly tired she was after this long week that she fell into her bed and she was dreaming this entire scenario.

This has to be a joke. Aliya thought. *I'm going to wake up tomorrow and all this is going to be a stupid dream.*

Aliya felt her world tilt. She held onto the bookshelf beside her trying to keep steady. She was not going to faint in front of her favorite author... Just in case all of this was actually real, that was.

Aliya took in deep breaths trying to wrap her mind around what was happening. It was all a little too much information for her but Aliya was determined not to faint.

That was, if Kiana - or rather, Sienna - was even the one that wrote the books.

"Who are you?" Enzo asked.

Sienna didn't answer. Instead, she only lifted her head and squinted her eyes as if wondering if he hadn't just heard her introducing herself.

Shaking his head as if trying to clear his own thoughts, Enzo asked again. "I mean, if you're from our world, how did you get here? Who are you? Is there a way we can get back to our world? I can't stay here forever."

Aliya tried not to look insulted at his tone, electing to remain silent. Earth might not have been perfect. But she liked it here. Although, Aliya couldn't blame Enzo. If she had a choice to pick between staying on Earth or exploring Indresal, she'd choose Indresal. Just for the adventure of it all.

"I don't know how you came to be here, my prince -"

"Please, stand up normally." Enzo interrupted her. He cringed as Sienna still had her head bowed. He was not used to this level of formality. Yes, his army respected him but their bond was more of a mutual admiration than one of reverence just for his position as the Crown Prince. "This conversation is going to be awkward if you continue bowing."

Sienna stood straight as she was told. Her eyes were still trained to the ground, however. She barely met Enzo's gaze. Her eyes flitted away every time she saw him. It was only then that Sienna seemed to notice the bruises on Enzo's face and body.

"My prince!" She gasped, holding onto her abdomen as she winced at the gashes. "You're hurt."

"And they won't heal." Enzo added.

Aliya eyed their exchange. It was as if she wasn't even in the room. Kia - No, her name was Sienna! - Sienna hadn't acknowledged her yet.

Should the wounds have healed by now?

87

Aliya knew that Enzo had accelerated healing powers, being an elf and all. She'd read of him getting wounded in battle only for him to be completely fine a few chapters later. But Aliya had always assumed that the healing took place in a matter of days or weeks. From what Aliya saw, Enzo had only been hurt a couple days ago. How fast exactly could his body heal itself?

Aliya began to question if her first aid was the reason he wasn't healing. She thought back to all that she did to contain his wounds. Nothing she did stood out to her, however. Then again, she hadn't considered that Enzo's wounds would probably need some elven or magical healing.

"What do you mean that they won't heal?" Kiana - No, she said her name was Sienna - asked.

Enzo only shrugged in response. Aliya noticed the wince that he'd tried to hide.

Sienna's eyes widened. She grabbed the chair she was just sitting on and rolled it towards Enzo. "Please sit." Was all she said before bolting out of the library.

Enzo and Aliya glanced at each other. That was not the welcome they were expecting. Aliya was completely prepared to go to jail. Her entire life flashed before her eyes when Sienna turned the light on. She was even trying to come up with excuses for the police so they don't throw her in the psych ward. But she'd never expected Sienna to be a part of Enzo's world.

"How do you think she came here?" Aliya wondered out loud.

"If I knew that, don't you think I'd have gone back to my world already?" Enzo muttered back.

Aliya gave him a deadpan expression and rolled her eyes. "Yes, thank you. Astute observation, Captain Obvious."

The two of them sat in silence for a few seconds before Enzo chimed in again. "Did you see her necklace?" Enzo asked.

"She was wearing a necklace?"

"How did you not notice the necklace?" Enzo's eyes scrunched in question. "It was right there hanging around her neck. It's not like you could miss the big crystal hanging from it."

"Well, seeing as I broke into my favorite author's house and she caught us, I was a little preoccupied with trying to not freak out or get thrown in jail."

It was Enzo's turn to roll his eyes. "She was wearing a necklace with a crystal."

"If you say so."

"Will you listen?" Enzo huffed. "That necklace is only worn by witches because they're the only ones that can access the magic in the crystal. Maybe she used her magic to create a portal to your world?"

"That's a good guess but maybe let's wait for her to come back and give us the answers herself."

It didn't take Sienna long to come back from wherever she was. She held onto a first aid kit as she walked towards Enzo and Aliya. As much as Aliya loved being near her favorite author, she was getting a bit miffed at not receiving any attention from Sienna.

Sienna opened the first aid kit. She tore a piece of cotton ball, dabbing it in a dark green, foul-smelling ointment. Aliya had never seen the cream before. She began to wonder if it was one of Sienna's concoctions.

Maybe it's a potion? Aliya wondered. That would make sense if Sienna truly was a witch.

Aliya's eyes slowly lifted to the pendant that Sienna was wearing. It was nestled in her bosom, making Aliya chuckle when she realized why Enzo might have noticed the locket. *Maybe she really was a witch.*

"I've already given him first aid." Aliya chimed in. Her voice tapered off in the end. "They still won't heal. Although I don't think some antiseptic wipes and tylenol will exactly help with magical wounds."

Sienna turned to look at her. Her eyes widened as if she was only noticing Aliya there for the first time.

Well, that certainly doesn't at all. Aliya pursed her lips, giving Sienna a tight smile. This was not the heartbreak Aliya was looking for. She revered Sienna as a writer. And to have the woman barely notice her even when she was the one of the only three people in the room... For some reason, that cut deep.

"Even if you did," Sienna said, examining the cut on Enzo's shoulder. "Some of these scrapes are inflicted by curses. None of the medicines of this world can heal him."

Sienna unwrapped the bandage from Enzo's right upper arm. Apparently, Aliya didn't exactly do a very good job. The gash looked just as gnarly as it did when Aliya first bandaged it.

Aliya winced as she looked at Enzo's pained expression and the now exposed gnarly gash on his arm. Unlike the time when Aliya was addressing his wounds, Enzo hadn't said a word or let out a moan in pain. Instead, he sat like a statue. His furrowed brows were the only sign of discomfort that he'd allowed himself to show as Sienna examined him.

Once she'd gotten a good view, Sienna closed her eyes, holding her palms together as if in a prayer.

What is she doing? Aliya wondered, looking between Enzo and Sienna. Before she could say anything, Aliya saw a faint purple glow from the necklace Sienna was wearing. *Is that magic?* She wondered.

Sienna had written about the magical system of Indresal in her books. It was elaborate, of course. It was at the core of Sienna's journey to gain her independence. But Sienna had never written about how she learnt her magic. Or why her magical abilities were so different from that of the other witches in the realm. But Aliya had just accepted that it was a fictional fantasy world where magic just existed and that some people could access it. Aliya never questioned the validity of it.

She never had a reason to do so before.

But now, seeing the glowing crystal hanging around Sienna's neck, Aliya began to wonder what else was possible.

Aliya's mind began to wander. Would the people of earth also be able to access the magic? Could she have access to those powers if she wore the necklace? Aliya began to imagine herself performing all sorts of tricks. She would definitely have the time of her life.

Aliya began to think of all the possibilities. What else is possible? Aliya stared off into the distance wondering about all the possibilities. How different would earth be if people would be able to access the magic?

Or would it be bad? Aliya wondered, thinking of all the attacks Sienna described in the book.

"Stay still." Sienna muttered, breaking the silence and bringing Aliya out of her thoughts. The wisps that were just contained to the crystal around Sienna's neck had flowed to her hands, swirling around and covering Sienna's hands in a faint purple glow. "This is going to hurt."

Hovering her hands over Enzo's wounds, Sienna closed her eyes and turned her hands into fists, as if she was grabbing something. For a moment, Aliya couldn't see any changes in the wound. It wasn't until Enzo grunted out loud that she saw the dark wisps wafting out of the wound.

Dark wisps that crackled as they came in contact with Sienna's purple ones. Enzo's grunts turned into low pained screams as he clutched the desk hard. Aliya's heart clenched at the sight of his eyes closed shut as he bit his lip.

Not being able to bear his pained screams any longer, Aliya stepped closer to him. She brought her hand up to his hair. She didn't even know what to say. Instead, Aliya just placed her hand on his other uninjured shoulder.

Enzo gasped as he released his hold on the desk and held tightly onto Aliya's hand on his shoulder. Sienna looked up, sweat trickling down her brow at the exertion of trying to remove the curse. Her eyes flitted down to Aliya's and Enzo's intertwined hands.

...And was that a smirk?

Aliya shook her head, trying to focus on Enzo. As most of the dark wisps escaped his body, the looser his grip became on her hand and the quieter his grunts became. When the final strands of the wisps escaped his body, Sienna encompassed the dark wisps with her purple magic, creating a ball.

Aliya watched in awe as the purple wisps intertwined with the dark ones, fizzing and crackling as they finally dissipated into the air.

"How many more times do you have to do that?" Aliya asked, sheepishly. She didn't know about Enzo but with how hard Enzo was holding onto her hand, she didn't know how long she could hold up.

"Looks like a couple more times." Sienna gave Enzo a once over. "He has other gashes."

"Give me a minute to recuperate. I can't do it just yet." Enzo panted. His forehead was covered in beads of sweat as if he'd just ran a marathon.

Sienna simply nodded before turning to Aliya. "I'm sorry. Where are my manners? You are..." She felt the sentence trail off waiting for Aliya to introduce herself.

Aliya's eyes widened. Her favorite author was finally acknowledging her. She gave Sienna a wide boxy smile and scratched the back of her neck as she gushed, "I'm Aliya. Nice to meet you. I love your books. They're my favorite stories! I guess it's not really a story. It's real life for you. I'm sorry for calling it that..."

Aliya rambled on, not noticing the look Sienna and Enzo shared. But no matter what, Aliya couldn't stop talking once she started. The words kept pouring out.

"...And that's why we were here. I promise I had no intention of breaking into your house." She continued, not hearing Sienna snicker along with Enzo. "But it was entirely his fault. I promise."

"What happened to loyalty these days?" Enzo muttered incredulously, cutting Aliya off.

Rolling her eyes at Enzo, Aliya turned to Sienna again. Clasping her hands together, Aliya bit her lip as fear began to creep up with her heart. "So, please don't throw me in jail. I promise to be out of your hair after we get the information we need."

Aliya took a deep breath at the end of her speech. With how fast she spoke, Aliya was sure Eminem would be proud of her rap at this point. She pursed her lips, waiting patiently for Sienna's response.

It was only when Sienna covered her lips, trying not to laugh that Aliya felt herself relax.

"Is she always like this?" She asked Enzo.

"She was actually a bit calm with me. I'm jealous she's gushing over you to be honest." Enzo sighed. "I'm getting used to it though. I think I might even miss it when I go back home."

Aliya didn't know what was going on but that statement from Enzo sent the butterflies in her stomach into a frenzy.

"That's going to be unfortunate, indeed. Unless you plan on taking her with you."

"I have college!" Aliya chimed in.

"Are you telling me that given the opportunity to explore Indresal, even if we told you that we can bring you back, you wouldn't want to go?"

That made Aliya pause to think. She'd always wanted to escape her life here. The monotonous routine of work, classes, assignments were nothing compared to the world of Indresal. The world of Indresal was her escape. It was hellish. It was devastating. There were never ending battles. There were people struggling to just live their lives as the battles waged on around them.

But within those battles against the darkness, Aliya found the light. The stories of the normal people, trying their best to live their lives as they fought the darkness that threatened to consume them. Just like the story Sienna wrote - the story of a young girl that escaped the massacre in Pheandra and grew to be one of the most feared witches in the realm.

Would Aliya miss an opportunity to visit Indresal given the chance? Could she?

Aliya bit her lip before looking at Enzo and Sienna. The two of them looked up at Aliya expectantly. Enzo more so than Sienna. The little hopeful expression on his face made Aliya's heart skip.

"In my defense, until one day ago, I thought the stories of Indresal were just that... stories." Aliya mumbled.

"Sweetheart," Sienna leaned forward in her chair. "In the end, we're all stories." Her loving chuckle at Aliya only seemed to make Aliya blush further. Her favorite author calling her 'sweetheart' was not what she'd expected to get out of this interaction, but Aliya wasn't complaining.

"Are you sure you'll be able to bring me back here?" Aliya asked.

"Are you sure you want to come back here?" Enzo asked, snickering under his breath.

She knew he was thinking of her life here. Her house and her car... She'd heard him call her car a death trap a couple times. The only response Aliya gave him was a slight narrowing of her eyes, mumbling all the curses she knew at him.

Sienna nodded. "I know I can bring you back." She glanced at Enzo for a moment before looking at Aliya again. "If you want, that is."

Aliya bit her lip again, peaking at Enzo before looking away again. His gaze didn't waver though. He continued to look at her expectantly. Although his smirk made Aliya want to smack him. He bent his head to look into her eyes. As if he was also waiting for her answer. Aliya gulped. She felt her heart speed up as she felt his gaze on her.

"I'll give you a moment to think it over." Sienna said and swiveled her chair towards Enzo. "Are you ready, my prince?"

That seemed to bring Enzo out of his reverie. He blinked, tearing his gaze away from Aliya. He'd stayed quiet the entire time making Aliya wonder what he thought of that proposal. Stealing himself for the pain again, he clutched the desk again and nodded to Sienna.

Sienna's hands froze mid air as the burglary alarm blared through the entire hour.

9

"So, those berserkers are nasty." – Aliya

NONE OF THEM SPOKE a word. The three of them waited patiently in the silence with bated breath to hear something. But for a few moments, the silence was deafening.

Aliya glanced at Enzo and Sienna - hoping they might have some answers. But they seemed to be just as confused as her.

Aliya felt her heart beat faster. Her grip on Enzo's chair tightened as she stepped closer to him. Her grip on Enzo's chair tightened as she stepped closer to him.

"Please tell me you were expecting someone." She pleaded with Sienna who only gave her a side-eye.

"If I were expecting someone, why would I turn the alarm back on?" Sienna hissed in response.

"That wasn't a false alarm then?" Aliya asked again, trying to think of anything but the worst. What were the possibilities of it being a coincidence that Sienna's house was being robbed the same day Aliya and Enzo visited?

Unless this isn't a robbery. Aliya's mind added unhelpfully.

"I just updated my system last week. No." She could detect a slight tint of concern in Sienna's voice. Sienna gulped, trying her best to stay brave. Aliya was thankful that at least one of them was being sane at the moment. Because, right now, her nerves were taking over.

Aliya turned around to look at Sienna and Enzo. Enzo winced as he lifted his hand to Aliya. A silent gesture for her to get behind him.

Without further thought, Aliya gulped, stepping closer to them as Sienna turned the alarm off. As if he sensed Aliya's uneasiness, Enzo slowly rolled his chair in front of her. Aliya turned off the lights to the library, hoping that the darkness would provide them some cover from the intruder.

They stayed huddled together, waiting patiently for what might have triggered the alarm. It didn't take them long to hear it though.

Somewhere in the distance, outside the closed office doors in the dark house, they heard a growl.

A deep, rumbling, guttural growl that sent chills down Aliya's spine.

If Aliya thought her reaction might have been intense, it was nothing compared to Enzo's or Sienna's Shock marred Enzo's features as they slowly morphed into horror. His grip on Aliya's hand tightened. He pulled her roughly behind him, shielding her from whatever it was at the door. That was nothing compared to Sienna's response, though.

"No, it can't be." Sienna gasped beside them. Her hand daintily covering her lips as she trembled like a leaf in the wind. She slowly rocked herself back and forth. Her eyes darted between the two French doors, as if wishing they wouldn't open.

The low growls slowly became louder. And with those growls came the scratches on the wooden floor. Like a hound stalking its prey. Step by step by step.

The scrapes on the wooden floor drew closer. Each scratch made Aliya's breath hitch, making her want to jump out of her skin. Whatever it was, Aliya didn't want to see it.

She stepped closer to Enzo and Sienna as the scratches grew louder. She knew from the shocked and terrified expressions the other two were sporting, those growls were what they least expected to hear.

"How are they here?" Sienna whispered, trying to keep her voice as low as possible. Her whole body shook as she tried to stand up.

"They might have followed me when I made a portal." Enzo replied. Although he didn't look too sure himself. His grip on Aliya didn't loosen however.

"But what are they?" Aliya tried to rack her mind of all the books she read. But in all of them, Sienna only described the growls for one beast - the berserkers. But there was no way that the berserkers could come into her world, could they?

Enzo just said they could have come in through his portal. Her mind added unhelpfully.

"Crown Prince Enzo al'Deran!" A booming voice came from somewhere outside the library making Sienna squeak.

Aliya looked down at Enzo. Even in the darkness, she could still feel his body turn rigid. His eyes burned with blinding rage - an expression that Aliya never wanted to be trained onto her. He fumed as he glared at the French doors. The doors seemed to be the only thing separating them from the berserkers and the man outside at the moment.

In her confusion, Aliya's gaze shifted from the door to Enzo, making her who it was that got that kind of reaction from Enzo.

"Isn't it one of your customs to greet even your enemies when they come to visit you?" The voice came again, this time a little further from the library. He was searching for them in the entire house.

He doesn't know where we are. A thought occurred to Aliya.

It was as if the man was searching through the house with his berserkers for the three of them. Every footstep the man and the berserkers made felt like a thud in Aliya's heart.

Good, he hasn't seen us in the library. Aliya thought, as she gulped. *He doesn't know where we are. We can escape!*

Hope began to bubble within her. They could escape. And she wouldn't have to encounter whatever it was that was scaring Enzo and Sienna.

"We need to leave now!" She whispered to Enzo and Sienna, trying to snap the two of them out of their reverie.

When neither of them budged from their positions, Aliya bent down to Enzo, shaking him. Enzo blinked for a moment, trying to smother his rage.

"Let's go!" She hissed again, not caring what his response was.

Sienna, however, was shaking violently. She hugged herself as her eyes darted everywhere. Her head snapped in every direction whenever she heard a small sound. Aliya didn't bother talking to her. Sienna didn't seem like she would listen to her at the moment. Instead, Aliya grabbed Sienna's arms, making her yelp. Pushing her towards Enzo, Aliya walked slowly towards the windows behind Sienna's desk.

"Where are you going?" Enzo hissed at her. When Aliya didn't respond, he hissed again. "Aliya! Come back! It's not safe!"

Aliya turned around, shushing the elf. "Anything's better than being stuck with whatever those are."

She fingered the rims of the windows searching for the hatch to open them. Just as she was about to open the hatch, though, she remembered Sienna saying she'd turned the alarm on.

"No." Aliya gasped. Breaking the alarm would grab the attention of the beasts outside. They wouldn't have enough time to escape.

"Did you turn the alarm off again?" Aliya asked. When she didn't hear a response for Sienna, Aliya turned around. Sienna continued to hug herself, her eyes wide as she stood beside Enzo.

"Sienna, we need to get out. How do we get out? Did you already turn the alarm back on again?"

The urgency in Aliya's voice was unmistakable. But no matter what Aliya said, nothing could seem to break Sienna out of her daze as she continued to shake violently.

Aliya groaned quietly in frustration when she couldn't find the alarm. She tried her best to move around the library making as little noise as possible. And neither Enzo nor Sienna seemed to be of any help at the moment.

She was going to have to figure this out herself.

If they couldn't get out of the windows, they needed to get out of the office door. Aliya thanked whatever fate was watching over her for the darkness. She palmed the bookshelves, using them as a guide as she walked closer to the library door. With every step she took closer to the door, she felt her heart pound. Her legs felt like lead as she dragged them with each step.

"What are you doing?" Enzo hissed at her again.

Instead of answering, she simply turned around to shush him.

When she finally reached the door, Aliya slowly leaned in, placing her ear against the wooden door. She flinched when she heard the booming voice again through the door.

"You can't run away from me forever, Enzo." The voice said, sending shivers down Aliya's spine. "How about I make you a deal? If you surrender, I'll leave the girl following you around, alone."

The girl following yo-. Aliya's eyes widened. The man was talking about her.

Her grip on the door handle tightened. The man was talking about her. He knew about her. How did he know about her? She'd never met this man before. She didn't even know that his man existed before today. If he even was a man, that was. Questions began to swirl around in Aliya's mind. She was beginning to spiral.

No, no, no! Stop! Aliya chastised herself. *Get out here first. Then we can freak out!*

Taking a few deep breaths to control her emotions, Aliya slowly walked back to Enzo and Sienna.

"Remember the window we came through?" She asked. Enzo nodded. "I left it open so we could escape through it. I don't think that guy is near the window. We can leave from there. Don't make any noise!"

The three of them held their hands forming a train as they slowly made their way to the door. Pursing her lips, Aliya opened the door as slowly as she could, hoping to everything that the door didn't squeak. She only let out her breath when she noticed that the door didn't creak when she opened it.

She didn't know how the other two were doing but with the protection of the door gone between them, Aliya felt exposed to the man hunting them.

The growls and stomps of the beasts seemed faint making her wonder where the beasts actually were in the house. She felt Enzo squeeze her hand slightly in reassurance as he walked closer to her.

Aliya tried to remember all the furniture they bumped into as they entered the house. She guided the other two, trying to avoid bumping into anything.

But it seemed that luck was not on her side.

Because the moment Enzo stubbed his boot on one of the cupboards making the sound echo in the silence, the moment his pained grunt sounded like a shout in the silence - that was the moment Aliya knew they'd been caught.

Shit! Aliya cursed when the snarls stopped for a moment.

Stopped for one moment before they picked up again. But this time as the beasts stomped down the stairs. They seemed to not care for the glass and furniture they crashed into as the berserkers tried to reach them. Running, scratching and crashing into the walls as they weaved through the house as the beasts tried to catch up to the three of them.

"Go, go, go!" Enzo screamed, not caring anymore to keep quiet.

What was the purpose? Their location had been compromised.

And without a thought in her mind, Aliya dashed, dragging Sienna along with her. Enzo wiggled his hand out of Aliya's grasp, making her look back in confusion.

"What are you doing?" She shouted at him. Aliya didn't stop however. She continued to run towards the kitchen where the open window was.

But with how big the house was, that open window was a couple turns away.

"Go!" Enzo shouted at them again. "I'll buy you time!"

Aliya wanted to protest. She really did.

But just as she opened her mouth, she saw the beasts turn the corner, snarling as they approached the three of them.

10

"Beast? Human? No, these were berserkers."
– Aliya

I T WAS AT THIS moment Aliya understood.

She understood why Enzo and Sienna looked so shocked and terrified. She understood the fear that radiated off their bodies the moment they heard the growls for the first time.

Because she was staring at the beasts now. No, not beasts.

She'd read about them in Sienna's books, of course. She'd seen the figurines and artist renderings of the berserkers. But none of them could capture the heart stopping fear Aliya was feeling at the moment. And for once, Aliya was glad Sienna left out the terribly gory details of the berserkers in her books. Because the sight in front of her right now chilled her to the bone.

Aliya had been enjoying her time with her favorite author and favorite character so much that she'd forgotten that if the good parts of Sienna's books were real... then, so would the bad.

Then again, who would think that the berserkers would come along with Enzo! Aliya complained in her head.

The berserkers were exactly as Sienna described them. They were human. Or at least they were human before they were forcibly turned into the raging beasts that they were by the Dark One.

They still had the features one would recognize on a human.

But the gnashing pointed teeth, the clawed hands, the protruding muscle and bones that made the creatures look more like beasts than the humans they once were. Even the way they moved on all fours was more beastly than human-like. Saliva - or rather, what Aliya hoped was saliva in the darkness - dripped through their teeth. Their growls only seemed to increase as they stomped towards the three of them.

Aliya saw the faint outline of a man standing behind the beasts. Dressed immaculately with his hands clasped in front of him and slicked back hair, he looked completely out of place in all the commotion.

It was only when Aliya saw a hint of a smile - or was it a smirk? - that she was able to snap out.

Turning on her heel, she dragged Sienna as the two dashed to the open kitchen window.

Aliya didn't care what she bumped into. She didn't even bother to hiss at the pain as she dashed into the tables and cupboards. If she were to survive this night, she could complain about her wounds later.

Instead, she dragged Sienna along with her, only peeking behind her a couple times to see where Enzo was.

She wanted to shout for him. She really did. But just as she opened her mouth, she heard a loud crash behind her. Glass shattered on the floor as the plates and cups from the cupboard fell to the ground. Aliya didn't stop running.

One more turn and they'd be in the kitchen.

Instead, Aliya snapped her head back to see what caused the commotion. Her eyes widened when she saw Enzo being slammed into the cupboard as he tried to hold back one of the berserkers. He grunted out loud as he struggled against its gnashing teeth. Trying with all his might to keep the beasts away from Aliya and Sienna.

The crash seemed to have brought Sienna out of her stupor. She wiggled her hand out of Aliya's grasp.

"Go to him!" Sienna shouted as a confused Aliya turned to her. "I'll get the car!"

That was all Sienna said before turning around the corner. Aliya could just as easily run with Sienna. She could be away from the danger. She'd never encountered anything like the beasts before. If she turned around, she wouldn't even know how to defend herself from them. She could just as easily helped Sienna with getting the car.

So, why did she turn around?

Aliya looked at Enzo again. He was an elf. He did tell her that he'd take care of the berserkers. He was a much more powerful creature than she ever could be.

But he doesn't have his powers on Earth! Her mind screamed at her.

That thought and one look at how Enzo was struggling was enough for Aliya to decide on which direction she wanted to run.

With the crashing sounds in the background, Aliya ran into the kitchen. She spotted a knife set on the kitchen counter in the faint light. Without thinking, Aliya grabbed the first two knives she could get her hands on.

It was only when she ran to Enzo that she realized she was holding onto a butcher's knife and a meat skewer.

No time to change now! Her mind screamed at her.

Enzo seemed to have heard footsteps as Aliya ran towards him.

"What are you doing?" He grunted out, still struggling against not one, but the two berserkers at the moment. Even in his struggle, Aliya could hear the alarm and panic in his voice as she approached him. "Leave!" He shouted at her.

"No! Not without you!" She shouted back. Although that only seemed to elicit a frustrated grunt from him in response. Aliya handed him the meat skewer.

Enzo looked at the skewer, perplexed, before jabbing it into the eye of one of the beasts. Its howls echoed down the hallway, loud enough that it sent a rumble through Aliya's chest. Aliya took the moment of confusion to slash into the other berserker.

Although that only seemed to shift the beast's focus onto her.

Aliya didn't let up, however. She swung the butcher's knife in every direction. Blood from the beast spurted all over, making her grip on the knife slippery. None of that seemed to stop the beast from approaching her, however.

Its gnawing teeth - or rather, its fangs - gashed at her, snapping anytime they were close to her arms. Aliya yelped every time the beast snapped its jaw. She didn't stop slashing at the beast, though. The beast's abnormal muscles rippled every time it lifted its arms to slash her. She yelped in pain as she felt one of its claws swipe at her thigh. Aliya could feel the thick liquid slowly trickling down from her wound. But she didn't dare look. The sight in front of her was enough nightmare fuel.

Instead, she elected to close her eyes and screamed, doubling her efforts. She held onto the knife with both her hands, making sure that her grip on the knife was steady as she waved it in every direction.

That wasn't exactly the best strategy but that was the only strategy she had at the moment.

"For someone so young, you fight valiantly." The voice said, from a distance.

Aliya had completely forgotten about the man till now. If she wasn't busy trying to survive the berserkers, she'd definitely wonder why the man hadn't attacked them himself. Because it was almost as if the man was playing with them. Chasing them. Trying to have fun instilling the utmost fear he could before killing them.

In all the commotion around them, the man was nowhere to be seen. Although, just from his words, Aliya could imagine the man smirking. The man was definitely enjoying this. In the rare moments that one of the berserkers let up, Aliya peaked at the man leaning against the wall several feet away. He watched them fight as if he was just watching a game, enjoying how Enzo and Aliya struggled against his beasts.

That sick bastard! Aliya screamed in her mind. But there was nothing she could do at the moment. Nothing, except injure the beasts enough for them to be able to escape.

With Aliya screaming her lungs out, she couldn't hear exactly what he was saying. "It's a shame to see such a fighter die."

Aliya was about to land another swipe when she felt another arm on her. She turned around quickly, screaming as she swung the knife along with her. Aliya stopped thrashing about when she saw Enzo's wide startled eyes staring back at her.

"It's me!" Enzo shouted as Aliya slowly lowered the knife she was holding in front of her. In her frenzy, she'd almost slashed Enzo. Her eyes widened in surprise to see him pulling her.

She only gave him her signature boxy smile as an apology. Aliya didn't have any time to apologize however. She felt Enzo cage her in his arms.

Aliya didn't know what he was shielding her from though. She'd already seen the berserkers. She was already fighting the berserkers. If he was trying to protect her from them, he was a few minutes too late.

It didn't take her long to realize what Enzo was protecting her from though.

Because only a moment after being engulfed by Enzo, she felt the blast as splinters from the wooden furniture flying around them. Aliya screamed from the shock. She closed her ears and eyes at the sudden loud noise. Enzo grunted in pain as his grip on Aliya tightened. She could feel him starting to slump onto her.

Aliya tried to turn back to look at him but his grip on her prevented her from moving.

"We need to leave!" She shouted at Enzo as another wooden shelf shattered, knocking the books off of it.

Enzo nodded weakly. Gone was the fierce Enzo that had taken on three berserkers. In his place was a much more silent - albeit, a bit lethargic - Enzo, pushing Aliya through the splinters and exploding furniture as he tried to protect her from the damage around them.

Aliya was sure she could hear the man cackling with every blast he'd sent out. If she had to guess, the man blasting at them either had a terrible aim or Enzo had been good at protecting them.

With every step they took, however, Aliya felt a sharp pain shooting from her leg. With her adrenaline of the moment slowly fading, Aliya could feel the pain from the slash the berserker left on her thigh. Wincing, she followed where Enzo was leading her.

As they reached the kitchen, Aliya searched once more for any weapons that they could use. But with her still being caged in Enzo's arms, there wasn't much she could do. She wiggled about trying to set herself free from his grasp.

She looked back in confusion when Enzo easily released her. Her concern for Enzo only grew when she turned back to see his hooded eyes closing slowly. She didn't have time to think about that however. Instead, she ran to the corner where she grabbed the knives before.

Pushing Enzo towards the window, Aliya threw the remaining knives on the stand, hoping that at least one of them would kill the beasts. It seemed that even though the beasts yelped, nothing was slowing either the beasts or the man down.

Aliya pushed Enzo out the window. Her hands grew slippery as she continued to push on his back. Aliya grabbed onto whatever she could hold and threw it at the beasts, trying to deter them - or at least shift their focus onto her. But no matter what she did, the berserkers pounced and growled at her.

Aliya almost heaved a sigh of relief when she heard Sienna shout. "Come on! Quickly!"

That seemed to spur Enzo on though. Because the moment he was out of the window, he grabbed Aliya's waist and pulled out of the house through the open kitchen window.

Aliya yelped at the sudden movement. Her eyes widened when she noticed the beasts advancing and closed the window once she was set back on the ground. With how fast the beasts were running after them, they smashed their heads onto the window glass, cracking it.

Aliya saw the man standing in the entrance of the kitchen. With a smirk that held a promise.

"Get in!" Sienna screamed at them, revving the engine to her car.

Aliya and Enzo only shared a glance at each other before running towards the backseat of the car. Sienna didn't bother to wait till they even closed the door. The moment she saw Aliya and Enzo in the backseat, she started driving. Tires squealed as she got off her driveway.

It was only when the car was several miles away from Sienna's house that all three of them relaxed.

Aliya could still feel the adrenaline and the blood pumping through her veins though. She looked outside the window, taking in a few deep breaths to calm herself.

None of them spoke a word. After all the commotion, the gashing, gnawing, and furniture blasting, the silence in the car was more than welcome.

"Let's never do that again." Aliya said, breaking the silence, to no one in particular.

"Let's." Sienna agreed. Her eyes never left the road. She didn't even turn back to see how Aliya and Enzo were doing.

When Aliya didn't hear anything from Enzo, she turned to look at him. Clutching her wounded thigh, Aliya leaned over to him.

"Enzo?" She asked, quietly.

His eyes were glazed over as he stared at the headrest in front of him. When he didn't respond, Aliya reached out to him, shaking his shoulder lightly.

His glazed eyes slowly turned towards Aliya. Although Aliya was sure she was not the one he was looking at. Enzo gave her a small smile before his eyes rolled over and he fell onto her lap.

Aliya yelped in pain as Enzo fell onto her wound. But her pain was momentarily forgotten when she saw the blood pouring out of his back.

Wounds from the splintered furniture that the man had been blasting at. This. This was what Enzo was protecting Aliya from. Aliya felt her breath begin to shorten.

No, He can't be dead.

"No, no, no, no." She chanted to herself like a mantra.

"What happened?" Sienna asked, looking back from the rearview mirror.

Aliya didn't answer, however. Not caring about the wound on her thigh, Aliya tried shaking Enzo. She held onto his cheeks, shaking him slightly, trying to get him to wake up. But nothing she tried seemed to work.

"Hospital. We need to go to the hospital!" She screamed at Sienna.

With her eyes wide and bated breath, she looked at Enzo's limp body laying in the backseat with her, hoping he'd be alive.

11

"Great. Back here again." - Enzo

"DRIVE FASTER!" ENZO HEARD Aliya shout at Sienna. Although her voice seemed distant and hollow.

Enzo's brows furrowed in confusion. That was not how Aliya sounded. Was she ok? Worry began to creep into his heart. He thought he had protected her well from the berserkers and Damon's attacks. But with how her voice sounded, Enzo wasn't sure anymore.

"Faster!" Another scream from Aliya. This one also sounded distant and hollow.

Enzo dared to look at her. His head felt heavy to even move but the jolt from the car in that moment seemed to help. He looked Aliya over, not noticing any bad injuries. Enzo felt like the weight was lifted off his chest when he noticed that she was ok. The worry in her eyes was ever present since he turned to look at her. But other than that, she seemed physically fine.

Was she still scared? Was it the berserkers? Questions swirled around in his mind - as muddled as it was. He couldn't think of anything else other than why Aliya was worried.

It's ok. He wanted to tell her. *We're safe now. They can't follow us now. We're far away from them.*

No words came out, however.

He wanted to tell her. He wanted to lift his hand to pat her shoulder. But every movement was lethargic. His hands - no, his entire body - felt heavy. None of his limbs were under his control.

Did Damon curse me? He wondered when neither of his hands moved. He moved his head to the side, slowly.

It was only then that he realized he'd not been sitting. No. Instead he was lying on someone's lap. No wonder none of his limbs moved the way he wanted them to. It took him a moment to realize that he was sleeping on Aliya's lap. She slapped his cheeks lightly, as if trying to keep him awake.

Through his blurry vision, he turned again and looked up to see Aliya. Tears streamed down her face. Her brows scrunched as she asked again for Sienna to drive faster. Her eyes only turned hopeful when she looked down to see him looking at her.

Although something on his face might have frightened her again.

"Don't close your eyes." Aliya said. The urgency in her voice was starting to worry him.

What happened? He wanted to ask. But none of the words came out... again.

Damon definitely put a curse on me. He thought.

He couldn't even open his mouth either. Enzo could feel his breath becoming shallow. Seeing Aliya this distraught was making him anxious. He wanted to tell her everything would be alright. That there was no need to be afraid... at least not now that they were far away from the berserkers.

But how was he to do that when he couldn't even think properly?

Enzo watched as the beautiful night lights from the buildings passed the car as Sienna whizzed through the streets. The lights were lulling him back into the land of dreams. Keeping his eyes open was becoming a chore. It'd be just so much easier if he just had a small nap. He'd heal in his nap.

With Aliya's voice echoing in his mind, Enzo took in a deep breath.

Everything will be alright. You'll be alright, Aliya. He thought before letting the sleep consume him.

Enzo jolted awake.

The woodsy smell, the greenery that surrounded him, and the hard rocks digging into his back was a harsh contrast to Aliya's soft lap he fell asleep on. No, this was very different. Enzo looked around and scowled.

He was surrounded by the forest. His back ached from the roots and pebbles that dug into him when he was unconscious. Enzo grunted as he twisted trying to soothe his sore muscles. He let out a content sigh when he felt a couple of his bones crack. Only for him to scowl when he realized where he was.

Enzo was back in the land of his memories.

He was back in the scene of the last battle he fought in before coming to Earth.

With a humph, Enzo tried to stand up, trying to find a safe shelter for the night. It didn't help that he was surrounded by the remnant of the battle that was fought just a few hours ago. He was surrounded by the tall trees swaying with the warm breeze. Wood crackled in the distance from the flames of the battle they'd fought. What was once a thick forest covered in foliage that made it hard for sunlight to reach the forest floor, now was nothing more than just a clearing.

Enzo looked up to see the storm clouds slowly brewing above him. He needed to find shelter quickly.

But he couldn't move properly. His sides hurt from the splintered wooden bark that scraped along his chest. Blood slowly trickled out of his wounds staining his shirt underneath the armor. Enzo gritted his teeth trying not to hiss or make any noise. Biting his lip in pain, he clutched tightly onto his wound. He didn't move from his position, however.

He took a moment to listen for the beasts once again. All he could hear, however, were the sounds of the forest.

Enoz didn't know how long he could hold up in this current position. He didn't know how many people were still trapped in the forest with him.

But most importantly, with the wood crackling beside him as the ambers burning within it, it was hard for him to hear any other sounds from the berserkers.

That made Enzo more nervous. The hair at the back of his neck stood on edge as Enzo patiently waited for any sound that indicated where the berserkers were. For the enormous beasts that they were, they were surprisingly nimble.

Enzo sucked in a breath as he peeked from behind the trunk. When he didn't see any movement, Enzo slowly stepped out of his hiding spot from behind the tree. He plotted for a way to get out of the forest. But all of his choices came down to creating a portal to get him out.

He could do it.

He should have done it long ago.

But creating portals would mean drawing attention to his location. His superficial wounds had already healed. The gashes were a different story however. And with the amount of blood he was losing because of the gash, he didn't know if he had enough energy to create a portal right now, let alone sustain one long enough for him to get through. He didn't even have enough energy to save himself if the berserkers were to find him at the moment.

So, instead, he trudged through the forest. Walking gingerly, he tried his best not to step on any twigs or dried branches. Panting and wheezing, Enzo winced with every step he took. His ears twitched with every sound he heard. Never once did he let his guard down.

Which was good because he was starting to hear suspicious roars and stomps in the distance.

He only stood still for a moment, trying to locate the source of the growls. The sounds were mixed with the fires blazing in the forest, making it difficult for him to know where the berserkers were.

Enzo whipped his head in every direction, his ears twitching searching for where the growls and stomps were coming from. He heard it only a moment later.

A low rumble that made his heart tremble. The earth shook with each stomp of the beast's hoofs.

But none of those noises stopped his stride.

Enzo kept walking. He used the noises as his guide, limping in their opposite direction. He didn't dare open any portals. They hadn't noticed him and he'd very much like to keep it that way.

Enzo didn't know how long he'd been walking like that. He could feel his pace slow down. His breath was becoming shallower with each passing minute. His boots dug into skin, making him wince with every step he took. Enzo made it a point to avoid the twigs and branches from scraping against his skin. He had enough scratches on his body already and didn't want to add any more.

Come on. Come on. Come on. Enzo chanted to himself.

The sun had long started to set drenching the woods in darkness. That, combined with how blurry his vision had gotten, Enzo stumbled over every rock and root.

He hadn't heard the horde in a while. And yet, Enzo didn't dare to stop.

Enzo hissed as he clasped the bark of the tree in support. He knew there would be blood on his palms with all the scrapes from the bark but he didn't care.

Panting, he tried lifting his leg over the root. Enzo couldn't even feel his leg catch on the root, given how delirious he was. His eyes widened as he saw the ground approach quickly. Enzo let go of the bark, bringing his hands forward to shield his face from the fall. He grunted out loud when he felt the impact of the hard forest floor on his forearms.

Taking a moment to recuperate, Enzo looked around, trying to gauge where he was. He hadn't been paying attention for most of his escape. But he had to be somewhere close to the outskirts of the forest…

…unless he was walking in circles, that was.

Enzo tried his best to keep his eyes open. With how quiet the forest was, this was a battle he'd soon lose.

It was only when Enzo felt an arrow whiz past him that he jolted awake. He didn't know how long he'd been sleeping. The darkness surrounding him told him that he'd been passed out for a while. He snapped his head around, trying to see where the noise was coming from. Except the sight around him made him scramble back on all fours.

In the distance behind him were the hoard of beasts, snarling and scratching as they stampede through the forest. How hadn't he heard the beasts? They were right behind him. Was he that delirious?

They weren't advancing towards him however. Before he could wonder why, Enzo felt another arrow whiz past him.

In the darkness, the arrow whistles were the only ones that indicated what was happening. Somehow, the beasts were being ambushed by the soldiers. Enzo dared to peak behind him to see the beasts struggle against the onslaught of arrows barraging over them. Their vicious snarls turned into howls of pain and yet, they didn't stop trying to move forward.

The beasts scratched and crawled over one another, trampling the ones in front of them as they clawed to move forward... even if it was just an inch.

Enzo laid low on the forest floor. He crawled to where he heard the arrows coming from. He did not dare to fight against the beasts. All his weapons were scattered around the battlefield somewhere. Only a fool would go against the beasts without any weapon. And given how he couldn't even create a portal, Enzo wasn't that desperate to die at the moment.

He hoped beyond anything that the group raining down the arrows was his cousin's army and not a trap. He didn't know how long he'd been crawling.

"We found him!" Enzo heard someone shout.

Enzo lifted his head. There was no light for Enzo to see who the voice was. One of the soldiers stepped forward. The soldier bent down to Enzo's level, trying to avoid the arrows still sailing above them. The soldier's brown uniform was marked with the Illadoran Insignia. In that moment, Enzo could have wept tears of joy at the rescue.

Enzo could feel his shoulders slack as the weight began to lift off his shoulders. He let out the breath he didn't know he was holding as he slumped to the ground, thanking whatever stars or power that was watching over him that night.

A slow smile spread across his face as he let his exhaustion consume him. Letting the haze take over, Enzo closed his eyes, letting himself fall into a deep slumber.

12

"We have a plan... I think." – Enzo

I T WASN'T UNTIL THE next morning that Enzo even woke up.

He groaned as he stretched his muscles, wincing when he felt his pain intensity with every movement. Holding onto his shoulder, Enzo craned his neck as he stretched.

Enzo wondered how long he'd slept. The sun had already risen, sending rays of sunlight through the thick foliage. Birds chirped around him, flying from tree to tree. After the battle from the day before, just watching the birds felt like a luxury for Enzo.

Enzo took in a deep breath of the warm morning breeze before looking around at the makeshift camp. Straw grass was laid out haphazardly on the forest floor. Several wooden cots were laid out side by side on the straw.

Each of the cot had at least one wounded soldier. Some of them even had two or more, depending on how serious the injuries the soldiers sustained.

Elves, mages, and humans walked past Enzo, not even giving him a sparing glance. They had much more important things to worry about as they attended the wounded and dying soldiers all around him.

The witches moved from one cot to another, tending to the wounded soldiers. Most of the injuries Enzo could see were gnarly, making him wince internally. No matter how many times he'd gone to battle, Enzo would never get used to the sight of what the battles cost them.

Moans and grunts filled the air as the witches tried their best to heal the soldiers. Enzo could see the toll it was taking on both the soldiers and the mages though. The unshed tears as they bandaged a broken or amputated leg. The soft smile they gave the soldiers that were at death's door. The urgency they had to move from one cot to another trying to save one soldier after another. Desperation clung onto the air in the infirmary.

This... this was the sight that Enzo rarely got to see.

Anytime he came back from the battle, he'd always been carted off to the palace infirmary. Only he and a couple of his Generals were allowed to be in the palace infirmary though. His soldiers were always taken care of in the palace grounds.

In one corner, Enzo saw a group of men and women huddled together. Squinting his eyes, Enzo saw the glowing white crystals around each of their necks. Magic from each of them intertwined as they made the potions the healers used on the injured soldiers.

Enzo got off his cot, struggling for a moment to maintain his balance. He looked down at himself, assessing his damage. Sometime during the night, they'd removed his shirt. He didn't know where they left it for him to search for it now. But Enzo didn't care about it for now. His gash was irritating him already. His chest was covered in bandages covering a green ointment. His left shoulder and palms were covered in the same bandages.

He tried turning his hands into a fist. But the bandages restricted the movement Enzo pursed his lips.

That's not going to do. Enzo thought, scowling when the bandages hindered his movement. Not caring what the healers thought, Enzo removed the bandages on his hands.

He mentally thanked the mages and his fast healing abilities when he noticed only a dark scar in the place of all the gashes he had on his palms only the night before.

Not bothering to put on a shirt, Enzo slowly made his way around the camp. The more he looked around, the more he began to wonder if his cousin had made it out alive. There was no sign of him anywhere in the camp.

As his curiosity got the best of him, Enzo stopped one of the healers. She was a short stout woman, carrying a tray of bloodied bandages. Enzo could see the sweat beading her forehead. Her eyes carried the weight of the sadness, of all the loss she'd seen, as she gazed up at him.

She blinked a couple times as if trying to get out of her thoughts. Shaking her head slightly, she bowed slightly, as much as the heavy tray she was holding allowed her, and asked. "Yes, your highness."

"Prince Aryan? Where is he? Is he safe?" Enzo asked, straight to the point. He didn't want to delay the healer any more than necessary.

The woman nodded. "Yes, your highness. He's in the General's tent." She said, pointing to the tent a short distance behind her.

Enzo gave her a curt nod before heading in the direction the healer pointed him. Even from this distance, Enzo could hear the arguments from the General within the tent even before he entered it. Enzo nodded to the soldiers guarding the tent from anyone entering.

When the soldiers didn't let him in immediately, Enzo said. "I'm Crown Prince Enzo of Ravendore and Prince Aryan's cousin. I need to speak to him."

He didn't usually use his title this way. But desperate times, desperate measures...

The soldiers' eyes widened when they noticed who the man was. Bowing to him, the soldiers opened the tent flap, allowing Enzo to enter. The tent was almost barren, save for the large table in the middle. His cousin stood at the head of the table, looking down at the map laid atop it. Three of his generals surrounded him. All of them looked down at the map, firing off suggestions for retreat or plans for attack.

But either way, it seemed that none of the men were coming to the same conclusion.

Enzo stood to the side, observing the discussions. None of the people in the tent seemed to have noticed Enzo come in as they continued with their discussion.

"That is a terrible plan!" One of the Generals, a dark curly haired man standing beside his cousin shouted, shaking his head. "If we attack them here," He pointed to the map. "They'll be able to enter through the pass here." He pointed to a different area on the map. "We're already short on soldiers. So, even if we send most of our soldiers to the attack, we're basically giving them a free reign to attack our camp."

Prince Aryan nodded beside the General. He was quiet for a moment, not talking while the other Generals bounced strategies between each other. His dark brown eyes focused on the map as he rubbed his chin. His hair, which had been short the last time Enzo saw Aryan, had grown longer as the dark locks framed his face. The beard growing on Aryan's face made Enzo wonder if Aryan has even been taking care of himself.

Not that Enzo was one to talk.

Aryan's eyes darted from one corner of the map to the other. Enzo knew his cousin well enough to know he was going through all the battle strategies he'd learnt thus far.

"Or we can lure them into a false attack somewhere in the middle and then ambush them from both the left and right." Enzo chimed in, as if that was the most obvious solution.

Enzo gave them a cheeky smile as every head in the tent turned towards him.

"You're finally awake." Prince Aryan said, trying to suppress a relieved smile. "I thought you'd died." He waved his hand.

"I was planning on it, actually." Enzo rolled his eyes. "But my mother can be scary. She'd bring me back to life just to give me a lecture. And I would like to avoid that if I could."

The two cousins pursed their lips, as if laughing at a certain inside joke.

"I would have if it wasn't for your men." Enzo said, bowing his head slightly in gratitude. He walked past the Generals and stepped closer to his cousin.

"Most of my men would have died if it wasn't for you getting them out in time." Aryan held his head up high as he looked Enzo straight in the eye.

A moment of silence turned into two. A slow smile spread across the two cousins' faces. Without a word, the two embraced. Enzo didn't care for the wound on his chest as he hugged Aryan tightly.

"It's good to see you again." Aryan whispered in Enzo's ear. Hugging him for a moment longer, Aryan let his cousin go. He tapped Enzo's uninjured shoulder twice, as if trying to make sure that his cousin was really there, standing in front of him.

Giving his cousin a somber smile, Enzo looked down at the map of the forest laid out on the table in front of him. All the Generals stood around the table with their heads bowed. None of them spoke a word.

That was until Aryan chimed in again.

"I have to agree, I like your plan better." Aryan said, tapping his chin as he thought. None of the Generals chimed in with their opinion, however.

"We just need a small distraction." Enzo nodded. "That is, if Damon is still there."

"We received information that Damon hadn't moved from there since last night." Aryan answered.

"Why?" Enzo muttered, mostly to himself. Aryan simply shrugged in response though.

"He's refused to leave this forest since he arrived." Aryan said.

Enzo's brows furrowed in thought. He bit his lip as he asked out loud. "How long has he been here?"

"About three weeks now." One of Aryan's Generals chimed in.

"That's when we got the first reports that our messages weren't reaching your army." Enzo mumbled, loud enough that everyone around the table could hear. "Could it be that Damon has placed some kind of blockage to isolate you?"

Aryan's Generals mumbled among themselves. "That is a possibility." One of them finally said. "We haven't been able to receive any messages or help since Damon arrived."

"How were you able to get in then?" Aryan turned to his cousin.

"Unlike the messages, I just need to know the destination of where I'm going to get there." Enzo shrugged.

Aryan nodded, satisfied with Enzo's explanation. He turned back to the map, muttering to himself.

"I can have a couple men here for the distraction as we concentrate our forces on the attack from the left and right." Aryan nodded.

"And if you give me twenty men and about five witches, I can guard the left." Enzo said, rubbing his chin.

"I'll be to the right then." Aryan mumbled, more to himself.

The rest of the meeting, everyone in the tent made sure the detailed plan was foolproof. They didn't have any room for mistakes. Especially with how few men they had.

No, they needed to protect their men and attack Damon al'Kara where it hurt.

And this plan was the best for now.

Enzo spent the rest of the day walking around the camp, preparing for the battle that evening. He finally laid down on the cot in his cousin's tent. He still needed to regain what energy he could before the night. He'd be of no use as he was now.

And so, that was what Enzo did.

Settling into the cot and making himself comfortable, Enzo fell into a deep sleep.

13

"I should not be catching feelings." -Enzo

ENZO WOKE UP WITH a start, blinking hard as he looked around the room.

Room?

He didn't have to ponder about it though. Just by the softness of the bed he was laying on, Enzo knew he'd woken back up from his dream. Awake only to realize that he was on Earth. With Aliya. That everything he'd dreamt thus far about the battle in Indresal was just that...

A dream.

His mind reeled back to the night before where he escaped Sienna's house with Aliya. He remembered Aliya's fear and her shrieks. With how groggy he was feeling at the moment, he wondered what might have caused Aliya to shriek as such - especially when they were safe in Sienna's car.

Where is she?

Enzo groaned and winced when the light from the window gave him a sharp pain in his temples. Rubbing his eyes, Enzo lifted himself onto his shoulder. When the movement became restrictive, Enzo looked down to see his shoulder bandaged and wrapped around his chest. A thick, green, pungent substance that made Enzo gag was slathered within his bandages.

And if he had to guess, the bandages and the ointment was Sienna's work.

His body was sore in places he didn't know he had muscles. Enzo strained and stretched his back to hear a couple cracks. He sighed at the temporary relief it provided. The relief that was only short lived, however. Enzo winced when the badges on his thigh moved, reminding him of the gash he'd received from the berserker.

That pain was enough to wake him up completely.

Memories of the night before flooded his mind. Enzo remembered sneaking into Sienna's house, fighting the berserkers, coming face-to-face with Damon, and most miraculous of all... they'd somehow escaped.

He still didn't know how though.

He'd gotten Aliya out of the house and she'd somehow gotten him in the car. Enzo looked down at his bandages again.

Oh, so that's why she was worried. Enzo thought as the realization set in. *Makes much more sense now.*

Enzo thanked whatever fates were watching over them the night before because he was sure if it were to happen again, at least one of them would have died - most probably him, but he wasn't going to think about that.

Taking a deep breath, Enzo looked around the small rustic cabin bedroom.

The bedroom was no bigger than Aliya's living room. He was sleeping on a simple wooden bed with carved wooden posts on each corner of the bed. In front of the bed was a small closet. The door to the closet was slightly ajar, giving him a view of the clothes hanging in there. Beside his bed was a small wooden desk on which stood an intricately carved candle holder.

Enzo stopped looking around the room when his eyes caught the chair sitting beside him. Seated on the chair was a very sleepy Aliya. Enzo chuckled as Aliya's head bobbed with her sleep. None of her head bobs woke her up though. He wondered how tired she must have been.

Aliya licked her lips and rubbed her nose. She moved around in the chair, trying to find a comfortable position before settling back into her slumber again.

She'd surprised him last night. He knew she was brave. But he never expected her to put her life on the line to save him. Fighting beside him with whatever she could. If they weren't in the middle of the fight, he'd have laughed when she handed him the meat skewer.

He remembered how she slashed through the berserkers. She screamed like a banshee as she cut gash after gash at the berserkers. Although her fighting stance was abysmal.

Enzo winced as he remembered her holding onto the knife with both hands, her grip faltering as the berserker's blood made it slippery. She could have cut herself during the fight. One slip of her hand would have been enough. It was only a miracle that she hadn't cut herself during the fight.

No, the berserker did that for her. Enzo thought.

His gaze wandered down to the bandaged gash on her leg. Her scream when the berserker's claw latched onto her thigh... Enzo felt a shudder crawl down his spine. He'd decided then that no matter what happened to him, he would get Aliya out of the house safe and in one piece.

Enzo remembered enveloping her in his arms as he moved her out of the house. He made sure that none of the blasts Damon threw towards them hit her.

The blasts hit him though. Enzo could still feel the faint sting in his back. Sienna's ointment must have helped with the healing. Not as bad as the night before, but enough that it still reminded him of the danger that prevailed outside the cabin.

Exactly who are you? Enzo wondered, looking at Aliya, a loving smile playing at his lips. In the short time he'd come to know her, she'd stuck with him through thick and thin. Even when danger stared them in the face...

No, not without you! Her words echoed in his mind.

Well, if you're going to come with me, you're going to have to learn to fight, my little one. Enzo said. He couldn't help but swell in pride as he watched Aliya sleep in the chair. Enzo let out a tight smile. *Yeah, I'm going to have to teach her to defend herself.*

She had the bravery to take on an entire army but with only the knowledge to get herself killed. Enzo shook his head.

Watching her fight the night before was like watching a child waving a stick at a berserker. No, Aliya was definitely going to be needing a lot more training if she was planning on coming with him to Indresal.

That reminded him, Aliya had yet to answer Sienna's question. Was Aliya even willing to come to Indresal? Enzo knew he was being selfish in wishing that she would say yes. He'd only known her for a couple days at most, but Aliya had already become one of the people he cared about the most.

Enzo leaned forward and softly brushed back the strands of hair on her face. She looked peaceful in her sleep.

No! Not without you! Her words echoed in his mind again as he gazed at her. Those words were the only ones swirling in his mind at the moment.

His gaze softened as his eyes trailed Aliya's features. Her innocent expression with her wide doe eyes that were currently closed, her plump lips slightly ajar, her unruly curly hair that was falling onto her face...

Which might be tickling her now that he saw her scratch her nose where the hair touched.

Aliya looked much younger than she really was.

That brought on Enzo's guilt ten-fold.

She had her entire life in front of her. He shouldn't have dragged her into this mess. He shouldn't be wishing that she'd follow him to Indresal.

But there was no going back now. Damon knew of her existence. So, if he couldn't catch Enzo, there was a very good chance that Damon would go after Aliya.

And that was not a thought that Enzo wanted to entertain even in his dreams.

When Aliya's head bobbed again, Enzo got up from the bed. Slowly making sure that he wasn't making sudden movements to disturb Aliya, he stepped closer to her. He bent down to her level and tucked the loose strands of hair behind her ear, not knowing that simple action brought a big smile to his face.

Gently, he hooked one of his arms behind Aliya's shoulders and another behind Aliya's knees - taking care that he didn't hurt her thigh any further - and slowly lifted her. He didn't even wince when his shoulder bothered him from lifting her. Enzo only stopped for a moment to make sure that Aliya wasn't awake. When he was certain, Enzo turned and placed her gently on the bed. He brought up the thin blanket, covering her up to her chin.

He traced her cheeks with his knuckles, giving her a soft smile. Enzo didn't realize how close he was to Aliya. It was only when he heard someone clear their throat behind him that he jumped back.

Enzo turned to see Sienna giving him a knowing smile.

"I was just placing her on the bed." Enzo scratched the back of his neck. He could feel the blood rushing to his cheeks as he tried to look anywhere but at Aliya or Sienna. When Sienna didn't respond, he looked at her to see her knowing smile only widened.

"I thought she might be more comfortable on the bed than the chair."

Why am I explaining this? Enzo wondered. Although the words didn't stop.

"Oh, I'd assume the bed would be much more comfortable. Especially after she spent the entire night sitting on that chair beside you." Sienna suppressed a smile. "It's not even a very comfortable chair."

"She was beside me the entire time." Enzo didn't know why but that brought a little flutter to his heart. He did hope that Sienna didn't notice the smile that didn't seem to want to leave his face though.

"Yup." Sienna said, popping the 'p'.

Enzo plopped himself on the chair beside Aliya who was now soundly sleeping without a care in the world. He felt Sienna take his arm in hers, removing his bandages and cleaning his wound. But through that, Enzo's gaze didn't seem to waver from Aliya.

"You know, this is her world, right?" Sienna whispered.

That brought him back to reality. Blinking a couple times to come out of his daze, Enzo simply nodded.

"She cannot come into our world." Sienna whispered.

He didn't need the reminding. "Then why did you invite her to Indresal?" His gaze didn't waver from Aliya's sleeping face.

"That was before I remembered the berserkers." Sienna scoffed lightly. "This world," Sienna pursed her lips looking at Enzo. Enzo turned to look at Sienna when she paused. "It has a way to distract you. It has a way to make you forget. I found peace here. Peace and happiness that now, when I look back at Indresal, I only remember the good times I had with my family."

Enzo didn't interrupt her. Instead, he just gazed upon Sienna with a tight smile. He was starting to understand that feeling.

"The berserkers were so far in the back of my mind that I completely forgot their true horrors when I suggested that to her." Sienna said.

Enzo gave her a tight smile, nodding as he looked down at his hands. "I know. I just keep thinking."

His words were cut short when Sienna said, "Don't." Enzo turned to look at her stern expression. Her expression left no room for arguments. "Don't do that to yourself. She belongs here. In this world. Her world. She might think she knows of our world because of all the things I've written in my books. But what I've written only scratches the surface of both the good and bad within our world. She wouldn't be able to survive."

Enzo let out another sigh. As much as he hated to admit it, Sienna was right, of course. Aliya would not survive in Indresal. No matter how much he would try to protect her. He could just lock her in his castle. He could teach her how to fight or even kill. That'd ensure her protection. But just the thought of taking her freedom away made him want to vomit.

No, she wouldn't survive in Indresal.

But that didn't mean that Earth was any better…

"She's not even safe here." He said.

When Sienna looked at him quizzically, he continued. "Damon knows of her existence."

The name of one of the most feared Disciples being uttered so casually sent a shiver down Sienna's spine. Enzo saw her visibly shudder as he mentioned the Disciple's name.

"He won't bother her if you can take him back to our world." Sienna urged.

"But I don't know how to take him back to our world." Enzo complained. His head snapped to Aliya when he realized he'd raised his voice. When Aliya didn't move, he continued. "I don't know why but my portals are not working. I can't create them. So, how can I lead her away from Damon? How do I even protect her when I can't seem to protect myself in this world? My powers are gone. And I never got a chance to fully recover." He hissed back at Sienna.

His words, his fears, his concerns all seemed to pour out. There was no stopping them now. But it was only now that he noticed that most - if not, all - of his concerns centered around Aliya and her safety. He was no longer concerned about himself. He'd been through the worst and came out of it surviving.

But Aliya...

No. Sienna was right. She knew nothing of their world. He was not the heroic character Aliya seemed to revere in the figurine. No, he was flawed.

So very deeply flawed that he wondered if Aliya would look at him the same way if she came to know.

And yet, she still loves you. His mind added, unhelpfully.

It was only when Enzo noticed Sienna's bewildered expression that he stopped. He lifted his eyebrow at her, as if to ask, "What?"

"Did you rely on your power so much that you forgot that you had all the training in your high palace?" Sienna asked. Gone was the reverence that Sienna regarded him with when he first met her in her house. No, instead, now she was sporting the same incredulous face his mother would portray when he'd say something stupid.

Sienna's brows furrowed as if trying to understand his concern. "Figure out a way." She hissed at him. "That girl might need you soon. In this world. So, I don't care if you don't have your powers. Figure out a way. Because there's only so much that I can do."

With that, Sienna grabbed the bowl of ointment and other potions and stormed out of the bedroom, leaving Enzo to stew on his words.

14

"Idiots. I am dealing with idiots." – Sienna

S IENNA PLACED THE BOWL of bandages and ointment on the kitchen counter. She could feel a dull pain forming by her temples. Groaning, Sienna massaged her temples trying to ease her pain. But nothing she did seemed to dull the pain. In fact, it only had the opposite effect.

Sienna groaned again as she bent over the counter. The events of the night before, the action - or adventure for the lack of a better term - the adrenaline, her lack of sleep, everything was catching up to her. Sienna groaned again, this time cursing Aliya and Enzo.

I'm dealing with idiots. She thought to herself. *Two idiots.*

Of all the places they could go to, the two of them had to come to her for help.

It's not like they had that many options. Sienna scoffed.

Of course, she had to write those books. Of course, she had to add in as much detail about her world as possible. Details that clued Enzo that Sienna was of their world.

Of course, they'd come here. Her mind added unhelpfully. *They literally had no place else to go to for help.*

That didn't stop her from cursing her situation at the moment, however. Her house in the city was ruined. If the Disciple knew of her place in the city, she and her family were no longer safe there.

We're safe here. She tried to calm herself. But her nerves didn't seem to want to listen.

Sienna had already warned her wife to not go back home, redirecting her to the cabin. So her wife was safe as well. There was no reason for her to feel like she was in danger anymore.

She was safe.

Her family would be safe - once they came back to the cabin, that was.

But her nerves didn't calm down. Realizing how hard she was gripping the wooden kitchen counter, Sienna flexed her hands, trying to release the tension from them. Craning her neck, she took in deep shaky breaths - a technique her wife taught her to regulate her heartbeat. When that didn't help, Sienna bit her lip.

I'm safe. We're safe. We're no longer in Indresal. We're on Earth. We're no longer in Indresal. She chanted mentally.

But even after three decades of her life, the horrifying images of the battle, the bloodshed, and the rampaging berserkers didn't want to leave her mind.

It'd been seven years since she'd escaped with her family from Indresal to Earth. Seven years of peace. Seven years of not looking behind her shoulder every moment. It took her Seven years but she was finally comfortable with her life here. She no longer cowered at loud noises. She no longer had to constantly look over her shoulder.

Life on Earth was simple.

Why now? She lamented. Her life on earth was perfect.

Sienna didn't stop taking deep breaths. Her body stiffened when she felt a warm hand engulf hers as she didn't let go of the counter.

Looking up from the hand holding hers, she saw Enzo giving her a solemn look. A sad smile pulled at his lips as he moved his hand from hers and onto her back. Enzo rubbed slow circles on her back, shushing her.

"What are those sounds?" Enzo asked, lifting his head as if he was thinking. "Are those birds? Are we in the middle of nowhere?"

"What?" Sienna asked, breathily. *That's his question now?*

"Why did you even get a cabin in the middle of nowhere?"

"So that me and my family can escape from the city sometimes." Sienna replied, her eyes squinting as she wondered what he was getting at.

"Ah, I didn't know you had a family." Enzo murmured.

"You were rummaging around in my house. You didn't see any pictures then?" Sienna mumbled back.

"We weren't exactly rummaging-" He said but was cut off by the questioning look Sienna gave him. "Well, we were trying to find a book. But I couldn't exactly see all the pictures in the dark. And after that, I was a little preoccupied to go sight-seeing around your house."

Sienna rolled her eyes. "Why are you asking about my cabin now? Aren't there bigger things to worry about?"

Enzo didn't reply.

Instead, he looked down at her hands that were gripped tightly onto the counter just a moment before. Except, now they were free beside her.

Looking back at Enzo's sad smile, Sienna realized just what he'd done.

He had successfully distracted her. She could feel her heart beat normally. She was even breathing normally. Her hands were no longer sweaty. Sienna looked up, giving Enzo a small smile in gratitude.

Enzo bent down to her height, bringing his face closer to hers. With a cheeky smile, he searched her face before chuckling as he booped her nose.

Sienna rolled her eyes, smiling widely. *Children.* She shook her head.

Children? That thought made her pause for a moment. Enzo was no more a child than she was. In fact, he was older than her. But with how he looked and acted, anyone would have believed it if Sienna said Enzo was younger than Aliya.

"So, where did you say you were from?" Enzo asked. He walked towards the couch in the living room, craning his neck to the side. Enzo winced when he heard a crack.

He spread himself on the couch taking up almost the entirety of the couch that would normally seat three people.

"Pheandra." Sienna replied.

She saw a dark look pass over his face as his jaw clenched. Sienna knew exactly what he was thinking. She'd seen that look before. That was the look of anger, sympathy and pity that the people of Indresal gave her whenever she told them where she was from.

Pheandra was a kingdom that was surrounded by mountain ranges. Ranges that provided them a natural barrier against the world and the war around them. For hundreds of years, they'd been lucky to stay out of battle.

That had been a mistake.

Because all those years being secluded from the rest of Indresal gave them a false sense of security. A security that the Pheandrans believed that they were protected from anything that was happening around them.

They cared not for the war or any political disturbances that happened around them. They kept to themselves - sometimes, enough that the other kingdoms around them forgot that they still existed.

That had been their mistake.

Because what the Pheandrans didn't realize in their seclusion was how strong the Dark One was getting.

If they did, they probably would have probably prepared for the attack. But the years of negligence and lax in security and defense meant that the people of Pheandra were fresh for the plucking when the Disciples and the berserkers attacked.

But Sienna didn't know that. She was just a child when the first attacks started. Barely ten years of age.

All she remembered was that when the attacks started, the three rivers that ran through the kingdom of Pheandra were drenched in the blood of her people. The pristine snow capped mountains that surrounded her kingdom were littered with berserkers and the bodies of her people.

"When did you leave Pheandra?" Enzo asked, bringing her out of her thoughts.

Sienna blinked, trying to clear her mind. She scoffed before she answered. "More than three decades ago." She said.

Enzo's eyes widened. "When Pheandra fell?"

His words came out as a question but his expression told her that he already knew the answer. Sienna simply nodded.

"You left Pheandra with your family." Enzo said, but it came out more as a question. But looking at Sienna's sad expression he might have realized that he was wrong. So, he asked again, slowly. "What happened to your family?"

Sienna gave him a tight smile as images of the night she barely escaped filled her mind. "My parents died trying to save me and my brother."

Her voice was low as the images filled her mind.

Eight year old Sienna, silently sobbing as she ran, clinging to her father's arm tightly. She had tripped a couple times already. Her knees and legs scraped and bloodied from all her falls.

But her father never stopped the breathtaking pace at which they ran through the cobblestone streets. Shouts and screams filled the streets as the growls from the berserkers trailed the fleeing people. People around her pushed her in every direction as they tried to escape the onslaught of the berserkers. In the commotion, Sienna couldn't see her brother and her mother. She remembered the tears streaming down her face as she wailed for her dad every time someone pushed her.

Finally her father must have gotten enough, because Sienna remembered her father picking her up. She remembered clinging to her father's neck, hiding her face in the nape of his neck. Sienna could still remember the woodsy scent mixed with sweat from her father at that moment. She only looked up for a moment.

That apparently was a mistake because Sienna was able to see the berserkers rampaging behind them. Her little eyes widened as she clung tighter onto her father. Not being able to see all the berserkers and their bloodlust anymore, the young Sienna shut her eyes and screamed into her father's neck.

She wept silently as her father ran down the streets. Sienna didn't know where they were going. Because chaos reigned everywhere she looked. There was not one place she could see that was safe from the berserkers tearing down her town. The only safe place she knew of at that moment was in her father's arms. Her father hugged her tightly as he dashed through the streets and alleyways. Sienna had her head buried in her father's neck, not daring for a second to look behind her.

Sienna didn't realize when she and her father were rejoined by her mother and brother again. They were all together... And for that moment, even in the chaos, she had hope that everything would be alright.

Hope that seemed to be squashed as the night drew closer.

Sienna only let go of her father after they'd run the entire night, finally seeking shelter in a lone cave in one of the mountains surrounding Pheandra.

When she finally let go of her father, Sienna clung onto her brother. She didn't let go of his hand the entire night. She could still remember her parents telling her brother something. But for the life of her, she couldn't remember what they said. Even now, their voices sounded hollow and distant.

But no matter what, Sienna didn't let go of her brother's arm. Clinging onto him as if her life depended on him. Which, for that night, it did.

That was the last time Sienna saw her parents alive.

The last time she felt her mother's soft caress on her cheeks as she tearfully kissed Sienna. And the last time she felt her father's hug.

It'd been so long since that evening.

So long ago that she'd forgotten how her mother and father looked. No matter how much she tried, she couldn't remember. She couldn't remember their features even if she tried. If anyone were to show her a picture of her parents right now, she would definitely not recognize them. But she did remember a few things about them.

She remembered her mother's love.

Sienna could still feel her mother's lips on her forehead - her mother's last tearful kiss before heading out of the cave to face the berserkers.

Sienna remembered her father's tight grip on her as he carried her through the crowded streets as people shoved each other to get to safety. She remembered his desperation to keep his children safe - even if he knew he couldn't come out of it alive.

It was only later, when Sienna was much older, that she'd come to realize how the Disciple and the berserkers came through the undefended mountain pass.

And the Disciple that led the charge to tear through her kingdom...

Damon al'Kara.

Sienna realized she'd been in her head thinking of that night the entire time. She looked up at Enzo giving him a sad smile when his wide eyes turned soft at his realization.

He was a prince. He probably studied about that night.

The night Pheandra fell into the hands of the Dark One.

Sienna knew of the stories that were spread over Indresal about the fall of Pheandra. About the rampage. About how there were only a handful of people that survived that night. News had gone out to all the seven remaining kingdoms.

Pheandra had fallen.

The message echoed in hushed voices through everyone in Indresal.

Just like that. The Kingdoms that once didn't bother or care for the Kingdom of Pheandra shook at their core at how easily it fell.

They mourned the loss of Pheandra. It was only when Sienna was older that she realized that the other Kingdom's mourning was more because of their fear. A soul-shattering fear as they made contingencies on what they'd do if something like Pheandra happened to their Kingdom.

And so, Pheandra became a lesson. Relegated to the status of myth or a legend or at best, a cautionary tale.

The people of Pheandra - or rather, the last remaining survivors of Pheandra - fled the region to other kingdoms. Scattering around Indresal, trying to escape any attacks, integrating into the customs of the various kingdoms that gave them solace.

No one knew if the remaining Pheandrans were still alive.

Even if they were, no one knew how many of them were left. With their Kingdom gone, their houses demolished, and their loved ones either killed or turned into Berserkers for the Dark One, everyone in Indresal pitied the last remaining members.

So, Sienna understood Enzo's shock. He was finally seeing one right in front of him. One that was not only alive but a Pheandran that managed to not only escape the wrath of that fateful night, but also managed to escape Indresal. Sienna gave him a proud smile.

She was a survivor.

A fighter.

She'd seen death in its face and walked away, smirking.

Sienna saw the wheels turning in Enzo's mind as he gaped like a fish with his eyes wide. But just as he opened his mouth to ask another question, they heard a car stop outside the cabin.

Enzo tensed, looking around. He only relaxed when he noticed that Sienna wasn't on her guard.

Instead, Sienna walked to the front door of the cabin, opening it wide. And in walked a woman, slightly shorter than Sienna herself. The yellow floral sundress she was wearing complimented her dark skin. Her long, thin braids were held together like a bun atop her head. She held onto a small, sleeping child.

Sienna didn't care that the child was sleeping. She hugged both the woman and the child, not letting go of them for a long time. When she finally did, Sienna clutched the woman's cheeks, giving her a chaste kiss on her lips. Sienna leaned her forehead on the woman's taking in the moment for a couple seconds longer.

With a hand on the woman's shoulders, she turned to Enzo with a proud smile.

"Meet my wife, Anya, and my child, Sanya." Sienna said with a wide smile.

15

"So, even Princes can be idiots." – Sienna

SIENNA TRAILED BEHIND HER wife. The two of them walked to their child's bedroom leaving Enzo alone in the living room and gently placed the sleeping child in her crib.

Once they tucked Sanya in her cot and made sure that their baby was sound asleep, the two of them walked back out into the living room just as quietly.

Sienna and Anya stood by the door to their child's bedroom. Anya gazed between Enzo and Sienna. Enzo hadn't moved the entire time. Instead, he leaned forward, placing his elbows on his knees. His hands were clasped as he stared at the ground, deep in thought.

"Are you sure he's a prince?" Anya whispered, low enough that only Sienna could hear. "I thought he'd be more..." Anya stood straight with her head held high. She placed her hands on her hip, mimicking what she assumed was authority. But to Sienna, Anya simply looked cuter than she was.

Sienna chuckled but her chuckles quickly subsided.

Anyone would have asked that question if they'd seen Enzo. He looked haggard and deep in thought as if the rest of the world didn't exist. His loose shirt and baggy pants were torn and bloodied. His hair looked knotted as it fell across his face. Enzo just looked broken.

Sienna nodded. "Yup." She said, placing her hand on the small of her wife's back.

"Hello, I'm Anya." Sienna's wife introduced herself, snapping Enzo out of his thoughts.

He blinked a couple times before shaking his head. Finally, Enzo stood up, bowing low to Anya as a greeting.

"You didn't greet me like that." Sienna sulked folding her arms, making him smile a little.

"You wanted me to greet you after breaking into your house?" Enzo countered.

"You broke into our house?" Anya's head snapped from Enzo to Sienna and back again.

Sienna simply rolled her eyes and motioned her hands as if to say "I'll tell you later."

"Are you from Pheandra too?" Enzo asked meekly, as if he didn't know if it was rude or not to ask that question.

Anya squinted her eyes as she analyzed him for a moment. "No." She finally shook her head. Although she didn't offer any more information.

Instead, Anya kissed Sienna on her cheek before walking over to the kitchen. "I'll bring over some tea." She whispered to Sienna.

Sienna smiled as she watched her wife walk into the kitchen. When she turned back to Enzo, he gave her a soft smile with an expression that Sienna couldn't read.

Was that longing?

"You two look cute together." Enzo said as Sienna sat on the sofa opposite him. The two of them sat comfortably in silence again. Well, that was until Enzo looked up at her again. "How did you and your brother escape Pheandra?" He asked.

"Honestly, I don't remember." Sienna shrugged. "I don't remember anything after my parents left the cave. All I remember is that by the time I woke up, it was daylight and my brother was carrying me through the streets of Illadora."

"He carried you?" Enzo's brows were raised. "How old was he?"

"He was fifteen - about seven years older than me." Sienna couldn't help the slow smile that formed on her face as she thought of her brother.

He had her red hair that was longer at the top of his head than it was at the bottom. His piercing green eyes were always wide and mischievous. She always remembered her parents asking him to behave lest she learn all his mischievous ways.

Not that it stopped him from teaching her how to not get in trouble. She remembered him giving her piggy back rides everywhere and anywhere she wanted. He'd also promised to show her the short cuts around the village once she was grown up.

Not that the time ever came for that.

They left the village before that could happen.

But either way, Sienna always looked up to her brother.

"What happened?" Enzo asked.

"We were in Illadora for about a year. Never stayed in one place for more than a few weeks. We were both scared that if we stayed for more than a few weeks, we'd be stuck in another berserker attack." The smile Sienna had when she thought of her brother was no longer present.

Memories flooded in of their time staying in inns and taverns. Her brother would work at the tavern for their food and shelter. That would last a few weeks before they'd move again.

"We slowly made our way through Illadora and ended up in Eitish a couple years later." Sienna bit her lip. "We hadn't encountered a berserker attack in so long. We thought we would be safe in Eitish, at least for the time being. But it was only a year later that Eitish was attacked and we had to leave."

Sienna chuckled sadly, making Enzo cock his eyebrow. "That was the first time I saw my brother like someone. He was normally a charming person. But..." Sienna let out another chuckle. "Well, in front of the girl he liked, he became a blubbering mess. It was adorable, really." Her face scrunched as if she'd tasted something sour. "And annoying, really."

That earned a soft smile from Enzo as well. But before Enzo could ask her more questions, Sienna continued.

"We no longer trusted the land, you know." Sienna shook her head, still lost in her thoughts. "We promised each other we'll only be on the land if we absolutely had to. So, my brother took a job at the shipping yard. We spent about three years on the river, transporting food and goods from Eitish and Qadia. I thought life was finally getting better."

The somber look was back as Sienna's eyes danced between the wooden planks on the floor.

"But good things don't usually last long, do they?" Sienna looked up at Enzo, giving him a tight smile. Her eyes moved towards the motion in the corner of her eye.

Aliya rubbed her eyes as she yawned. She barely managed to not bump herself into the door as she walked out of the bedroom. When Aliya stopped yawning, she looked between Sienna and Enzo, electing to sit beside Enzo.

Sienna simply suppressed a smile in response. Aliya hadn't seen her smile but she was sure that if Aliya had, she'd been a blushing mess - like Enzo was right now.

Enzo cleared his throat bringing Sienna back to her story.

"The ports of Qadia were silent when we docked one day. There was no man or woman to be found. But the entire dock was filled with smears and splatters of blood. That was the first time I'd heard a port be that silent." Sienna shuddered slightly. "But there seemed to be a couple lone berserkers. When the berserkers charged at us, my brother - he was the Captain's assistant then - he..." Sienna took in a deep breath, trying to clear the knot behind her throat. "He pushed me back onto the ship and untied the ropes. He was left on the dock along with a couple other sailors. That was the last thing I remember of him."

Silence filled the cabin as Sienna took a few seconds to mourn her brother.

She could feel the stinging in the back of her eyes. Tears formed but she refused to shed them. Her hands turned into fists as she tried to control her emotions. Sienna took in a couple deep breaths as her memories came flooding in again.

She didn't want to tell Enzo all of it though. He didn't need to know all of it. He didn't need to know how she became a mage.

No one needed to know that.

That was a story she'd rather take to the grave.

"I honestly don't know how I got through the next few years. But I was wandering through the streets of Qadia a few years later. That's where I met Anya."

Sienna gazed lovingly at her wife who was still rummaging in the kitchen.

The sun glistened against her dark black skin. Her doe eyes crinkled at the edges as she gave Sienna a soft smile. The long braids adorning the top of her head in a bun were decorated with small white flowers, making Anya look ethereal.

When Anya heard her name, she smiled as her gaze met Sienna's. From the corner of her eyes, Sienna noticed Enzo peeking at Aliya.

"But a few years ago, I came across a book. It contained the ancient knowledge of the witches before me." Sienna said. That wasn't exactly the complete truth but Enzo didn't need to know that. "The book talked about alternate universes. Alternate dimensions. Universes that were more dangerous than Indresal. Universes that were much safer than Indresal. But it was written in the ancient tongue. So, it took me almost five years to translate it."

"But you did, didn't you?" This time it was Aliya that interrupted her. Aliya's eyes were wide as curiosity bubbled within her. She clutched the sofa as she sat at the edge of the seat unaware of Enzo's frown.

Looking between Enzo's frown and Aliya's excitement, Sienna wondered, almost incredulously. *How is she so blind?*

But Sienna answered either way

"Yes, I did finish translating it." Sienna lifted her arms pointing to herself. "I'm here, aren't I?"

"So, where's the book?" Aliya said again, this time earning an eye roll from Enzo.

Sienna winced. It seemed she didn't need to answer as Aliya gave her a tight smile.

"It's back in your other house, isn't it?"

Sienna simply nodded.

"I can go get-" Aliya wondered out loud but she was interrupted by a furious Enzo.

"Don't even think of finishing that sentence."

"But we need the book to get back." Aliya protested, looking as if she was only a few arguments away from hitting Enzo. She then turned to Sienna. "Unless you remember how to get back to Indresal."

Sienna shook her head. "We're going to need that book unless you want me to mess up that spell." She simply said.

"See!" Aliya pointed to Sienna as if she'd just won the argument. "We need the book. I can go get the book. What's there to argue about?"

"Did you forget that we were just chased out of that house?" Enzo countered.

"Do you really think the bad guy is going to be staying in that house, sipping tea waiting for us like a Bond villain?"

"Like who?" Enzo's brows scrunched.

Aliya only rolled her eyes and shook her head in answer.

"What makes you think the book is still there?"

"It's not like the berserkers were there for the book. They were there for you." Aliya gestured at him.

"And how do you know that?"

Is he serious? Sienna wondered, bewildered. She'd been looking between Aliya and Enzo as they argued. But she had to agree with Aliya here. The berserkers were there for Enzo. Not for her book. *Is being near her really messing with his mind that much?*

Finally getting tired of their bickering, Sienna chimed in.

"How about the two of you go?" Sienna raised her voice. "Aliya can search for the book. And you can protect her if you're so worried about her." Aliya gave Enzo a satisfied smile, as if she'd just won an argument. Sienna mumbled to herself. "And I can get a moment of peace away from you kids."

"I am perfectly fine going alone." Aliya mumbled but stopped when Sienna gave her a warning glare.

It's like I'm babysitting two kids. Sienna exhaled exasperatedly. *Even Sanya doesn't give me this much trouble.* She thought about her kid.

But Sanya was only five years old. Sienna began to wonder if this was what she had to look forward to as Sanya grew up. Her eyes widened. Sienna was never this petulant, was she?

When Enzo and Aliya didn't utter another word, Sienna continued.

"Good, so it's settled then. The two of you are getting the book together."

16

"She. Is. Infuriating!". - Enzo

ENZO LEANED AGAINST SIENNA's car with his arms folded. Sienna had given them a change of clothes. Old ragged and loose shirts of hers that seemed to fit him. His loose gray t-shirt flapped with the breeze, making him shiver slightly. He finally got a good look at the cabin from the outside and he had to admit. The cabin was beautiful.

The one storey log cabin looked natural and rustic as it blended into the surrounding woods. From this distance, Enzo could see the moss growing on the roof of the cabin. With the rustling leaves, swaying trees, and the chirping birds, this was the most peaceful place he'd ever been since he...

Well, since he was born.

If there ever was a chance of the war being over in his lifetime, if there ever was a chance that he could settle down peacefully, this would be the place he would choose. His ears twitched when he heard running water in the distance.

Is there a river nearby? He wondered. *Maybe a pond or a waterfall?*

Shaking his head, Enzo looked towards the cabin front door where Sienna and Aliya were deep in conversation. Although Sienna looked like a mother giving her daughter all the precautions before her daughter left the house. Enzo saw her wrap something around Aliya's wrist, although he was far enough away that he couldn't clearly see what it was.

"This is the key for the cabinet. You remember where the cabinet is, don't you?" Sienna asked Aliya. Aliya nodded, grabbing the keys.

She gave Sienna one last smile before bouncing down the steps on the front door.

"And not a scratch on my car!" Sienna shouted as the two of them got into her car.

Although Aliya rolling her eyes was the only response she'd gotten. "It's not like we're going to crash it." She mumbled as she pulled the car out of the driveway.

"It's also not as if we don't have two beasts and a maniac chasing us." Enzo said.

Stopping the car for a second, Aliya bit her lip as if she was thinking. "You know... touche. But we have something that the maniac doesn't." Aliya seemed to take Enzo's confusion as an invitation to continue. "This," She patted the steering wheel. "This, my friend, might look like a regular SUV to you. But this car is a Lamborghini."

A low purr from the engine startled Enzo as Aliya drove down the road. "If we have them tailing us, this will help us escape."

Enzo's face contorted in confusion at her reply.

None of that made any sense to Enzo, however. But the manic glee on Aliya's face as she drove down the winding roads was enough for him to just stare at her and not question anything she said. She could have spoken another language for all he knew.

But something about this car made her happy. So, he was going to let her stay this way.

The two of them drove in silence. Aliya followed the directions from the map on her phone. The directions from Aliya's phone were the only sounds that interrupted their silence. Aliya didn't even bother to play some music, enjoying the way the car glided on the roads.

She must really like this car. Enzo thought. He had to admit that the car was smooth. Although, with Aliya driving like a maniac, he thought it'd be better if he held onto the handles.

Enzo gazed at the passing woods. The blurring greenery gave him a sense of peace that he hadn't had in a long time. He could finally see why Sienna chose this world to move into.

Compared to Indresal, Earth was... well, it was boring.

However, after a lifetime of war, running from berserkers, and struggling to even survive, boring was equal to heaven.

Enzo didn't know if the war would be over in his lifetime. He really hoped it would be. At least then he could come back to Earth. Maybe then he would be able to meet Aliya again.

His heart felt heavy at that thought.

By then, she might have already moved on from him. If he thought his heart was heavy when he thought of leaving her, it was nothing compared to thinking of her moving on from him.

Would she even remember me then? Enzo began to wonder.

He was only a few hours away from getting the book - meaning, he was only a couple days at most from going back to Indresal. Enzo took in a deep breath taking a peak at Aliya beside him.

Two days at most that you can spend with her. Enzo thought.

Enzo felt a dull ache spread through his chest. He was starting to like spending time with Aliya - although, he didn't know how she felt.

Maybe I can take her to Indresal. He wondered. But as soon as that thought made its way through his mind, he squashed it.

No, bringing Aliya would only endanger her. All the images of how she could be harmed ran through his mind, sending a shiver down his spine. *No, she cannot come back.*

But he couldn't help but wonder. Maybe he could get her to stay in his castle. Maybe she'd just be safe in his castle. There hadn't been any attacks on his kingdom. He'd been very diligent in protecting his people. Enzo could protect Aliya too.

She'd just stay in his castle, safe and sound. And at the first hint of danger, he'd use the spells in the book to send her back to Earth.

No, you're being selfish! He chastised himself, taking a peak at Aliya from the corner of his eyes again.

But he didn't feel any guilt at being selfish though. The more time he'd been spending on Earth, the more he was starting to realize that there was more to his life than battle after battle. Whether she wanted to or not, Aliya had shown him that. And the more time he'd been spending on Earth, the more he'd begun to consider her his solace. And he wanted to take what little solace he had back with him to Indresal.

She'd be his peace. Maybe he could just show her around and then let her come back to her life here.

But is that what she'd want? His mind added unhelpfully.

Enzo was brought out of his thoughts when he heard a small chuckle from Aliya. He turned to see that she was suppressing a smile.

"What is it?" Enzo asked, smiling. Her chuckle was contagious.

"When we first went to her house, we were basically sneaking around for the book. But now," Another chuckle. "Now, she's just handing it to us."

Enzo shook his head, smiling at the turn of events.

"Do you think she'll let me borrow the book?" Aliya thought out loud, her tongue sticking slightly out from her lips again. "I want to see if I can do a few spells."

"You want to see if you're a mage?"

"I could be a mage. Maybe a healer? Oh, I could even be an assassin!" Aliya looked almost offended. "You'd never know."

"And what would you do if you found out that you were a witch?" Enzo crossed his arms again, a small smirk playing on his lips. He didn't know what the medicine Sienna placed on his shoulder but he couldn't feel the pain anymore. For that, he was very thankful.

Aliya shrugged. "I don't know. Maybe I could come to Indresal and help with the war."

That sobered him up. "You want to come to Indresal?"

It was as if she heard his inner turmoil. However, her confirmation that she wanted to join him in Indresal did little to soothe him. Enzo should be happy. This was what he wanted. But hearing it directly from Aliya, made it all the more real.

"Why not?"

"Because it's dangerous."

Aliya scoffed. "As if this place isn't dangerous." She mumbled.

"Indresal has been in a constant state of war ever since I was born." Enzo tried to reason with her.

But her deadpan expression as she turned to look at him only made him wonder if he'd judged Earth a little too quickly.

"You're not coming to Indresal." Enzo said with a finality. He heard Aliya mumble to herself but it was low enough that he couldn't understand what she said.

Suddenly a thought occurred to him.

"Are you saying that you wanted to come to Indresal because you wanted to meet all your favorite characters?" Enzo asked.

He knew she'd always thought of his story as just that... a story. Now that it was confirmed that he wasn't just stories, Enzo wondered if she was being adamant just so she could be a part of it.

One look at her guilty expression and tight embarrassed smile said as much.

Before Enzo could say anything else, Aliya brushed him off as she sighed.

"Well, my favorite character died though." She said, as she bit her lip. "Or maybe I should say my favorite person died."

That confused Enzo even more.

Aliya had pictures of him. She had his figurines, his drawings and his paintings all over her house. What did she mean her favorite character is dead?

Am I not her favorite character? He looked at her incredulously. *No, that can't be.*

Enzo felt a stab of jealousy. He pursed his lips as he tried to discreetly clear his throat. Who else could be her favorite? He bit his bottom lip, trying to look as calm as possible. He just hoped that Aliya didn't see his hands balled into fists. No matter how much he tried, he couldn't seem to control that.

Adjusting himself in the seat, he wondered if he could ask her who her favorite character was.

No, you don't need to know that. His pride answered for him.

But his curiosity was another matter, altogether. The more his pride told him that he didn't need to know, the more his curiosity got the better of him.

Adjusting himself again in his seat, he tried to be as subtle as possible as he asked. "So, who's your favorite character?"

He didn't care to turn his head to look at Aliya. But even then, he scowled when he saw the wide smile spreading across her face from the corner of his eyes. A light blush tinged her brown cheeks, making him roll his eyes.

"Chan." Aliya's smile widened even more, as if that was even possible. Enzo racked his mind to see if he knew anyone by that name. He didn't have to wonder long though. "Sienna's brother. He was the one that got her out of Pheandra and took care of her the entire time. Well, that was until he died, of course."

"But you have my figurines in your house?" He asked, as if Aliya had betrayed him by saying Chan was her favorite. Enzo had never felt this sort of betrayal before. To be fair, he'd much rather prefer the politics and the betrayals in battle than this. Enzo crossed his arms, sliding down his seat as he sulked.

Aliya shrugged. "You were a close second."

"Second?!" His voice came out as a squeak. "Unbelievable." He rolled his eyes.

"Well, I didn't get much of your story in the books anyway." Aliya muttered, trying to defend herself.

"Not everything about everyone's life can be found in books, Aliya!" Enzo raised his voice. Although he wondered what was comical when he heard Aliya snicker. She was definitely enjoying this. "Sometimes, you have to get to know the person before they become a favorite character."

Enzo couldn't hold his contempt any longer. Especially not after he'd known the story of Sienna's brother.

Of course.

The one person that she fell for and he couldn't even compete with his story.

Enzo sneered as he rolled his eyes.

It's ok. His mind added. *At least she doesn't completely remember his name. I'm still her favorite.* And as if that wasn't petty enough, he thought again. *And I'm alive.*

Aliya's snickering didn't stop though. She did have the wherewithal to stifle her laughs, however. That only seemed to make Enzo sulk more.

Enzo didn't speak to Aliya for the rest of the ride.

Instead, he folded his hands, watching the buildings pass as he sulked at not being her favorite character.

17

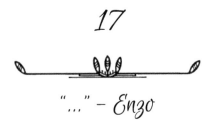

"..." – Enzo

I T TOOK THEM ALMOST three hours to get back to Sienna's house.
Three hours of complete silence.

A silence imposed by Enzo as he still sulked that he was not her favorite character. Not that it stopped Aliya from teasing him everytime he looked at her. He had long since stopped sulking. But hearing her chuckle every time he looked at her was enough for him to continue the charade.

By the end of the ride, Enzo only remained silent to hear Aliya chuckle.

Aliya slowed down to a stop as they turned into Sienna's neighborhood. It was already late afternoon by the time they reached her neighborhood. And Enzo just wanted to get the book and go back home.

"Why are we stopping here?" Enzo asked.

"We practically trashed her house while we left. If any of her neighbors saw us when we escaped, they might have called the police." Aliya said. "I'm already a broke college student. I can't afford the police being on my tail in this economy."

Words.

Aliya said words.

But Enzo only understood some of it.

Enzo looked at her quizzically. He might not have understood a word she'd said but if she was sure there might be other people checking Sienna's house, Enzo would follow Aliya's judgment. But to Enzo, everything looked normal.

Much to her concern, there wasn't anyone outside Sienna's house.

The driveway that they left the night before looked the same. From the outside, the house looked normal. There wasn't even a single sign to show that there had been a fight inside the house the night before.

He turned to see Aliya biting her lip, deep in thought. She still pulled into Sienna's driveway cautiously. As if one wrong move was all she needed before she could drive them away from here.

"It looks safe now, Aliya." Enzo whispered.

He saw her audibly gulp, making him wonder if she was worried about being caught by others or if she was scared from the night before. Enzo placed his hand over hers on the steering wheel, nodding at her in reassurance.

As Aliya stopped the car in the driveway, the two of them got out.

This time, instead of walking to the kitchen window, the two of them walked to the front door, unlocking it with the key Sienna gave Aliya.

Enzo pushed Aliya behind him before entering the house. The two of them almost gasped at the destruction within the house. There wasn't a single piece of furniture that wasn't trashed or knocked off its place. Splinters from the broken wooden shelves and cupboards laid strewn everywhere. Shards of glass littered the ground. Paintings were tilted as they barely hung onto the walls. Streaks of blood lined some of the walls giving him flashbacks to the night before.

This was their evidence of their gruesome fight with Damon and his two berserkers.

But as terrible as the house looked, it was the silence that gave Enzo comfort. Silence meant that Damon and his two berserkers were no longer in the house. And that was exactly how Enzo liked it.

It was only when he deemed everything was safe that Enzo turned to let Aliya in. Although she didn't seem to appreciate him pushing her behind him.

Aliya folded her arms, rolling her eyes. She dashed him lightly as she walked past Enzo and entered the house.

"Where did she say the book was?" Enzo asked, trailing behind her like a lost puppy.

"In the library."

"We were just in the library last night. Couldn't she have gotten the book then?" Enzo mumbled.

"In case you forgot, we were a little preoccupied last night."

Enzo rolled his eyes, watching his step as they made their way to Sienna's office which also doubled as her library.

"You know, I'm still wondering..." Aliya muttered out loud, trailing off in the end.

"Wondering what?" Enzo asked, his interred piqued.

Aliya stopped walking and turned around. Her tongue peaked between her lips again. "Your name." She said as if that answered his question.

"What about my name?" Enzo asked, flipping the shelf that fell down.

It was empty. All the figurines that were once on the shelf were now on the ground. Enzo scowled. He'd hoped the book would be here so they could get it quickly and leave.

"Your name was the first one Damon called when he first entered the house."

"Yes." Enzo dragged out his answer, not understanding where she was going with this.

"How did he know you'd be here?" She asked, tilting her head. Her gaze was distant as if she was thinking of all the possibilities.

That gave him a pause. Aliya did have a point.

How did Damon know where Enzo was going to be?

Aliya didn't wait for an answer before turning around and heading for the office again. But Enzo couldn't.

"It's like he knew you were going to be here." Aliya mumbled more to herself as she continued to walk to Sienna's office.

Questions kept buzzing in his mind. How was Damon even tracking him? It wasn't as if he was letting Damon know of his location. If Damon was entering a random house, he wouldn't have known Enzo was in it. But by calling for Enzo the minute Damon entered Sienna's house, he'd revealed that he knew Enzo was in there.

When Enzo noticed that he could no longer see Aliya, Enzo shook his head as he rushed to the library in Sienna's office.

Why doesn't she stay still in one place? Enzo groaned.

Sienna's office seemed to be the only room that wasn't trashed like the rest of the house. As they entered the office, Aliya headed straight for Sienna's large wooden desk. Enzo chuckled as he watched her struggle with the desk.

"I swear, when I get my own house, I'm going to have a library just like this one." Aliya muttered to herself.

"The house that you live in, that's not yours?" Enzo asked, bewildered.

Aliya stopped tinkering with the desk for a moment to look up at Enzo, bewildered. "Again. I'm a broke college student." She said, as if that answered all his questions.

When she finally got the desk cabinet to open, she let out a loud, "Tada!"

Enzo chuckled at her antics. He walked closer to the desk. He'd been keeping an eye out for the beasts and Damon. It didn't matter how much he checked though, after last night, Enzo couldn't let his guard drop.

"For a book as important as this, I'm surprised she just used a simple safe." Aliya muttered.

"Sometimes the best way to keep something safe is the simplest one."

Aliya gave him another deadpan look. "I could open this with a blow-torch." She said, simply, pointing at the metal safe with both her hands.

"And in doing so, you will burn the book within it. People would just get a charred book with incomplete spells. The book would be of no use to anyone."

Aliya shrugged. "Not if you only concentrate it only on the lock, you won't. You're basically handing the book to your enemies by keeping it in here."

Enzo's brows furrowed. Was she thinking of something else? What other technology does this Earth have that they could control fire as such? All the tactics that Enzo knew of wouldn't help with getting the book out of the safe intact.

Concentrating the fire on the lock? He wondered. *Can the people of this world do that?*

In Indresal, only certain elves and fire mages could control the fire. And even then, concentrating their fire power would require years of practice. Did the people of Earth master this ability that quickly? Now, he really wanted to see that.

Enzo bent over the desk to look at the book as Aliya opened the safe. There was only one thing in the safe. It was a simple black leather journal with embroidered designs in the corner.

"And the journal doesn't even have a lock!" Aliya said exasperatedly.

Groaning loudly, Aliya grabbed the journal and slammed the safe shut, not bothering to close the safe again.

"Let's go!" She said, cheerfully. Aliya skipped the entire way out of the house making Enzo chuckle at her antics.

Although his chuckles died down quickly when he realized they'd have another three and a half hours drive back to the cabin.

Three and a half hours in that... car.

He'd very much prepare to portal himself back to the cabin. But with his powers not working in this world, this... car should do. No matter how fast or smooth it drove. The only solace was that it was more time to spend with Aliya. Time that he'd not have when he goes back to Indresal.

Enzo threw his head back, groaning, preparing himself for the ride as he got into the car.

18

"I thought he was going to be taller." – Aliya

THEY'D ALREADY BEEN DRIVING for two and half hours.

Aliya didn't know how many times she'd zoned out as she drove down the winding roads. Concrete buildings that surrounded them had long turned into lush greenery. Even the noise reduced the closer they got to Sienna's cabin. The hustle of the city was nowhere to be found as they got closer to the nature around them. There were barely any cars driving with them.

It was peaceful.

And with how smooth the car was driving, she felt herself relax more. Aliya shook her head a couple times, trying to wake herself up.

Not that it helped with the consistent yawns that made her tear up. It didn't matter how hard Aliya blinked to rid her eyes of the tears, she could still feel her eyelids drooping.

When none of her tactics helped, Aliya turned on the music, not caring what played. She sang along to all the songs that played, only stopping when she heard Enzo chuckle.

"What's so funny?" She asked, chuckling along with him. It wasn't exactly her fault that his laugh was contagious. And was that a small dimple?

Sienna didn't describe the dimple when she wrote about Enzo. Then again, anytime Sienna spoke of Enzo in her book, it was during battles and his strategies where he'd trick his enemies and save the people. There wasn't an occasion for Enzo to smile - much rather laugh - as he was doing now. Aliya admired him. Her gaze softened as he looked at Enzo from the corner of her eyes.

That was, until he said, "Your voice is atrocious."

Although, that only prompted Aliya to sing louder, making him laugh harder.

This man beside her was slowly getting into her. If they'd met under different circumstances, Aliya could definitely see herself being friends with Enzo... and who knows? Maybe something more. Aliya shook her head slightly.

No. Stop! She chastised herself. *He needs to go back.*

Although a small part of her hoped that he would offer her to join him when he goes back to Indresal. It didn't matter now though. She was going to enjoy what little time she had with him for now.

Aliya chuckled again when she heard Enzo laugh again.

"You're terrible at singing." Enzo said.

Instead of singing louder this time, she said, haughtily. "Music is meant to be enjoyed." She said haughtily. "And I enjoy music by singing."

"Yes, well, when you start singing, I can't enjoy it." Enzo said, chuckling.

Aliya didn't hesitate to smack his arm, harder than required. "You can plug your ears then. Because I am not stopping." She chuckled.

With one hand on the steering wheel, she acted out the song as she sang... horrendously. Aliya gave out a satisfied grin when she heard Enzo's pained yelp as he rubbed the area she smacked.

"Eyes on the road, woman!" Enzo giggled again. "You're going to get us killed."

Enzo lowered his window, smelling the crisp clean air. The two of them calmed down letting the music fill the silence. When Aliya yawned again, her eyes flitted to the gas tank that was almost empty. It was only when she turned into a gas station that Enzo chimed in.

"Why are we stopping?" He asked, looking around.

"We need gas." Aliya said. When she noticed his quizzical expression, she continued. "Cars run on gas. It's what gives them the energy to move forward. The gas for this car is almost empty and we need to fill it."

"That sounds primitive." He said, making Aliya scoff.

"Well, if your powers were working, we wouldn't have to use this primitive vehicle." She snapped back.

Aliya was really starting to question why he was her favorite character. He looked so good on paper. He was mysterious, smart, dashing, heroic, and everything she wanted. But actually meeting him was a completely different story. He hadn't stopped complaining about Earth from the moment he stepped foot on it.

Never meet your heroes. Aliya scoffed again. *Maybe he'll stop complaining once he's back in Indresal.*

That gave her a pause. He was going to go back to his world. And she wanted to go with him. She'd tried to bring up the subject on their way to Sienna's house. But his lack of response made her dejected.

Maybe he just wants to protect you. Aliya thought hopefully. Scenarios of all the fanfics she'd read began to play in her mind. That thought lasted for only a second before she snapped herself back to reality.

Stop being delusional. He might be a prince but this isn't a fairytale. He's not going to whisk you off your feet after meeting you for a couple days.

171

"And we can get that here?" Enzo asked, snapping her out of her reverie. He looked around the gas station again, as if judging its entire existence.

Maybe he was.

"We have another hour and a half to drive back." Aliya said as she stopped. "Are you hungry? We could get something to..."

She didn't need to complete that sentence. Enzo's wide pleading eyes gave her the response she needed. Enzo was a conundrum. He was a nuisance complaining about everything one second, and the next he looked at her as if she had the answer to every puzzle in the world.

"Hold on." Was all she said. She paid for the gas and handed her credit card to Enzo. "That building there..." She pointed to the convenience store in the distance. "They have all the food we could need for the ride back. Here, take this." Aliya handed him her card. "Get anything you want. And when you're done, please don't just walk out." At Enzo's confused expression. "There will be a cashier at the front. Give him this card, yeah?"

"This card?" He flipped the credit card Aliya gave him. An eyebrow raised as he looked at the card as if it'd just accused him of committing a crime.

"Yes, that card. You can buy anything you want with it." Aliya said. "Just don't buy the whole store. I don't have the funds for that."

Aliya chuckled as she saw Enzo's eyes light up. He quickly got out of the car and flipped her card again before heading inside the convenience store.

Shaking her head, Aliya turned to finish filling the car. She took in a deep breath, as she looked at the surroundings.

The green trees looked vibrant against the dark cloudy skies. The trees swayed with the wind gusts. Aliya could smell the moisture in the air. A few seconds of admiring the nature around her, she realized something.

She couldn't hear any animals. No sounds of the birds chirping, or the frogs croaking, or even the crickets chirping. Aliya could feel the hair stand in the back of her neck as a cold shiver ran down her spine.

Is there a tiger nearby? She wondered before shaking her head at her stupidity. *No, there are no wild tigers in america.*

She remembered one of the documentaries. What she also remembered was that she needed to be on guard when the forest was quiet like it did at the moment. That could mean that there was a predator nearby.

Maybe there's a different predator nearby. Or well, maybe one escaped! Or maybe it's a bear.

Aliya edged her way to the gas nozzle, squeezing it tighter as if the gas would fill the car quicker. She could feel her heart beat quicker.

She was about to call for Enzo, when she heard a voice behind her.

"Hello there, child." A deep gravelly voice startled Aliya, making her squeak.

She turned on her heel, wide eyed, staring at the man in front of her. His gray hair was cut short and neatly gelled. There was barely a strand of hair out of place. He was taller than Aliya by more than a foot, making her tilt her head to see him. His wrinkles were the only ones that betrayed his age. Aliya looked back to his chiseled face. For someone who was setting off all the alarm bells in Aliya's mind, he had one of the kindest eyes she'd seen.

If she didn't know any better, Aliya would have smiled, treating this man like she would have done to anyone else. But unfortunately for him, Aliya knew who he was.

Damon al'Kara

Aliya knew he was dangerous. Especially with how Enzo and Sienna reacted to hearing him in Sienna's house the first time. She knew she should be afraid of him. But Aliya held her ground, not stepping back even when Damon walked closer to her.

"It's normally considered respectful to greet people when they greet you." Damon said. His brows furrowed as if he was curious. "Unless the customs here are different."

Aliya gave him a sarcastically sweet smile. "Oh, they're not." It took everything within Aliya to not step back. "Unfortunately, my parents only taught me to respect those who deserve it. And you tried to kill me yesterday. I say you don't deserve it."

"That's too bad." Damon said, shaking his head as if what Aliya said was of the utmost travesty. "They should have also taught you to practice caution on who you should raise your voice to. And who you should fear. And most importantly, who you should defy. And my child, I am not one you should be defying."

Aliya narrowed her eyes. "Was that supposed to scare me?"

"Well, it doesn't matter if you don't respect me." Damon shrugged. "It's not your respect I need. Your fear should be enough for me to get what I want."

"I am not scared of you."

"That's completely fine. But maybe you're afraid of them?" Damon turned around to look at the dark alley beside the convenience store.

It took Aliya a moment to adjust her vision to the darkness in the alley. But when she did, Aliya couldn't help but gasp out loud.

Blending in the darkness were two large masses that sent chills down her spine. Aliya's eyes widened. She felt her throat go dry as she shuddered. Even with how far the beasts were, she could hear their rumble. Her head snapped back to Damon. Aliya tried her best to maintain her composure but with the berserkers only a few feet away and Damon in front of her, she was trapped.

Enzo. Her mind screamed. He was still in the convenience store. He hadn't come out yet. *Good. Don't come out yet.*

Damon must have noticed how scared she was. He gave her a genuine wide smile.

"I just need a little information from you, my child." Damon bent down slightly to her height. "Where is Enzo?"

"I don't know who you're talking about." She cursed herself when she realized how her voice shook.

"Don't play with me, child. I'm giving you a chance here."

Aliya pursed her lips, trying to weigh her options. Damon probably had already seen them together. As chaotic as the night before, Aliya was sure Damon could recognize her from Sienna's house. Letting out a defeated sigh, Aliya dropped all pretense.

"You want me to betray him. I am never going to betray him." Her voice still shook. But the conviction in which she said surprised both her and Damon.

Damon lifted his eyebrow. He looked as if he was... no, that couldn't be.

Why does he look proud?

"So much loyalty for someone you've only met a couple days ago." Damon tsk-ed. "He doesn't deserve it."

"Then, who does? You?"

Damon only chuckled in response. "You would make a good Disciple." He mumbled, only loud enough for Aliya to hear.

Aliya's expression soured at what Damon said. She could hear the berserkers moving closer to her. Her body shook in fear but she stood her ground. Not moving an inch. If she was going to die in his hands, she was not going to give him the satisfaction of showing him exactly how afraid she was.

"Where is he?" Damon asked, letting go of all pretense. He was no longer smiling. His voice was deeper, almost a growl as he stepped closer to Aliya.

Aliya could feel her breath shorten. She had to get out of here. Somehow. She couldn't even look into Damon's eyes any longer. Instead, she'd chosen to look at his chest. Just as she gulped, trying to accept her fate, she heard the gas nozzle sound as it stopped.

Aliya didn't think. She didn't give Damon a chance to respond either.

She grabbed the nozzle. Removing it from the car, she lifted it up and pointed it at Damon. Aliya pressed the nozzle, spraying the liquid onto Damon.

Damon's exasperated sigh almost made her chuckle.

"Is this little liquid supposed to keep me away?" Damon asked. "You think this... liquid is going to stop me?" Damon's nose scrunched at the smell of the gas on his clothes. He looked back up at Aliya as if to say "Really?"

But his exasperated expression slowly turned into curiosity when he saw Aliya's smile widen.

"Do you know what this liquid is?" Aliya chuckled. "It's petroleum. Highly flammable, actually. One spark. That's all it'll take for you to burn into a crisp."

Her smile slowly faded when Damon stepped closer to her. His evil smile marring his kind face. When he stepped a couple steps closer, she felt the gas sprinkle on her clothes as well.

Well, that's unexpected. She thought.

He was foiling her plans. If she was to go through her threat of lighting a match now, they'd both be doused in flames. Aliya scoffed. He actually thought that little step forward was going to scare her.

Aliya didn't stop the nozzle from spraying on the two of them though. Instead, Aliya stepped closer to Damon.

The petrol sprayed on both of them, drenching them completely with the flammable liquid. Aliya fumed. Her anger shone through her eyes as she gazed back up at Damon. With how close they were, Aliya had to lift her head to look up at Damon.

And his proud expression was only angering her more.

Gazing deep into his eyes, she asked. "I have nothing to live for in this life." She seethed. Aliya felt the pang in her chest as she said that but chose to ignore it. Now was not the time. She stepped closer to Damon. They were close enough that the nozzle almost touched Damon's chest. "Can you say the same?"

Damon didn't answer. But he just smirked, gazing down into her eyes with pride.

Aliya waited for a moment longer. When she didn't get any response from Damon, she nodded, satisfied.

Still holding out the nozzle towards Damon, Aliya stepped back. "Enzo!" She shouted, hoping he'd be able to hear her from this distance. "In the car! Now!"

She didn't dare move her gaze from Damon. It was only when she heard the front door to the convenience store chime that she stepped towards the car. In the corner of her eye, she could see Enzo hesitate for a moment.

"It's ok." Aliya said loudly, sneering at Damon. "I've got this under control. Get in the car."

Aliya stood beside the car, still pointing the nozzle at Damon. When she heard the passenger door shut, Aliya gulped. With one swift motion, she opened the driver's door and threw the nozzle in the distance.

"Go, go, go, go, go!" Enzo shouted as he watched the berserkers running towards them.

Aliya didn't need to be told twice. She screamed while slamming her foot on the accelerator.

Even in the chaos, she saw the smirking image of Damon in her rearview window.

19

"I promised myself not to use magic again." – Sienna

"**W**HAT'S TAKING THEM SO long?" Sienna mumbled as she walked back into the house.

This would be the tenth time she'd gone outside waiting on Aliya and Enzo. "I'm sure I gave them the correct directions." Sienna wondered out loud. She was sure she'd given them the correct directions to her book. "No, if it was the wrong direction, Aliya would have at least called."

Running her hand through her hair again, Sienna plopped onto the sofa unceremoniously. She hadn't stopped mumbling to herself for the past hour. Aliya and Enzo should have been back by now. And not hearing from them was putting her on edge.

None of the scenarios her mind played were ideal. She tried her best to not think of the worst case scenario. Not that her mind cooperated. Every second that followed with Aliya and Enzo walking through the front doors made Sienna more nervous.

She groaned as she placed her arm over her eyes. She desperately needed some sleep. Sienna hadn't slept the entire night. She'd been taking care of Aliya and Enzo. And now that was taking a toll on her. She felt her eyes droop as she stifled a yawn.

Even with her eyes closed, Sienna felt her wife's eyes on her.

"I can feel you smirking." Sienna said out loud without opening her eyes.

"They're going to come back. Stop worrying." Anya chuckled. When Sienna didn't respond, Anya continued. "So, that was the Crown Prince of Ravendore."

Sienna nodded.

"He doesn't look much like a prince." Anya muttered.

That brought a chuckle out of Sienna. "I thought the same." She removed her arm from covering her eyes and leaned forward on the sofa. "He actually looked much better from a distance."

It was silent for a moment, until Sienna looked up at her wife. The both of them couldn't control themselves anymore and burst into a fit of giggles. Sienna couldn't stop chuckling from the absurdity of it all.

She'd thought that after all this time - after five long years - that they were safe from anything related to Indresal. But it seemed that trouble wanted to find them wherever they were. As the chuckles slowly died down, Anya gazed at her lovingly.

"What?" Sienna asked. Even after all this time being married to Anya, her wife never failed to make her blush, especially with the way her wife was looking at her right now.

"Are you really going to help him get back to Indresal?" Anya asked. Any trace of laughter was long gone.

Sienna could sense the fear slowly radiating off her wife. They'd been through too much as a family. Any decision she was going to take was going to impact all of them. And that felt like an additional weight on Sienna's shoulders.

Sienna solemnly nodded, looking at the ground. "I have to." She slowly looked up at Anya, hoping she'd understand. "You know I have to. Especially after how he saved us."

Images of her last week at Indresal ran through her mind.

Sienna and Anya had already made plans to escape Indresal to Earth the next week. They lived peacefully in the village in the outskirts of Illadora. Surrounded by forests, it was one of the most secluded and safest places in Indresal. But if all the events throughout her life had taught her anything, it was to never trust safety.

Because one day or another, that safety could crumble.

So, they prepared. Day in and day out, Sienna translated that book. That was her only job. She wanted to get out of Indresal with her family and if there was even a sliver of chance for her to do it, she'd take it. The joy she'd felt when she finally realized there was a world without berserkers, Sienna leapt at the chance.

It took Sienna and Anya two years to prepare for their departure. They'd even adopted a baby. The baby was coming into their village from one of the war torn kingdoms. One look at the child and hearing that her parents died trying to protect her, Sienna couldn't hold back from wanting to protect her.

That was their child.

Their Sanya.

Everything was going according to plan. Everything was perfect.

That was until the berserkers attacked.

They hadn't planned for that.

Even in the chaos of that night, Sienna could remember, the berserkers cornering her and her family in the dark alley. They could have died that day. They would have...

...If Enzo wasn't there on his campaign to save the village.

He'd redirected the berserker away from Sienna, Anya and Sanya. They didn't wait any longer after the attack that night.

Instead of running out of the village with the rest of the people, Sienna dragged her family to the secluded part of the woods where she'd hidden her books and translations. The moment she reached her spot, Sienna didn't hesitate. She didn't look back. Not caring for one moment who might see them. Her family's safety was her priority.

And she created the portal. Summoning all the strength and power she had in her. Letting the power coarse through her, from the pendant she always had hanging around her neck, through her veins as she felt nature bend to her will.

She still remembered the fizzle and crackle of the portal being opened as she held her breath. It was only when she and her family walked through the portals that she was even able to breathe.

Sienna shook her head, trying to clear her mind off the images that were running through it. She looked up to see Anya gazing at her, sadly.

"I know." Anya said. She moved closer to Sienna, gently caressing Sienna's cheek. "Just promise me you'll be safe. Promise me you'll come back."

At that, Sienna smirked. "I always come back."

Anya deadpanned, not appreciating the humor at the moment. Seeing how serious Anya was being, Sienna sobered.

"I promise, I'll come back." Sienna bit her lip. She didn't know if she should ask it. Especially considering the gravity of what she was asking. Finally, taking in a deep breath, Sienna asked. "Promise me you'll wait for me?"

There were so many things that could go wrong in helping Enzo. She was leaving the solace of her new home and the comfort of her family to help him.

Anya didn't let any of Sienna's dark thoughts fester. The minute Sienna asked her question, Anya nodded, whispering a resolute "Yes."

The two of them sat in silence for a moment, listening to the nature around them. With their child sleeping and them being quiet, they could hear the birds chirping around them growing slowly silent by the setting sun. All they could hear were the leaves rustling in the wind, the frogs croaking, and the crickets chirping. The faint smell of petrichor told them that it might rain again.

"Have you ever thought about going back?" Anya asked as she looked out of the window. "Back to Indresal."

"No." Sienna's answer was simple. She didn't need to think about it. Earth was where her family was safe. So, even if she did miss her home, Earth was where she was going to be.

"But don't you miss it?" Anya asked.

"My longing to go back to our world is nothing compared to my love for you and our child. And definitely nothing compared to my desperation to keep you safe."

"What if this was after the war-"

Sienna didn't give Anya a chance to complete her sentence. "Where is this coming from? Are you missing Indresal? We are safe here. We will stay here. I will come back here after I help Enzo. The war in Indresal hasn't stopped in centuries. There's no way that it'll stop within our lifetime. Only a miracle can stop that war. I don't see a miracle coming anytime soon."

Anya didn't respond. Instead, she simply took in a slow, deep breath, looking at Sienna before turning to gaze outside melancholy.

Sienna and Anya let the silence between them permeate. Although this silence was much less comfortable. The two of them stewed in their own thoughts only occasionally looking at each other.

Seconds turned into minutes as Sienna began to get antsy again. The sun was beginning to set. And yet there was no sign of Aliya or Enzo.

"Where are there?" Sienna groaned out loud, making Anya chuckle.

"Those two were eyeing each other. We might be a little while before they choose to come back."

Sienna looked at her wife horrified. "They better not be in my car then."

"My dove, I don't think you should have high hopes for that." Anya said, making Sienna groan louder.

"I wonder if they even got the book." Sienna mumbled.

"You could check the security cameras. If they went through the front door, you'll see if they have the book." Anya shrugged. When Sienna didn't answer, Anya turned around to see her sheepish expression. "You didn't think of the security cameras, did you?"

Sienna wanted to smack her forehead. She could have easily checked on the two of them as they searched the house. And yet, that idea hadn't occurred to her. Sienna brought her phone out of her pocket. She sighed as she was about to open the app.

Her finger hovered over the app but she didn't press it. Instead, she kept looking at the app, horrified as a thought occurred to her.

Anya might have noticed because she asked, "What is it? Are they ok?"

"We're tracing what happened in our home from here." Sienna stated simply, as if that explanation was enough.

"Yes..." Anya trailed off.

"I've been wondering how the *Disciple* knew where to search for Enzo." She mumbled the word 'Disciple'. "What if..." Her eyes widened even more. "What if he'd been tracking Enzo the same way?"

Anya thought for a moment. "You're thinking of a tracking spell? But when would he have the chance to..." Anya trailed off again. But she seemed to have understood as Anya shared the same horrified expression Sienna had.

Sienna nodded in response.

"Do you think he's tracking them right now?" Anya whispered, not daring to ask the question any louder, as if she didn't want it to be true.

Sienna didn't wait to answer.

She dashed out of the house. Grabbing the keys to Anya's car, she only stopped to say, "Protect yourself. Protect Sanya. You know where everything is. If you find anything suspicious, remember the clearing we first came in?" She waited for Anya to nod. "Good. Anything suspicious at all. Get there! I'll be back for you."

That was all Sienna said before driving off in the car.

20

"Between a rock and a berserker." – Aliya

ALIYA DIDN'T STOP SCREAMING as she drove off from the gas station.

The image of Damon in her rear view mirror grew smaller. That made her happy. But the reflections of the berserkers chasing their car did not grow smaller like she'd hoped.

That did not make Aliya smile.

Aliya stepped on the pedal, trying to speed the car. Although, it only seemed that the berserkers were keeping up with the car.

"How fast can they run?" Aliya screamed in the chaos. She turned around to sneak a look at Enzo. When she noticed that he didn't have his seatbelt on, she screamed at him. "Seat belt! Seat belt! Seat belt!"

As if that was enough to save them from Damon and his beasts.

Enzo, who'd been holding onto the door handles thus far, could only seem to look around wide-eyed. When he heard Aliya scream at him, he brought out the seatbelt, locking it just as Aliya showed him before. He turned around to look at the berserkers following them.

"Apparently faster than this car can take us." Enzo shouted, making Aliya wince. "Go, go, go! Faster!"

Aliya didn't need to turn around. She could hear the growls from the beasts coming from behind them. In her panic, her mind began to think of all the mundane things around her.

How loud were they snarling? She wondered. *Or maybe they're running faster?* She groaned and slightly shook her head to clear her thoughts. *Now's not the time! Focus!*

The trees surrounding them whizzed past as Aliya sped through the winding roads. Every turn she made slammed the two of them against the car doors. Aliya still didn't stop or even slow down.

The car flew with every minor bump Aliya sped over, making her grunt when they landed. If they weren't going to be killed by the berserkers, at the speed she was driving, Aliya was sure they were bound to get into an accident.

Especially considering she'd never driven this fast before.

Enzo turned around again. "Aliya, faster!"

"What do you think I'm doing?" Aliya screamed back.

Aliya continued to drive, when she noticed a sudden movement in the corner of her eye. Taking her eyes off the road for a moment, Aliya turned to see one of the beasts running in the woods alongside the car. The beast seemed to have no trouble keeping up with the car.

But that wasn't what caught Aliya's attention.

No, what caught her attention was the man sitting atop the berserker. As if he was riding it.

Damon looked at her smugly as he watched her panic. Aliya gripped the steering wheel tighter. She'd floored the gas pedal. But it seemed that the beasts were able to ride in stride with the car. Aliya looked down at the speedometer.

109mph.

How is that possible? She thought, alarmed. *That shouldn't be possible. No beast should be able to catch up to this speed.* She looked back up at Damon alarmed. Her eyes widened when she realized there was only one beast with Damon.

"Where's the other berserker?" She screamed, trying to get Enzo's attention.

"Aliya, stop the car." Enzo said. Even in her panic, Aliya noted how calm Enzo sounded. That confused her further. It took her a moment to register what he'd said.

Although, that one moment of hesitation was where everything went wrong.

Aliya felt something slam into the passenger side of the car. She screamed as she felt her body slam into her side of the car door. As the pain shot through her left side of her body, Aliya knew she'd broken something. But she couldn't focus on anything else as their car tumbled off the road.

The car flipped in the air as it veered off the road and into the forest on the side. Aliya could feel the blinding pulsating pain from her broken arm.

But even in all the chaos of the flipping car, Aliya brought her hands up to protect her head. Her scream was muffled when she felt Enzo completely engulf her in a hug just as the car fell back to the ground.

The car didn't stop tumbling, smashing into the trees and smaller shrubs as it rolled into the forest.

In the havoc around them, Aliya could only think of one thing. With her one injured hand, she held onto Enzo as if he was her lifeline. With every bump and with her every scream, she could feel Enzo hug her tighter - holding tightly onto her back and cradling her head.

The flimsy airbags were the only things protecting them so far. Pain shot through every part of her body, with a new injury being added every time the car rolled again. Aliya could feel the tears pooling in the back of her eyes. The pain was becoming too much for her to handle.

She didn't know when her screams turned into loud sobs. With every jolt, sent another sharp blinding pain across her body. But even as the car tumbled, Enzo refused to let her go. He held onto her, grunting every time the car hit another tree.

Just as suddenly as the car began to tumble, it stopped.

It took Aliya several moments to recover from the tumble. Her sobs hadn't stopped. She was just glad that the car wasn't giving her new waves of pain. She couldn't think properly. Her mind felt jumbled. Wincing, she slowly opened her eyes but it felt as if the world around her was revolving. No matter how tightly she shut her eyes and opened them, she couldn't get rid of the dizziness.

"Are you ok?" Enzo asked. Aliya couldn't answer, however. He tapped her cheeks lightly.

Taking in a deep breath, Aliya tried to calm herself. But no matter what she tried, she couldn't stop the tears from pooling in her eyes, not even noticing that the tears were dripping upward towards her forehead rather than down her cheeks.

Aliya didn't know how Enzo handled his battle wounds because she certainly couldn't handle these car injuries.

She felt Enzo's hands gently cupping her cheeks. She winced slightly when she felt him turn her head towards him. It was only then that Aliya noticed that the car was flipped upside down. The only thing that stopped them from slamming into the top of the car were the seat belts that held them securely to the seat.

"You're injured." Enzo said, slowly, as if trying to get through to her. "You're in shock. But we need to get out of here, Aliya." He nodded at her, still talking to her slowly.

Aliya blinked slowly, trying to understand what he was saying but his voice seemed distant.

Injured must be an understatement. Because she could feel the blood seeping from some part of her head. She must have cut it when her head slammed into the car window. Her left shoulder hurt as she tried to move it.

Finally giving up, she chose to cradle her broken arm in her lap. Blood began to drip from the other cuts she'd gotten from the splintered car windows. Her face must have gotten some of the cuts, because Aliya felt a trickle trail down her cheek. She felt too tired to look over any other injuries she might have gotten.

But given how her entire body hurt, Aliya was sure she had more bruises. The upcoming days would be hell as she tried to recover.

If they got out of this alive, that was.

"Aliya, listen to my voice, yeah?" Enzo said, still slowly. Although Aliya could hear the desperation slowly creeping into his voice. "I can't lose you. Listen to my voice. You're going to be fine."

Aliya slowly nodded, making Enzo sigh audible.

"Good." He said.

Aliya groaned as she felt the thud from Enzo unlocking his seat belt and fell onto the roof of the car. She felt him gently hold onto Aliya's head as she fell beside him. Aliya yelped as another current of pain shot through her entire body.

"We need to get out now. We don't have time." Enzo said. Even with the thick fog clouding her mind, she could sense the urgency in his voice.

But before Aliya could move, she felt another jolt to the car. Aliya yelped, hitting her injured shoulder against the steering wheel. Her yelp turned into a scream as the car shook.

"What's happening?" She screamed.

Her eyes were closed. This was getting to be a little too much for Aliya. She could feel her breath shorten and choked back a sob. Curling herself into a ball, Aliya shielded her head, making herself as small as possible.

She felt Enzo crawl up to her. She felt him hanging onto her back. It took her a moment in the chaos to realize that he was shielding her body with his. Just like he had been when the car flipped.

Aliya turned her head to peek at him. Enzo gave her a small smile before winking at her.

"Berserkers found us!" Enzo screamed back at her. "This is fun, isn't it?" He asked, although there was no trace of mirth to be found anywhere in his face.

Aliya rolled her eyes at his sarcasm. "I'm having a splendid time." She gritted out through the pain. "How are we getting out of here?"

Enzo looked around. Aliya wondered if he could see anything with how much the car was shaking. All the items Aliya had stored in her car - many of which she'd forgotten she'd left in the car - fell down onto the roof of the car. Aliya looked around at all the items surrounding them.

Her eyes widened when she realized what else she had in the car.

Aliya wiggled under Enzo, trying to get him to loosen his grip on her.

"Where are you going?" He asked, eyes wide, alarmed. Enzo lifted himself a little, giving Aliya the space she needed to move.

"I have a bat in the back!" Aliya said, crawling out.

"What's a bat going to do against them?"

"Do you have a better idea?" She shouted back.

"Stay here! I'll get the bat." She screamed back at him.

Before Enzo could protest, Aliya grunted in pain as she reached back to the backseat. She could hear the glass around them slowly starting to crack, sending shivers down her spine. Aliya rummaged around the items that fell onto the roof of the car, smiling when she felt the baseball bat.

It was a metal baseball bat that she'd been using for protection whenever she had to work a late night shift. She'd never had to use it before.

There's a first time for everything. She thought.

Just as Aliya grabbed onto the bat, the window beside her in the passenger seat shattered, sending shards of glass into the car. Aliya closed her eyes, protecting her head as she felt the glass shower around her.

A gnarly claw from the beast swiped into the car from the shattered window. The beast did not seem to care for the sharp glass cutting into its skin, drawing out the blood from the scratches.

Aliya gripped the bat tightly, swinging on the beast's claw, making it yelp. But no matter how much she tried to beat the berserker's claw, it only seemed to draw the beast further into the car.

Enzo was probably tired as he watched her struggle against the beast. He crawled back into the passenger seat, beside Aliya. He grabbed the bat from Aliya and swung it harder at the beast.

"Find a way out. I'll take care of him!" He said.

Aliya gave him a tight nod. She rummaged through the back car seat, palming the side of the seat, searching for the level to open the seat leading to the trunk. But with how much the car moved, Aliya yelped as her hand pressed between the seat and the passenger door.

"I've told you, my child." Aliya heard Damon shout. "All you have to do is give him up. I'll leave you alone."

In the distance, she could see Damon smirking proudly, as if admiring his artwork. He crossed his arms knowing that if things continued the way it did, all he needed to do was wait. He looked at them as if this was the most boring thing he had to wait upon.

Enzo stopped slamming the bat onto the beast. He turned around to look at her, as if to ask, "What is he talking about?"

When Aliya only shook her head in answer, Enzo's brows furrowed in concern. "He's talking about me." That was more of a statement as he came to the realization.

"Shut up!" Aliya said, still struggling to find the lever.

"Just say the word, my child." Damon shouted again.

"You could have saved yourself! I would have been fine!" Enzo shouted.

"Enzo, shut up!" Aliya shouted again, not caring for what Damon was saying.

She wasn't going to give him Enzo. It didn't matter to her what the stakes were. Even if it meant her life on the line. She had nothing else to live for in this world anyway. Her family was gone. She only had her college, her job and her home to come back to.

Aliya knew that she was probably being impulsive at this point. But she didn't care. She tuned Damon out even as he continued to shout. Instead she focused on trying to find a way for her and Enzo to escape.

"And I will leave you alone." Damon shouted. "I give you my word. My promise. The promise of a Disciple is their bond."

"You're going to die if you stay with me." Enzo pleaded, his voice cracking. She could hear the desperation in his voice.

"I'm going to die even if I'm not with you. So, suck it up!" She'd finally found the lever. Grabbing onto it, Aliya used all her strength to pull it up. But with how much her shoulder hurt to even move, she struggled.

"Come on, child. You don't owe him your loyalty. What has he done that he deserves your love?"

Aliya shook her head, trying to block Damon. He was making it very hard though. If only he would shut up so she could focus on trying to get Enzo and herself out. She refused to listen to Damon. But now, more so, she refused to even look at Enzo's pleading eyes. Aliya ducked when the car seat bent forward. She turned around to look at Enzo.

"Go!" She screamed at him, pushing him as hard as she could into the opening to the trunk.

But instead of crawling into the trunk, Enzo grabbed tightly onto her waist, pulling her close. He pursed his lips, looking deep into her eyes. Time seemed to slow down as Aliya gazed into his eyes, trying to understand the emotion within his gaze. It was a little of desperation, gratitude and something else that Aliya couldn't place.

But Aliya didn't have time to actually ponder though.

Enzo pushed her roughly towards the opening into the trunk.

"What are you doing?" Aliya screamed. She turned around quickly, peeking out of the opening to find Enzo turning away from the opening, turning back at the beasts, swatting at them.

He's trying to save you. Aliya thought.

"Come with me!" Aliya screamed, the desperation clinging onto her every word. "Enzo please!"

Her heart ached as she felt the tears pool behind her eyes. "Enzo!" She screamed again.

But Enzo didn't respond. He was trying his best to let her live.

"No!" Aliya screamed again as she saw his hands move to the door handle. "Enzo, please! Come with me!"

Aliya reached out her hands to him. She could only claw at his shirt, her bloody grip loosening as the fabric of his shirt slipped through her finger. Nothing she said seemed to make him pause though.

"Enzo, please." Aliya pleaded. "Don't leave me." It came out as a whisper.

But just as suddenly as the car began to shake, it stopped. The sounds of the shattering glass, the metal creaking, and the tires bursting could no longer be heard. But what could be heard were the pained howls of the beasts. Leaves rustled violently as the trees shook violently from the impact. Branches fell all around them. But no matter what commotion was happening around them, none of it seemed to impact the car any longer.

Aliya took advantage of the quiet and crawled out of the trunk onto the backseat of the car.

She grasped onto Enzo, shutting her eyes and clinging tightly onto his neck with her good arm. Aliya held onto him tightly as if letting him go would mean that he would disappear. She sobbed against his neck, clinging onto him as tightly as she could.

Enzo didn't respond. He could only seem to reciprocate the gesture. Aliya felt his arms around her, hugging her tightly, making sure to not hurt her shoulder or broken arm any further. Neither wanted to let go of each other.

"Don't go! Don't go. Don't go. Don't go." Was all she could chant.

When Aliya slowly opened her eyes, still not daring to let go of Enzo, she looked through the broken car window. Aliya's eyes widened at the sight in front of her.

At that moment, she understood why the berserkers no longer tussled with the car.

And in that moment, Aliya understood exactly how powerful a single witch could be.

Especially a witch like Sienna.

21

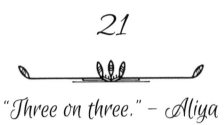

"Three on three." - Aliya

ALIYA'S TIGHT GRIP ON Enzo loosened only slightly as she gasped at the sight before her. Time seemed to slow down as Aliya watched the witch in action.

There, standing in the distance atop a small hill within the forest, was Sienna with her arms lifted high. Her hair flared around her as the wind blew against her. Her gown flapped against her body as the wind picked up. With the last flicker of sunlight behind her, Sienna looked like an angel descended upon the land to save them.

The crystal pendant that Sienna always had hanging around her neck shone brightly. Dark purple wisps wafted from the pendant, traveling up her shoulders and down intertwining with her fingers.

Aliya wondered for a moment what Sienna was actually doing. She couldn't see anything else move around Sienna. That was until...

A loud crash echoed around the forest sending the birds flapping away. Aliya yelped, searching the rubble beside Sienna for what caused the crash. It was only when she saw the dark purple wisps around the black mass under the rubble of the broken branches that she realized Sienna threw one of the berserkers down like a toy.

Sienna barely broke a sweat as she tossed the beasts around.

But nothing she did also seemed to work against the berserkers as well.

No matter what Sienna did, the beasts didn't take long for the beasts to recover from her attacks. Sienna threw blast after blast against the beasts. Nothing stopped them from advancing on her, however. They ran, dodging her attacks as they weaved through the splintered wood and broken branches.

It seemed that Sienna's magic was only angering them more. The closer they ran to Sienna, the more aggressive they became, snarling as they reached her.

"Get to the car!" Sienna screamed. "I got these two!"

In her daze, Aliya took a moment to understand what Sienna shouted. She looked around Sienna, only to find another car behind Sienna. But given the distance, Aliya began to wonder how they were going to get there with the berserkers and Damon out to get them.

But even more so, Aliya was still transfixed on Sienna. The magic that coursed through Sienna drew Aliya in like a moth to a flame. She'd only barely seen Enzo's portals - or rather what was sputtering for a portal before he lost his magic. But this...

... This was something else entirely.

Sienna commanded the elements around her. Her dark purple wisps poured out from her crystal, traveling down her arms, and pooling at her hands. She commanded the trees and the very ground she was walking on as if they were mere toys, making the forest work with her to protect herself from the oncoming berserkers.

Even with Sienna shouting for them to leave their position, Aliya couldn't seem to move. She stood behind the car, her mouth agape as she stared mesmerized at the sight before her. She didn't notice Enzo grabbing her hand, pulling her beside the car.

"Get down!" Enzo shouted.

Still transfixed on Sienna, Aliya didn't react to Enzo in time. Enzo must have noticed this as he pushed her to the ground. Unfortunately, in his hurry, Enzo wasn't exactly gentle.

Aliya fell down with a loud "umph". The force with which Enzo pushed her knocked the wind out of her. She didn't even have the chance to complain or groan in pain as she hit her injured shoulder and arm to the ground. Just as she fell, Aliya heard a whistling sound, followed by a grating noise. She looked up from her position to see a broken branch that flew past where her head once was.

Aliya's eyes turned wide. The door behind her was smashed with the branch now sticking out of it. She looked around to where the branch might have come from.

Damon! Her mind screamed at her.

In all the commotion, she'd forgotten about the biggest threat to them. Aliya looked around, searching for the man that was attacking from.

Enzo grabbed her waist, pulling her behind the car. She began to wonder how much protection a simple car can provide against magical beings. Especially with how Damon and Sienna were fighting. Aliya ducked into Enzo's arm as he guided her behind the car.

Once they were secure, Aliya peaked from the cracked window. The two of them crouched down, looking through the shattered car windows to see where Damon was throwing the branches from.

"Where is he?" Aliya asked, looking in every direction. But Damon seemed to have just disappeared.

"Shh." Enzo shushed her, making Aliya smack him lightly on his shoulder. "I don't see him either."

Aliya strained her ears, hoping to hear something from Damon that might give up his location. But all she could hear were Sienna's shouts as she tackled the berserkers on her own.

"We need to help her." Aliya hissed at Enzo.

"How do you suggest that?" He looked at her incredulously. "We're a bit stuck, if you hadn't noticed."

Aliya crouched again, trying to peek at the fight behind them again. Which was good, because Damon took that moment to fling another branch at the two of them. Aliya pushed Enzo away from the flying branch.

"He's right behind us!" Aliya shouted at Enzo. She could see the panic in Enzo's eyes as he watched the branch come in close contact with her once again.

With how focused Damon's attacks have been on her, Aliya began to wonder if she was Damon's target. His blasts have been taking out the trees and shrubs that were a little too close to her for her comfort.

Did my rejection really hurt him that much? She wondered. *No! Focus! Fight. Now.*

"I've got him." Enzo said, preparing himself to run. "You go get Sienna's car."

"You're not leaving me." Aliya's eyes widened in shock. Was he planning on being a sacrificial hero again? She really needed to talk to him to stop doing that. At least for her sanity that was. "We're going together."

Another branch crashed into the car again, making Aliya and Enzo duck. The car shook from the impact. Enzo held onto the car to stop it from tilting over.

"Will you listen to me just this once?" Enzo complained.

Another crash.

"Come out, child. Bring in the coward with you when you do." Damon shouted. They could hear the mirth in his voice. He was enjoying this a little too much.

Another crash. Twigs from the shattered branches flew all around them, making Aliya and Enzo duck trying to escape the flying debris.

"I am not leaving you." Aliya said. The conviction in her voice made Enzo look back at her. She could see his frustration build as his hands balled into fists beside him. "We're doing this together." She said again.

"Why must you make this so difficult?"

"I wouldn't have you if you weren't planning on sacrificing yourself at every minor inconvenience!" Aliya said back.

"Come out!" Damon said again. "This is getting a bit tiring. Have a little consideration for my age, will you?"

"This is a minor inconvenience?" Enzo asked, incredulously, as he gestured wildly at the battle around them.

Aliya pursed her lips. "Details." She said simply as she waved her hand.

Enzo huffed. He looked around, frustrated as if trying to find a way to get out of their predicament. Aliya took that moment to grab the larger shards of broken glass. Placing them to the side, she huffed as she tried to tear the corner of her shirt. But with only one good arm, it became difficult. When she finally gave up, Aliya huffed and asked Enzo for help. Enzo simply shook his head as he began to tear the hem of her shirt.

It was already blood soaked anyway. It was her favorite blouse too. A pale blue color with puffed short sleeves and a white collar. But now, it was marred with red from her blood and torn from the accident. It had somehow survived the berserker attack at Sienna's house.

The blouse wasn't so lucky now, however.

Aliya wrapped the piece of the blouse she tore off around the shard of glass. She handed one of the shards to Enzo and held onto the other.

By the time she was done, Enzo turned back to her. A curt nod from him was all she got in response before he held her hand firmly.

"How are we doing this?" Aliya whispered.

"Just follow me." Enzo whispered back. "On the count of three." He said before turning to look at Aliya once more.

"Three." He said.

They could hear Damon taunt them more. But now it was more of a background noise. Aliya had gotten to tuning him out. Damon's cackles grew louder the closer he got to them.

"Two." Enzo said again.

Aliya could still hear the snarls of the berserkers fighting Sienna in the distance. She began to wonder how long could Sienna keep fighting. Sienna had to grow tired at some point. Aliya could already hear her attacks slow down. They didn't have the same impact on the berserkers as they had before. The attacks were also coming in at random intervals rather than the coordinated attack that Sienna kept up in the beginning.

Aliya just hoped Sienna could hold off until her and Enzo reached the car.

With one final nod, Enzo grasped her good hand tightly. "One."

That was all he said before the two of them ran from behind the car.

Aliya tried her best to keep up with Enzo, running past the thick trees as they dodged Damon's attacks. Every dark wisp that Damon threw at them was close enough to hit them. Much too close for Aliya's comfort. Splintered from the shattered wood chafed at her exposed skin, making her hiss.

ONLY A PORTAL AWAY

Aliya didn't have time to numb the pain, however. Tears poured down with every step she took. Her pain was becoming unbearable now. But she couldn't think about it now. She had to escape. And so she followed Enzo.

She ran.

She ran with all she had in her alongside Enzo. Aliya felt the wind whistle in her ears - although that could also have been the injuries she'd sustained. She wasn't exactly sure at this point. Trees and shrubs around them exploded as they came in contact with Damon's dark wisp.

But no matter what, Enzo didn't let go of her hand.

Instead, he'd held her closer. Not stopping for one moment to even look back at Damon as they ran through the forest.

That seemed to be a mistake. Because the next attack was aimed directly at Enzo.

He didn't have time to respond as Enzo flew into the air. It was only Aliya's hand intertwined with his that stopped him from flying further away.

Aliya's eyes widened as she watched Enzo fall hard onto the forest floor. Blood seeped from the impact, making him scream in pain. Aliya tried to get him to stand. But nothing she did was helping Enzo.

She looked back to see Damon slowly stalking her. As if he'd all the time in the world.

That worried her even more.

That meant that Damon was sure Enzo wouldn't recover from his attack. Damon's feral look only seemed to confirm her worst fears.

Aliya looked between Enzo and Damon. Enzo still hadn't let go of her hand, still holding onto her just as tightly as before.

She weakly lifted her shard of glass, knowing well that little shard would do nothing to deter Damon. He seemed to have sensed her apprehension as well. Damon just smirked in response as he looked at the shard.

"I told you to hand him over, child." He said, chuckling.

"Don't come any closer." Aliya said, trying her best to sound fierce. But the small quiver in her voice betrayed her fear.

Damon's chuckle turned into a cackle sending shivers down Aliya's spine. Damon didn't stop sauntering towards them. Even the fight Sienna was having with the berserkers just a few feet away from them didn't seem to deter Damon.

And just for a moment, hope filled Aliya.

In their hurry to get away from Damon, she'd forgotten about Sienna. An idea began to form in her mind. She'd hoped that with all the powers Damon seemed to have, that telepathy wasn't one of them.

When Damon was only a few feet away from her, Aliya glared at him. "You'll never get him. I'll never let you have him." Was all she said before she shouted. "Sienna!"

She was glad that Sienna understood what she was planning to do. Because in that moment, Damon gasped in shock as he felt the wisp of Sienna's dark purple magic curl around him lifting him high into the air. Before he could recover, however, Sienna let go of him, letting him fall from the height.

Aliya took that as her opportunity to aim the shard at Damon. She only let out the breath she was holding when the shard lodged itself into Damon's stomach. The shard pushed in deeper as Damon fell to the forest floor, groaning in pain.

Taking that as her opportunity, Aliya placed her arm around Enzo's chest, lifting him. If anyone were to ask her how she managed to do that with one good arm, she wouldn't have been able to answer. But in the heat of the moment, Aliya dragged Enzo along with her.

She only looked back once as the two of them stumbled through the forest. Only making sure that Damon wasn't following them.

But Damon still laid on the forest floor, groaning as he strained to take out the glass shard.

This was her chance.

She had to leave with Enzo and Sienna if they were to survive.

22

"*Please stay alive.*" – *Aliya*

"**G**ET IN! GET INTO the car!" Sienna screamed at them.

She tried her best to hold off the berserkers from attacking Aliya and Enzo as they passed them. Aliya heard the beasts snarl at the two of them as they passed the beasts. For a moment, Aliya was worried if the beasts would charge at them.

But it seemed that Aliya didn't have to worry about them. They'd stopped attacking as viciously as they'd done before.

Instead, the berserkers alternated between attacking Sienna and looking back at an injured Damon. An injured Damon who'd been struggling to even sit up.

One less thing to worry about. Aliya thought as she dragged Enzo with all her might.

Sienna kept walking back to the top of the hill. With every dark blue wisp she threw at the berserkers, Sienna took a step back. Which was good, because Aliya couldn't find Sienna's car anywhere.

Aliya slowly felt Enzo lean more into her shoulder as the two of them ran up the hill. Or much rather, as Aliya dragged him atop the hill. His eyes drooped, as he stumbled on his feet. Blood from his head dripped onto his shoulder, staining Aliya's blouse even further.

He's supposed to be healing on his own. Aliya thought. *Why aren't his wounds healing on their own?*

That's when she remembered all the wounds that'd healed since he'd come to Earth were due to Sienna's potions or ointments. If Enzo were to heal now, they needed Sienna to get back.

Panic began to set in as Aliya looked at Enzo again. His eyes drooped even with all the effort he'd been putting in to stay awake. She could feel him try his best to not lean on her completely. Aliya increased her pace.

Aliya huffed with every step she took. Her lungs burned with the extra exertion. None of that stopped Aliya though. She continued to stumble through the roots and uneven forest floor. The darkness was making it even more difficult for her to see where the two of them were stepping. The light from Sienna's dark blue wisps of magic was the only guide for Aliya to see where she was going.

Enzo, for his part, tried his best to keep up with her. But trying as he might, every step he took felt like a drag. He couldn't even open his eyes completely to see what was happening.

When she felt Enzo's weight further lean on her, Aliya began to fear the worst.

Is he dying?

Aliya quickly scrubbed that thought off her mind. She didn't even want to entertain it. *No, he shouldn't. He can't!*

"We're almost there." She pleaded to Enzo. Although it sounded more like she was convincing herself.

In the corner of her eyes, Aliya could see the dark blobs of the berserkers retreat. They made their way back to what she assumed was to Damon.

When Sienna made sure that the berserkers were no longer attacking the three of them, she ran to Aliya. Sienna held onto Enzo's free arm, lifting his weight off of Aliya's shoulders slightly.

They could hear the snarls of the beasts in the distance. But the berserkers never attacked them.

Aliya didn't want to count her luck just yet though. They'd be lucky if they got out of there.

It was only when they got to the top of the hill that Sienna left the two of them, running to her car. Aliya saw Sienna turn the car around, holding the back passenger car door open. She kept scanning the woods behind Aliya and Enzo for the beasts of Damon.

But the snarling beasts only seemed to have retreated further into the woods.

Aliya could still hear the howls and whines of the berserkers behind her. Her only relief was that Damon and his beasts were wounded enough that it'd take them time to recover.

She didn't want to risk it though.

As they reached the car, Aliya pushed Enzo into the back seat. She didn't care if she was being careful with him or not. Her priority right now was to get away from Damon and the berserkers.

She pushed his legs out of the way before hopping in. "Go, go, go!" Was all she said before Sienna sped off.

Aliya let out a sigh of relief. She reveled in the peace and quiet. After that ordeal, she'd definitely needed it. There were no berserkers around to chase them. No Damon to taunt her.

Aliya heard a whisper coming from Sienna. "It's time." She heard Sienna say. After a few moments of silence, Sienna whispered again, this time with a conviction. "I will always be back, love. Wait for me. Tell Sanya I'll be back."

Aliya leaned over to see Sienna talking to her wife. Heaving a sigh of relief, Aliya sat back, leaning against the seat. She could feel her muscles aching from the soreness and the wounds.

But this silence, especially after their accident and fight with Damon... this was what she craved.

Aliya looked out into the darkness, watching as the trees passed them by. How had she gotten so caught up in this? One day she was a normal college student with two jobs, the next she was escaping one of the Disciples and his berserkers with her favorite author and favorite character.

I need to get a new favorite author. She thought to herself. *Probably a new romance author. At least that'll only leave me with angst and not broken bones.* Sighing again, she thought. *And probably another new favorite character.*

Aliya turned to look at Enzo. He hadn't moved from the position she'd laid him in. Her eyes narrowed as she slowly leaned into Enzo, hoping that what she was thinking was not correct.

Enzo looked too still to even be alive.

He hadn't even moved a muscle.

"Enzo?" She asked, quietly. When he didn't stir, she nudged him slightly, making sure she didn't agitate any of his wounds. "Enzo? Wake up."

Panic slowly began to rise when Enzo didn't so much as stir.

"Enzo!"

"What happened?" Sienna asked, still focusing on the road.

"He's not waking up." Aliya said, panic lacing every word. "He's not waking up! Do something!"

"I'm driving!" Sienna shouted back at her.

"I'll drive. You heal him!" Aliya tried to reason.

She leaned over to Enzo, shaking his head, trying to get him to say something. Aliya could feel his faint breath from his nostrils. But that was all it was... faint.

Panic rose within her again. Aliya felt the tears prickle her eyes as a knot slowly formed in the back of her throat.

"No, no, no." She whimpered, trying to get Enzo to wake up. "You can't die. Not now. Please. Wake up!" She pleaded. When Enzo didn't respond, she looked at Sienna, who was still driving. "Do something! Please..."

23

"Who said war was fair?" – Enzo

"**I**'M DRIVING!"

Enzo was hearing the hollowed voices again. Like in the distance as if they were talking through a tunnel. The voices seemed to echo through his mind.

"I'll drive. You heal him!"

There it was again. Another voice.

Although this one sounded surprisingly like Aliya. Was it really her voice? The last thing he remembered was holding Aliya's hand as the two of them ran through the forest dodging Damon's attacks. Everything after that just seemed... blank.

"No, no, no." There was that voice again.

Enzo could barely open his eyes. When he did though, he saw Aliya's worried face hovering over his. He wanted to tell her it was going to be alright. That they were going to be alright. But no words seemed to come out.

"You can't die. Not now. Please. Wake up!"

Aliya was screaming near his face. But why did it feel like she was talking from a distance? As if she was several feet away from him. Enzo felt it being a chore for him to keep his eyes open. He could barely open them as it was.

Maybe a small nap wouldn't hurt? He thought.

And with the last words from Aliya echoing in his mind, Enzo fell into a deep slumber.

"Do something! Please..."

Enzo and his troop of soldiers hid in the bushes and trees, camouflaging themselves as they waited for the signal for their attack.

Enzo looked around again, groaning lightly as he realized he must be back in the land of his memories. Taking a moment to collect himself, Enzo shook his head slightly as he tried to remember what happened. He gazed at his surroundings. The peace and stillness of the nature surrounding them was only betrayed by the nerves and anticipation in his thudding heart.

The soft morning light shone through the forest. But the camouflage the witches provided gave them ample cover. Seconds turned into minutes as Enzo waited patiently with his troops.

They weren't exactly his soldiers. They were soldiers that Aryan had lent him.

Three of the five mages that Aryan had given him stood beside him. Enzo's gaze flickered to the mages standing beside him. Mat, Ilyana, and Damyn stared straight with an unwavering determination, waiting for Damon al'Kara to show up with his berserkers.

The three of them stood ahead of the human soldiers acting as the first line of defense. If everything went according to plan, Enzo wouldn't have to put any of his soldiers in the line of danger.

The plan was simple really.

Aryan had already sent in spies to redirect Damon and his berserkers towards the soldiers in the center. Enzo hoped that Damon would take the bait. The bait was basically a few spies looking like forlorn villagers that had gotten stranded in the forest.

If Damon did take the bait and followed the 'villagers', he'd be ambushed on both sides by Aryan's forces from the right and Enzo's forces from the left as Aryan's Generals would take care of any remaining beasts in the middle.

The plan looked good on paper. It was soundproof. Damon would be surrounded with no chance for escape. Even his berserkers wouldn't be able to help him out of that trap. But they had only one issue though.

They were also going up against Damon al'Kara.

He was known to be the craftiest and the most cunning of all the Disciples. The oldest of the Disciples, rising to the ranks of the Dark One's circle of trusted allies. That worried Enzo even more.

But there wasn't anything he could do. At least not yet.

So, Enzo waited.

He waited for the signal that the spies would send out. Waiting for the ambush they'd prepared for the Disciple that was hunting them. Waited for the battle.

Seconds turned into minutes as Enzo kept his eyes peeled for any movement in the forest. The forest was quiet - never a good sign. Especially in the woods they were in. It was usually bustling with crickets chirping, frogs croaking, and birds flying about. But there was none now.

In their place was bone chilling silence. A silence that brought on with it the dread that Enzo hadn't felt in a while. The only thing that moved were the leaves of the trees as they swayed with the gentle breeze. For such a tense morning, it was a surprisingly warm and pleasant day.

Hopefully, that's a sign everything's going to go well. Enzo thought.

He didn't have time to think of anything else, however.

Because at that moment, Enzo saw a small figure wobbling as it tried its best to run towards them. Enzo blinked a couple times, trying to adjust his eyes to the sight before him.

A small figure ran towards them. Completely bloodied, the man waved his arms, as if trying to stop them from attacking.

What is he doing? Enzo wondered, worry marring his expression. The man was one of the spies sent out by Aryan. *Why is he waving?*

Enzo turned his hand into a fist, lifting it up for his soldiers. A signal for them to hold their attack.

Enzo leaned further from the branch as he tried to listen to what the spy was saying.

No one dared move a muscle. Everyone had one thought in their mind.

Was this another trick of Damon's?

Surely, that couldn't be it. That would mean that Damon knew of their plan. Enzo shook his head, trying to clear his thoughts and looked at the man running towards them again.

He could see the spy covered in blood. Gashes marred his entire body. It looked like the spy fought an entire battle by himself. The spy limped with every step he took towards Enzo and the soldiers. He was mouthing something. But the spy's weak voice did not carry the weight of the message.

A warning with only two words that filled Enzo with dread.

"He knows!" A tiny shout came from the spy. His voice grew louder with each step. "He knows!"

That was all he chanted. Those two words. The spy didn't have to clarify. Enzo understood the message loud and clear.

Damon knew of their plan.

But how could he?

No one other than Aryan, Enzo, and Aryan's Generals knew of the plan. Enzo hadn't spoken of the plan outside of the tent. Aryan would never speak a word about something this important. That only meant one thing. Dread pooled in Enzo's chest.

One among them were Damon's cronies.

Enzo didn't have time to stew on that thought for long. He had his soldiers to protect now. But just the thought of facing Damon and his horde terrified him.

Enzo only had twenty soldiers along with him. Of which five of them were witches. But none of those numbers of powers meant anything considering Damon's horde numbered in the hundreds.

They were sorely outnumbered.

They weren't supposed to be this outnumbered if they had gone with the plan. They wouldn't have been. Damon would have been blindsided. It would have been an ambush on Damon's forces.

Dread was slowly replaced with anger within Enzo. His body shook with unbridled rage. His hands turned into fists as he tried to control himself. There was only one way that Damon knew of the plan.

They had a mole within Aryan's forces.

The entire time Enzo was helping his cousin with the battle, the entire time his father had told him of the blackout of Illadora, Enzo wondered how one of the powerful kingdoms could fall so easily.

Now, he had his answer.

A kingdom that powerful could only fall from the inside.

Attack. Retreat. Attack. Retreat. Enzo wondered, weighing both his options at the moment.

He only had two options now. Attack and fight till the end. Or retreat and hopefully come back with reinforcements and hope that the next time, the plan would not be leaked to Damon. *That's a terrible plan.* He thought to himself.

If Damon had known of the attack before, he already had time to prepare for it.

They'd just lost their only advantage.

Enzo opened a portal near the spy, trying to bring him back to safety. He reached out through the portal, his hand hanging on the other end, reaching for the spy running towards him.

"Come on!" Enzo shouted, as the spy wobbled the few feet distance between them.

Enzo reached his hand through the portal, trying to catch the spy as he ran towards Enzo. The spy didn't stop wobbling. Every step he took towards Enzo only seemed slower than the one before. "Don't stop! Come on!" Enzo tried to encourage him.

It was only when the spy fell to the ground that Enzo realized what had happened.

In the distance was Damon with his horde, running towards them. The black wisps of Damon's magic surrounded the spy, crushing him as he fell to the ground, shouting in agony at the pain from Damon's magic.

And just like that, the spy was no more.

Enzo stood by his portal, wide eyed at the scene before him. The dead spy on the ground, his dead body still withering as it was surrounded by Damon's magic. Enzo looked up as Damon's wicked smile widened. When Damon lifted his hands, preparing himself for another attack, Enzo quickly closed the portal he'd opened.

Damon was here. He was here. Hearing the warning from the spy was one thing. But seeing the Disciple again, this time much closer than Enzo had ever gotten, was another situation altogether.

But there was not going to be another time to directly attack one of the Disciples. Especially one as powerful as Damon.

Enzo looked around at his soldiers. They'd heard the spy shout the warning. Enzo could see their apprehension, their confusion, their fear. But most of all, he could see their determination. Their determined faces was enough for him to decide.

Attack.

He still had to give his soldiers a choice.

"No one is going to think less of you if you choose to leave now." Enzo said. When no one moved, he continued. With a determined nod, Enzo balanced himself as he stood on the branch. If they were going to fight the Disciple himself, they might as well give it their all.

"I know you're afraid." Enzo said, looking at the scared faces of his soldiers. There was no use in hiding anymore. Especially when Damon knew of their location. "And to be honest, I am too." That brought on a low murmur among the soldiers. "We all know that there's only one way the Disciple could have known about the attack. So long as that traitor is alive, our families, our lands, our homes, our kingdom is no longer safe. So, today we fight. We fight for our families. We fight for their safety. We fight for their protection from the Darkness." A cheer rose from the soldiers. "Protection from evil." Another louder cheer. "From the evil that calls itself Damon al'Kara."

A loud uproar rang through the soldiers as they readied their battle gear.

24

"How am I still alive?" - Enzo

E NZO'S SOLDIERS WAITED WITH bated breath.

The ground beneath them shook as the horde of berserkers came closer. The trees the soldiers were sitting on began to sway with the force of the stampede, approaching the soldiers like a black wave laying destruction to everything in its path.

Enzo counted down mentally, waiting for the perfect moment for him to send in his soldiers.

Five.

The screeches from the berserkers were unlike anything he'd heard before. Even from the distance, Enzo could see that the hordes that were charging at them were different. These beasts were much larger than the berserkers Enzo had fought before.

Four.

The berserkers cared not for anything that laid in their path. It didn't matter how big the trees were. It didn't matter how far the soldiers themselves were. It seemed that nothing deterred the beasts from their path.

Three.

And right in the middle of the horde was Damon al'Kara. Sitting atop one of the beasts, riding it into battle as if he was riding a horse. Enzo's face was scrunched as disgust marred his face. The beasts were once people. And here Damon was... treating them worse than actual animals.

Two.

Enzo turned his attention back to the oncoming horde. Their stomps made Enzo's heart thud loudly in his chest. He had to take a few breaths to calm himself. Enzo peeked behind him to see his soldier jittery and shake as the berserkers came closer. It was now or never.

One.

"Charge!" Enzo roared.

Arrows rained down on the advancing beasts. The beasts' viscous snarls turned into pained howls when the arrows pierced their thick flesh. Although the fallen injured beasts only made the other berserkers stumble. The arrows only seemed to slow down the horde stampeding towards them.

Enzo climbed up the nearby tree to get a better view of the battle. His eyes flitted around the forest, trying to find berserkers that might have escaped the wrath of his men's arrows. When he did, Enzo created a portal in front of the beasts. Not expecting the portal, the beasts ran straight through them.

Which only made Enzo smirk.

He created another portal above Damon, who'd been watching the battle as he sat on his berserker in the distance. And just like that, Enzo dropped the berserkers that ran through the first portal down onto Damon and the beasts that surrounded him.

As the berserkers rained from above, the confusion among the beasts and Damon was almost instant. The beasts stumbled against each other. Enough that it almost threw Damon off his beast. The commotion seemed to only last for a moment though.

It still didn't stop the horde.

Although, it did slow down the mass advancing towards them.

I can't just keep throwing them back. Enzo thought, trying to come up with a new plan. He looked around at his troop again, eyes widening when he realized he hadn't been using the biggest advantage he had. Enzo gathered his five witches to stand by him.

"Mat!" Enzo called for one of the witches to stand beside him. "When I give you the signal, rain fire on them."

Enzo didn't wait for any affirmation from the witch. Mustering up all his strength, Enzo opened a portal leading to the berserkers in the middle of the horde. As the beasts ran towards them, Enzo only uttered one word. "Now!"

And with that word, Mat screamed as he blasted the fire. Mat's crystal shone bright white, almost blinding Enzo, as the magic coursed through him. The inferno that left Mat's fingertips was nothing short of spectacular. Enough that it would have made Enzo gasp out in awe if they weren't in a battle.

But they were.

Fire blazed from his fingertips with a ferocity that it drowned Mat's screams. And Mat's deadly fire sprung from his fingertips, into the portal, blazing the oncoming swarm of berserkers. For just a moment, Enzo could hear the shrieks and screams from the berserkers. That was a sound he'd rarely heard from the berserkers.

As the berserker lines slowly thinned, Enzo smirked. His plan had worked!

Enzo tried to muster enough strength for another portal. He could feel his strength slowly drain the longer the portals remained open. Keeping them open was becoming almost painful. Enzo could feel his arms shake as he lifted them to create another portal either way, opening this one behind another section of the berserker lines.

Enzo lifted his hands again, creating a couple more portals in front of Damyn and Ilyana. With a look and a nod, the crystals around the two witches shined a bright white light. White wisps crawled down their hands, encircling their arms, intertwining with their fingers as the magic coursed through them.

Torrents of wind gushed down from Damyn into the portal, hitting the berserkers. Enzo smirked. The beasts were no match for the torrents of gusts that Damyn poured down. Every beast that came in contact with Damyn's gale flew, crashing into the other berserkers around it.

The pandemonium that ensued within the berserkers was nothing short of amusing.

Enzo really would have laughed out loud if he wasn't a part of the battle.

The beasts stumbled and crashed against one another. Their commotion only seemed to slow down their onslaught however. But that was enough to give Enzo hope.

Damyn had changed his tactics. With one hand he let the gale rain down on the berserkers through the portal Enzo made for him. With his other hand, he redirected his wind through Mat's portal.

His gusts of wind combined with Mat's fire creating a fire tornado, blazing through the berserkers. The shrieks of the berserkers only intensified. Their pained howls filled the air, drowning even the roar of the fire and gale from both Mat and Damyn.

Enzo didn't even have to look at Amenya to see that she was causing her own sort of destruction.

The white wisps encircled her arms from her crystal as she strained to lift the burnt branches from Damyn and Mat's reign of destruction. With a flick of her wrist she turned them into shards and sent them hurtling towards the berserkers that had escaped the onslaught from Damyn and Mat.

If any of the berserkers had escaped the fire and gale from Damyn and Mat, they had to deal with the shards from Amenya. And even if the berserkers managed to somehow escape from Enzo's three witches, they had to deal with his soldiers.

Arrows rained down on the few berserkers that managed to make their way past the devastation that the three witches caused. So much that there were barely any berserkers attacking them, much less ambushing them as they'd done in the beginning.

Enzo and his forces were advancing on the berserker. Slowly gaining the ground they'd lost. They were gaining back their land. This was their home and no number of berserkers were going to take that from them. And if the enemy did try...

...Well, they could see what was happening now.

There was no chance for the berserkers to escape.

They could slowly advance on the berserkers. Enough to probably get to Damon.

We can win this. Enzo thought. Hope bubbled within him, threatening to spill out as a maniacal laughter as he watched the berserker forces thinning.

By the end of this battle, they'd either have a dead Disciple or a captured alive one. Enzo hoped for the second option. That way, at least they'd try and gain some information from Damon.

But that was his wishful thinking. He didn't really think Damon would give them any information. But the thought was good right now. That thought gave him hope that they were going to survive the battle.

So, he held onto it.

Ensuring that his portals held strong, Enzo ordered his witches to rain down destruction again. He couldn't help but smile as he saw the berserker horde thin with every wave of power his witches sent through the portal. Each blast knocked the berserkers off their tracks. The beasts flew in every direction knocking against the forest trees.

And for a moment, it seemed that only the pained yelps and howls of the berserkers permeated in the air.

Enzo chuckled maniacally. He could feel his energy drain slowly with each passing minute. He hadn't completely healed from the night before. And this was straining what little energy he had. With how weak he was, keeping one portal open would have been a chore. But now, he was controlling four different portals. Trying his best to keep them open.

He honestly didn't know how he was doing it either. Especially with the number of portals he was trying to control in his weakened state. Unfortunately, he also didn't know how much longer he could hold them open.

Straining himself a little more, he created a portal high in the sky, giving him a bird's eye view of the battlefield below.

A slow smirk formed as he saw his plan working.

His witches' attacks were thinning the hordes of beasts running in the back while his archers and soldiers fought the remaining beasts from the front. The air around the battlefield stunk of blood and charred flesh.

Gone was the chilly morning air as the fires blazed around them. In its place was the heat bellowing from the roaring fire around them. The gusts of wind only served to spread the fire, engulfing the enemy forces. The only reason Enzo and his soldiers could still see the forces was because Damyn created an air bubble around them. Smoke swirled around them, not affecting any of Enzo or his soldiers.

Enzo couldn't help but feel proud at the moment.

Yes, Damon had known of their original plans.

But Damon certainly underestimated how steadfast the Illadoran soldiers could be.

Enzo looked into the portal for a moment longer, trying to formulate another plan. One that could get him closer to Damon. He hoped he could blindside Damon with his attack.

But Enzo didn't.

No... he couldn't.

That one moment of pause Enzo took in the battle was a moment too long.

Enzo fell to the ground, shouting as pain shot through his entire body. He gritted his teeth, trying to control his pain. He tried to understand what happened. One minute he was standing and admiring the battle where he knew that his victory was almost certain; and the next, he was on the forest floor, clutching onto his sides and his head in pain.

Enzo swore in that moment that he could hear the lights and see the sounds with how hard he'd fallen to the ground.

He grunted and groaned as pain radiated through his body. Blinking hard, Enzo shook his head slightly as he took a moment to clear his mind. The dull headache he'd been sporting all morning flared, making it hard for Enzo to even open his eyes.

It was only when he heard the screams of his soldiers that Enzo opened his eyes as he still clutched his ribs.

And the sight before him only filled him with dread.

25

"Out of the frying pan. Into the fire." – Enzo

I F ENZO COULD HEAR at the moment, he'd hear the screams of his soldiers mixed with the snarls of the berserkers above them.

The screams would have mixed with the roaring fires of the burning forest around them creating a noise louder than any thunderstorm. In the distance, he would have heard the faint cackling from Damon as all of Enzo's forces grunted and screamed in their struggle.

But Enzo couldn't hear properly at the moment.

He was unfortunately thrown on his back. His head hit the protruding thick tree root, making the loud ringing noise from his ears the only sound that Enzo could hear.

If Enzo could look around, he'd have seen his witches and mages straining themselves to create a bubble of protection big enough to encompass all of his troops.

Enzo would have seen his mages' powers mixing together, creating a bubble of fire, water, and air, strong enough that the berserkers struggled to get through to the soldiers in the bubble underneath. He'd have seen the berserkers snarling, piling on top of one another as they surrounded the bubble in every direction. Making Enzo and his troop's escape essentially impossible.

Enzo would have seen his soldiers - even when fallen on their backs - were still fighting as valiantly as ever. Any berserker or one of their gashing claws that made it through the defense bubble the mages set up were chopped, making the injured berserkers howl in pain.

But no, Enzo couldn't see any of that.

His eyes shut close the minute his head the protruding tree root. Enzo curled up for a moment, grunting hoping the pain would fade.

What he could feel, however, was a small trickle of blood trailing from his head, down between his fingers clutching onto the wound and onto the forest floor.

When Enzo was finally able to see what was happening around him, his eyes widened as he let out a scream. He looked around, mouth agape at all the carnage around him.

His soldiers, disregarding their own bleeding wounds, fought on, desperately trying to keep the berserkers away from them and the other soldiers. His witches and mages screamed in frustration every time a part of the berserker or the berserker itself broke through their protective bubble.

But none of his troops gave up. No matter how badly they were hurt. No matter how tired they looked and felt.

Enzo took in a deep breath trying to calm himself. He needed to get his people out of there.

But how? He asked himself as he looked around helplessly.

No matter where he looked, berserkers surrounded them. They were truly trapped. The protective bubble his mages made was the only thing keeping them safe at the moment. But how long was that going to last? His soldiers and mages were already getting tired, straining against the beasts.

They weren't going to last much longer if this continued.

Enzo leaned on his elbows, wincing when pain shot from his wounds. He tried his best to lean as far away from the snarling berserkers as he could. Keeping an eye on the beasts above him, Enzo crawled towards his mages. He had an idea for their escape. But he needed their help.

Enzo didn't stop crawling on his back until he bumped into Damyn, Ilyana, and Mat. His mages only glanced at him for a moment before straining against themselves to maintain the protective bubble they'd built up.

From this distance, he could see his remaining soldiers clashing their swords with the berserker's claws that had broken through the protective barrier. Of all the soldiers that Enzo had brought with him for this battle, only ten of them remained.

And he'd be damned if he didn't save his troops... or at least what was remaining of his troops.

"I have a plan." Enzo shouted at his mages. The gnarly sounds from the beasts and the screams of his men almost drowned his voice.

Once he was sure his mages could hear him, Enzo continued. "Keep the bubble strong. I'm going to create a portal and get them out first." Enzo nodded in the direction of his soldiers. "And then starting with Ilyana, I'll be sending you guys through the portal."

"That's suicide!" Damyn shouted back. He turned to look at Enzo, his eyes wide in alarm.

"Do you have a better plan?" Enzo screamed back.

"How will you get out once you get all of us out of here?" Ilyana asked, raising her voice above the chaos around them. "You'll be trapped in here with them."

"Or worse, the beasts will rip you apart." Damyn said, still alarmed at the plan.

"No, worse would be if they turn him into a berserker himself." Ilyana said. "Best case scenario, he'll die."

Enzo looked at Damyn and Ilyana incredulously. He should be glad that there were people around him that gave him the truth. He should be glad they told him how dire the situation truly was. He should be...

But now was not the time.

Now, he was just focused on trying to get the remaining members of his troops to safety. He'd already lost a lot of people. And he'd be damned if he lost any more. So, Enzo just elected to ignore them. His life wasn't his priority at the moment.

"This barrier is barely holding on with the three of us." Mat shook his head wildly as he continued. That caught Enzo's attention. "Send one of us out and the barrier might as well just be a piece of paper for the beasts to tear through."

"You'll be sentencing not only you but Damyn and Mat to die as well." Ilyana screamed back.

Although this time, it seemed to be more from the strain of using her powers. She was right, of course. Her hands were already shaking from the strain of maintaining their protective bubble as it was. So were the other two.

That still didn't deter Enzo. He simply shook his head, pursing his lips. He was still going through the plan. There was just going to be a slight modification...

"We're doing this." He said, determination lacing every word. "With every soldier I send out through the portal, reduce the size of the bubble.

It'll be easier for you three to control it And it'll be easier when I send you away one by one."

The three mages still looked skeptical. To be honest, Enzo didn't know if that plan would work. But it was worth a try at least.

And so, Enzo started.

He brought his hands in front of him and took in a deep breath. Waving them around in a circle, Enzo could feel the fire burning in his chest. His power trickled down his arm as a purple glow surrounded his hands. The air in front of him crackled as the fabric of space tore open to create the portal.

On the other side, he could see the palace grounds. His palace grounds. The palace grounds of Ravendore.

The contrast in how the grounds looked was almost jarring. There were barely any people walking about the palace grounds at this time in the day. Enzo swore he could hear the birds singing as a silent warm breeze swayed the trees in Ravendore. It was quiet. It was peaceful. Something that Enzo, currently in a battle with a snarling horde trying to save him men, envied.

Safety was only an arm's reach away.

They could all escape from this massacre. They'd all be safe... or rather, all that were remaining.

"Brace yourselves!" Enzo shouted to his men.

Only a couple of them turned to see what Enzo was talking about. The rest were still fighting the rare berserker limbs that escaped the bubble and reached down to claw them. Their blades swished in every direction. Hoping that the beasts' claws would stay as far away from them.

With the human sized portal in front of Enzo, it didn't take them long to understand what Enzo was planning. They quickly alerted the remaining men. And although the others didn't turn to Enzo, their relieved expression was all the response Enzo needed. They knew what was going to happen.

Enzo didn't give them time to prepare.

Instead, he quickly moved his hands down and then to his right. And just like a marionette obeying the puppeteer's every command, the portal traveled across the ground towards Enzo's men, swallowing them. Teleporting them to a safe location.

As the soldiers fell through the hole one by one, leaping through the other side, Enzo looked over to the mages beside him. He nodded. His signal for them.

And just like they spoke about, Enzo could see the protective bubble they'd been safely under slowly shrink. With every soldier that leaped through the portal, the bubble became smaller.

Enzo looked at his mages. He could see the sweat dripping from their temples. Their clothes clung onto their bodies like a second skin. He could see their arms tremble as they tried to maintain the protective bubble.

Even when working together, even with shrinking the bubble, it seemed harder as the time went on. And with how many berserkers were able to reach into the bubble, Enzo's mages were clearly struggling to maintain the integrity of the bubble they'd created.

In all honesty, it was also getting difficult for him to maintain the portal as well. He didn't have enough strength to maintain a portal this long to begin with. And with the number of people that had to go through...

Enzo's hands trembled just like his mages. He could feel his heart beat faster. Enzo tucked his hands and legs closer to himself, trying to shrink as far away from the beasts.

With the bubble shrinking around him and that the berserkers right on top of them, it seemed futile though. Their snarls and gnashing teeth and claws were closer than ever.

Enzo looked at his men again.

Five more. Enzo told himself. *Come on! Leap through the portal. It's right there.*

But none of them seemed to even make a move towards the portal.

Instead, they clashed with the beasts' claws that reached for them through the bubble. They screamed as the beasts' claws sank into their flesh.

In the distance Enzo could see the sizzling bubble shrink, moving ever so close to the men. If his men didn't jump into the portal now, they'd be left outside of the bubble. Left to fend for themselves.

There's no fending for themselves! Enzo was alarmed.

There truly was no fending for themselves once his men were outside the protective bubble. With the number of berserkers, his men would be long dead before they even could bring their swords to protect themselves.

No, if he had to save them, they had to jump into the portal now.

With the bubble closing in, Enzo let out a shuddering breath and shouted. "Leave them!" He tried to gain their attention. "Leave them! Get through the portal now!"

With a slight turn of their head, Enzo could see the reluctance in their eyes.

He was still their prince. And they were still his troops. And he was just telling them to abandon him. He could understand their conflict. But now wasn't a time for them to contemplate if they had to stay with him.

"You need to jump through the portal. Now." Enzo's voice wasn't much louder than the berserkers above them. But his commanding tone left very little to be challenged.

His soldiers gave each other one last skeptical look before turning to Enzo and nodding.

Even from this distance, Enzo could feel their relief as one by one got ready to leap through the portal. Jumping just in time as the protective bubble shrunk past them.

Enzo's eyes were wide. He bit his lips, hoping all the five soldiers made it to the other side safely. It was only when the last soldier jumped through the portal that he let out his breath.

And just as Enzo and his mages had planned, the bubble grew ever so smaller by the minute.

It was time to get his mages out of here. Damyn let out a chuckle when Enzo turned around to face them.

"That was an insane plan." Damyn said. He looked like he couldn't believe that Enzo's plan had actually worked.

To be fair, Enzo couldn't believe that his plan had actually worked...

Or rather, half of his plan had actually worked. He still had to get his mages and himself out of this chaos.

"That was a terrible plan!" Ilyana shouted. Even if Enzo hadn't looked at her, the incredulity in her voice made him chuckle at what her expression could be.

"It got them out, didn't it?" Enzo chuckled. "Your turn now."

Just as he was about to move the portal over to his mages, he heard Mat shout. "Again, that's suicide"

"Let me take care of that detail." Enzo shouted back. "I don't plan on dying today."

Before any of them could protest, Enzo brought the portal over to Damyn. Enzo didn't give them any time to prepare.

Instead, he dragged the portal below each of his mages. Watching as Damyn fell into the ground through the portal.

It was only when Ilyana and Mat couldn't see the fire in the bubble surrounding them that they realized Damyn had gone into safety.

Ilyana didn't have any time to look alarmed. Enzo dragged the portal below Ilyana, not giving her a chance to protest. He knew he was going to get an earful from her the next time he saw her. But that was a worry for another day.

"Wait!" Mat said, looking at Enzo skeptically.

It was only his powers holding them safe within the bubble now. But with Mat going through the portal, Enzo would be stranded. Left alone to fend for himself against the horde of berserkers that they were surrounded by.

"The minute I step through there, there's nothing that's going to protect you." Mat pleaded.

"Let me worry about that." Enzo said.

Although Mat's expression implied that was the wrong thing to say.

"Why can't we jump together?"

Enzo pursed his lips. His muscles and body strained with every minute that the portal was open. Why couldn't Mat just leap into the portal. He didn't need this conversation now.

"Because I am having a tough time just maintaining the portal as is. If I come down with you, I don't know if I'll be able to maintain the portal to Ravendore and we'll be torn in space. And I'm sure you don't want that now." Enzo said with the most sarcastic smile he could muster.

"Are you telling me you're having performance issues right now?" Mat chuckled.

Enzo scowled and rolled his eyes. "Now, jump! I'll be right behind you!"

Looking at Enzo seriously, Mat said. "Your plans are stupid!"

That wasn't exactly the way to talk to a prince but Enzo was going to let it go for now.

"Tell me exactly how stupid they are once I come back." Enzo smiled. The smile did not reach his eyes though.

The two men nodded at each other.

And in that moment, Enzo realized he'd never experienced true horror before then.

Because the moment Mat jumped into the portal to safety - to Ravendore - was the moment Enzo was no longer protected by his mages' magic.

And with the loss of protection, He saw the berserkers descend upon him like a rain of hungry teeth and sharp claws. Enzo wanted to jump right behind Mat. He knew he should have jumped right behind Mat.

But the shock of the berserkers descending upon him was too much.

Enzo brought his hands up, instinctively. Unfortunately for him, that also meant that the portal he'd maintained for so long to send his soldiers to Ravendore was no longer open.

So, with the berserkers' descending upon him, Enzo did the only thing he could think of at the moment. He no longer cared how he would escape. He no longer cared where his portals would take him. Enzo waved his hands one more time, making the air sizzle in front of him as the portal opened.

He didn't care where the portal led. At this point, the portal could lead him to the Dark One himself and Enzo would be thankful to be thankful to be away from the berserkers.

Just as he was about to jump, Enzo shouted when he felt the claw of one of his berserkers sink into his thigh, tearing his skin.

He didn't stop to check though. There would be time for that and that time wasn't now.

Enzo slashed the berserker's claw with his dagger before jumping into the portal.

He swore he could feel his body traveling through all the dimensions before landing onto the solid ground with a thud.

He grunted, holding closely onto his slashed thigh. Leaning back on the ground, he looked up.

His eyes widened in shock when he realized he was still in the forest though. The birds sang the tunes of nature as leaves of the trees above him danced to their tunes with the quiet breeze. He could hear the frogs croak and...

Was that...?

Was that running water?

Either way, of the nature surrounding him, Enzo noticed one thing more than most.

There were no berserkers. There was no Damon al' Kara chasing him. There was just Enzo. Enzo and nature. He wasn't being chased. He wasn't being hunted.

He was safe...

...for now.

26

"Someone's persistent." – Enzo

1 *0, 9, 8...*

Enzo counted down slowly. Not daring to count out loud lest any creatures in the woods heard him. He couldn't hear the berserkers anywhere near him. But he didn't want to risk it either way.

7, 6...

He needed to move. Try to get as far away from the berserkers as possible. He needed to go back to his troops in Ravendore. Enzo still couldn't believe he saved his remaining troops. A brilliant stroke of luck. That was all that was. Just pure luck. And now, he had to save himself.

5, 4...

He tried moving a couple minutes ago. But his body ached in places he didn't know he had muscles. With how much his body was protesting, Enzo could only lay down and stare at the green canopy above him.

And so, he started counting. Allowing himself just five minutes to lay on the ground. Gather what remaining strength he had left. He was going to need it if he wanted to create a portal to Ravendore.

Although with every passing second, his dread only increased. Even with him laying completely still on the ground, his muscles hadn't relaxed. The serene forest sounds should have calmed him. They should have relaxed him enough that his body could heal itself.

But Enzo couldn't stop thinking.

What if the berserkers were close by? What if one of them got away from the horde. What if they were silently hunting and I can't hear them?

Questions swirled through his mind. Enzo shook his head several times to get those thoughts out of his mind. But nothing he did seemed to work. Those thoughts seemed to linger. He needed to get away from here. Put some safe distance between him and the beasts and Damon. Only then, he'd be able to breathe properly.

So, Enzo gave himself a little time.

Some time for himself to calm down and then he'd make a portal for himself to Ravendore.

3, 2, 1.

Enzo grunted as he got up... or rather tried to get up. He must have fallen on his chest when he got through the portal. It seemed that any small movement was enough to shoot pain down his spine.

"That's not ideal." Enzo murmured to himself. It wasn't exactly a humorous situation. But humor was all he had at the moment.

Just standing up alone made him feel like the world was spinning. He pursed his lips feeling queasy. Enzo grabbed onto the tree trunk beside him, taking in deep breaths, trying to steady himself. It was only when he peeled his eyes open to look around that he realized where he was.

In the commotion and chaos of trying to escape from the berserkers, Enzo had portaled himself back to the base camp.

A very abandoned base camp.

There was not one person, elf, or witch to be found anywhere in the camp. It was as if everyone had just left everything behind and abandoned the camp. Which was probably something that they did.

Especially with how the equipment, tents, and weapons were strewn about. All the tents were slashed as if the people inside were in a hurry to escape the wrath of whatever was chasing them. The cots that once housed the injured were overturned. Blood of the injured soldiers still clung onto the beds. Small clay pots and glass vials were strewn about the camp. A sign that even the mages had abandoned the camp.

What happened here?

That would have been the question Enzo would have asked... that was if he didn't see the claw marks marring the tree trunks. The fabric of the cots were slashed tearing the cloth rendering the cot useless.

They were attacked here too? Enzo asked himself, horrified.

His eyes widened in shock at the scale of destruction. There was nothing in the camp that remained intact. Nothing.

In the distance he saw black streaks like veins covering the forest floor, reaching above to the tree trunk. It looked like a small black hole, swallowing all light around it. Enzo had never seen such a thing before. Was that... thing there before? How had he not seen it then? He didn't know what they were... nor did he want to find out what they were either.

Of all the destruction to the camp, there was only one thing that let him breathe calmly. There were no dead bodies here. None of the soldiers were left behind. They might have been injured. They might have fought back. Either way, they escaped.

And now it was Enzo's turn.

He brought his hands up in front of him, willing the flutter of energy in his chest to trickle out to his hands. But it seemed that all the energy in his body was being used to repair the gashes and injuries he'd gotten during the battle.

Enzo could feel his gash on his thigh slowly stitch itself up. He could feel the scrapes on his face slowly heal, just leaving behind a trail of dried blood. Which was all good. Except now, he barely had enough energy to conjure up a portal to escape.

The air in front of him sizzled as the sparks of the portal formed in front of him. But Enzo couldn't hold on much longer. His arms shook as he expended his strength. Just as the portal was about to open in front of him, Enzo's arms gave away.

And the air in front of him that would have opened up into a portal, just laid... calm. As if it hadn't been sizzling just moments before.

"Hm, that's a shame really." A voice came from a distance behind Enzo, startling him.

He whipped around, only for his eyes to widen in shock when he saw who it was. There, standing in front of him, was none other than Damon al' Kara.

Without his berserkers.

Not that Damon needed his berserkers to defend himself. If all the stories that Enzo grew up with were true, Damon had just been holding back his power this entire battle. Essentially toying with Enzo and his troops.

But that still begged the question...

Where were his berserkers?

Am I being surrounded? Enzo wondered. He didn't dare move a muscle. Nor did he dare to take his eyes off Damon.

No.

Instead, even with bated breath and a thudding heart, Enzo simply feigned courage and raised a brow.

"I thought you'd be more powerful than that." Damon mused, loud enough that Enzo could hear it even from this distance. "But I guess, you, being able to conjure up a portal even looking like you do at the moment, takes enormous strength."

It's true that he looked horrible with all his injuries at the moment. But Damon didn't have to point it out. It was pretty rude, honestly.

Enzo shrugged, trying not to wince when pain shot through his ribs.

"I could give you a few tips if you'd like." Enzo said, trying to be as nonchalant as possible. He just had to keep Damon talking for a little longer. He'd get his strength back and escape from here. But until then...

Damon chuckled.

"I don't need much to kill you, boy. But thank you for the offer." Damon said, nodding.

"You're not going to kill me." Enzo said. He didn't know where that confidence in his voice came from because he certainly wasn't feeling it. But even with the fear being latent within his heart, Enzo knew what he said was true.

Damon was not going to kill him. He had several chances. And if one of the most powerful Disciples wanted to kill someone, they were as good as dead. But here Enzo was. Still breathing.

Bruised. But still breathing and alive. So gloriously alive.

He didn't know why Damon spared him but that was a thought for another day. Now, Enzo had to escape.

Enzo took a step back lazily, trying to put as much distance between him and Damon but not trying to look scared at the same time.

"And how do you know that?" Damon asked, intrigued.

"Because if you're truly as powerful as they say you are, you'd have killed me by now." Enzo shrugged, taking another step away from Damon.

Was baiting Damon really the best strategy? Enzo didn't think so, but he was in too deep. There was no going back now. Just a few more seconds and he'd be able to make another portal and escape.

"Or maybe I have other plans for you." Damon suggested.

That made Enzo pause mid-step.

What other plans could Damon have for him? It didn't take long for Enzo to stew on that question, however. His eyes widened in shock when he realized. Blinking a couple times, Enzo tried to recover from his shock as much as possible.

"So," He stated simply, trying to look as nonchalant as possible. He was not going to show how much Damon affected him. Damon's presence alone was nerve-wracking. "Were you planning on turning me into your pet or..." Enzo lingered at the statement before continuing. "Were you going to take my power as well?"

In all the stories Enzo had heard about Damon growing up, one thing stuck out the most. Damon's powers were similar to the Dark One. If the Dark One could take the life force of a person, Damon could take the powers from someone and use it as his own - leaving only a shell of the former person behind.

And honestly, Enzo didn't know which was worse.

Moral dilemma aside, it had just clicked for Enzo how dangerous the situation was for him.

If Damon had gotten a hold of him... If Damon had the chance to take Enzo's powers... If Damon could turn the husk of a man Enzo would be without his powers into a berserker...

There would be no hope for this war in Indresal.

With all of Enzo's powers absorbed into Damon, he could move his berserker horde anywhere in the continent. Damon would be able to attack any kingdom at any point. And with how powerful Damon already was, none of the kingdoms would stand a chance.

Damon's smirk was the only answer Enzo got. A smile so vile that Enzo could see the rest of the war play out in his mind if he was caught by Damon. Enzo's heart thudded in his chest as he thought about his mother and father... his kingdom... his people. He could feel a thin line of sweat falling from his temple.

There was no way that Damon would spare any of them. Enzo couldn't think of one person that could survive. It'd be a massacre. It didn't matter the person - old or young, man or woman. It wouldn't matter.

The only thing Enzo was sure of was that any healthy person would be turned into a berserker. That would only increase Damon's horde. And with how big Ravendore was, the Dark One's horde of beasts would almost double.

The fall of Ravendore would foretell the fall of Indresal to the Dark One.

Enzo couldn't let that happen.

No, he wouldn't let that happen.

If Enzo wasn't in a hurry to get away from Damon before, Enzo sure was now. He took another step away from Damon.

Damon finally seemed to move from his position, stepping closer to Enzo. It was almost as if he glided across the forest floor with how gracefully Damon stepped by the tree roots and twigs laying on the forest floor. His long robes covered his legs, making it look like he was gliding across the forest floor.

"I wouldn't do that if I were you. You have nowhere to run…" Damon stepped closer once again. "And you definitely can't hide from me for long."

As if on cue, Enzo heard the growls of two of Damon's beasts stalking up to him. Their menacing growls only made Enzo more anxious. They looked nothing like the beasts that'd just attacked Enzo and his troops. These beasts looked different. Bigger. More threatening.

Only two? Enzo wondered. *Where are the others?* Enzo shook his head lightly, trying to get out of his thoughts. *No! Even two berserkers was two berserkers too many.*

Damon was right. He couldn't outrun Damon and his berserkers. Not in the condition Enzo was in. Enzo gazed over Damon and the two berserkers standing a little distance beside the robed man.

"You're right." Enzo said. "But you're also wrong."

That was all Enzo said before turning around and bolting. He didn't turn back to look if Damon and his berserkers were following him.

Enzo didn't know where he was running to. He just needed to put some distance between him and Damon before he could open a portal. He didn't want to bring Damon and his berserkers with him wherever he was going.

So he dashed. Not caring if the branches and twigs scraped at his flesh. Not caring if his shoes dug into his ankle with every step. Not caring if his lungs burned from breathing so hard. No, he just had to get away.

Turning the corner near a tree, Enzo saw the same dark spot he'd seen before. The small black hole with tendrils creeping up along the trees and forest floor surrounding it, that seemed to swallow the light and everything around it.

Enzo didn't stop running as he raised his hand. He felt the flutter in his chest, a feeling that crept down his arms. He saw the air in front of the dark hole sizzle as the space itself opened up to create a portal. It was dark on the other side. So dark that Enzo couldn't make out where the portal led him to.

But that didn't matter at the moment. He just needed to get away from Damon and the two berserkers chasing him. He hadn't turned back to look at how close they were either.

All Enzo hoped was that if Damon and the two berserkers were close by, Enzo would still be able to go through the portal to safety. And he'd be able to close the portal fast enough that the only thing that Damon and his berserkers could go through was the dark hole behind Enzo's portal.

Even with the bright evening sunlight in the forest surrounding Enzo right now, the darkness on the other side of the portal looked inviting. Providing him the safety that had eluded him since the beginning of this battle.

Just a few more feet.

Enzo could hear the snarls of the berserkers close by. His heart rate sped up, anxious that all of this would be for naught if the berserkers caught up to him at the last minute. Enzo ran like no other.

Not bothering about the berserkers' snarls that were moving closer by the second.

Not caring if any of Damon's attacks would hit him.

He'd already felt Damon throw something at him. It'd been stinging his back ever since he'd felt it. But Enzo didn't dare turn around. Not now.

He just needed to escape into the dark on the other side of the portal. And then he could worry about anything Damon had done to him.

Just a couple feet more! He told himself, hoping the berserkers didn't catch him.

Enzo's prayers seemed to have been answered. Because just a couple seconds later, he leaped into the portal. His body tumbling through the space and through to the other side. He felt different traveling through the portal.

Something felt different.

This portal was unlike anything he'd gone through before. It felt like he was traveling between the two locations a lot longer than he'd ever done before. But he had no time to wonder where he ended.

Enzo grunted as he fell onto the hard forest floor. That was what the darkness covered. A thick dark forest that allowed for no moonlight to enter its canopy.

He quickly turned to see Damon and his berserkers getting ready to run into the portal. Enzo didn't waste any time. He didn't care if they leapt into the portal. Because just at that moment, Enzo lifted his hands, closing the portal before Damon and the two berserkers could even enter the dark forest.

Enzo's hands hovered in the air even after the portal closed, as if waiting for something to happen. As if all of this had been Damon's trick and he'd hear the berserker's growls any second. He couldn't believe that his plan had actually worked.

... Which seemed to be the theme for his battle against Damon so far.

Seconds turned into minutes and yet, Enzo didn't dare move from his position. His hands were lifted, hovering in the air, in anticipation for... something. His eyes darted from one corner to the next.

Enzo could feel his heartbeat slow down. It was only several minutes later that Enzo even dared to relax. He could feel his body sway as the rush of adrenaline slowly left his body. He tried to step forward, to grab onto something. Anything that would give him support.

But the only thing that he could see was the forest floor quickly approaching as Enzo fell to the ground... unconscious.

27

"Oh, so, that's how I got here." - Enzo

ENZO FELT THE DROPLETS dripping onto his face.

His eyes fluttered open as he brought his hand up to shield himself from the droplets. With how sore his muscles were, Enzo began to wonder how long he'd been unconscious for.

But the light - or rather the lack thereof - told him that barely much time had passed since he'd fallen unconscious.

Enzo groaned as he sat up, leaning himself on his elbows as he looked around. Or tried to look around in the darkness. There wasn't much he could see. There was barely any light coming through to the forest floor. For a moment, Enzo wondered if it was because of the thick canopy above him or if the night was moonless.

Could be both. He thought.

Tall, thin tree trunks surrounded Enzo everywhere he looked. Water dripped from the leaves of the swaying branches. Enzo shivered under the gentle night breeze. He grunted, sitting up straighter, and brought his arms together, warming himself.

Enzo's brows scrunched in confusion.

No part of this forest seemed familiar to him. Not the trees. Not the random lights that passed by the forest every so often. Not the low rumbling that accompanied the lights that lit up the forest every time they passed. Enzo wondered what they were. He'd never seen anything like it before.

If the lights were from horse carriages, they were moving a little too fast for his taste. He didn't know of any transport that would go that fast.

Maybe they're not carriages. He wondered.

The low rums of something passing by outside of the forest echoed within the forest. The random lights that passed through the forest. They couldn't be horse drawn carriages rattling outside the forest. Enzo knew of the riders lighting the lamps to guide them through the darkness in their journeys. But whatever the sounds outside the forest were, they couldn't be any horse drawn carriages he knew. Not with how fast they were going. It had to be something else. And the low hums every time the transportation went by him...

It was unnerving to say the least.

What was familiar, however, was the wet forest ground.

The petrichor assaulted his senses, bringing him a sense of calm Enzo didn't know he needed. Enzo smiled. After smelling the stink of the berserkers for the past few days, this pleasant naturistic scent was most welcome. Enzo's smile only grew when he heard the frogs croaking and crickets chirping.

It didn't matter what the sounds and lights were to Enzo anymore. If the frogs and crickets weren't bothered by them, Enzo wouldn't be bothered either.

And most importantly, even after falling unconscious for however long, Enzo was still in the same place... and alive.

That meant Damon hadn't followed him. And he didn't hear any growls or snarls from the berserkers.

He truly was safe.

Enzo let out an elated chuckle. After all that time of running, Enzo truly felt free. He'd escaped Damon and his berserkers. He'd survived... somehow. And now, he just had to get back to this kingdom.

But first, he had to know where he even was.

Enzo stood up slowly, letting his muscles get used to the strain. He looked down at himself.

Most of his injuries were healed. Although, he could still feel the gash on his chest troubling him. He didn't want to open his armor to see how badly he was injured that his body was taking this long to heal the wound. No, he'd go back to Ravendore and let the healers do that job with that one.

But first, he needed to get out of this forest.

Enzo limped across the forest. He didn't care which direction he went. The forest had to end somewhere. He clung onto the trees, pushing himself every time he felt his legs shake or felt the world sway a little. His breath came out as short huffs the more he exerted himself. Enzo clung onto his chest with one hand, hissing every time his shirt scraped against the gash.

He didn't know how long he'd been walking. He didn't know if he was even getting out of the forest or worse... deeper into it. The only sign that gave him hope was the trees thinning out and sparsely populated the more he walked.

Enzo continued to walk, or rather, stumble his way through the forest. His head hung low as he felt dizzy with every step.

He'd only come to a stop when he realized that there were no trees surrounding him. He stopped mid step and turned around. All the trees stopped growing a few feet away from him. Almost as if someone had cut it to make a clearing.

Enzo turned around again. But nothing prepared him for the view in front of him.

The roads were made of materials that he'd never seen before. Light shone off of tall poles brightly lighting the dark passages. So much that even in the moonless night, Enzo could see everything. Enzo looked at the lights again. There was no fire coming from them.

Where is that light coming from? Enzo's brows were scrunched.

That was when he saw the houses the lights were illuminating. He was used to seeing houses with thatched roofs. Houses made of mud or clay houses in the desert. But none of the kingdoms he'd ever visited had houses that looked like these.

Where am I? Enzo wondered.

He'd traveled with his father to several kingdoms ever since he was a child. And never once had he seen any house that looked like the one he was standing in front of.

Enzo rubbed his eye, wondering if he was seeing things in his delirium. When he opened them again, the house was still there.

No, it's real.

He shook his head. Either way, a house meant safety. He could at least seek shelter for the night before going back to Ravendore the next morning.

Enzo looked at the rounded road. At the end of the rounded road stood a house. Alone. With no neighbors.

Ok, that's good. He thought. The less people that see him, the better.

He limped to the house, trying to be as inconspicuous as possible. He stuck to the shadows, hoping no one would see him.

This kingdom was very different from all that he was used to. And Enzo hoped to all the gods above that he didn't just portal himself to the Dark One's kingdom.

The Dark One doesn't care to build houses like these for his people. Enzo's mind reminded him.

No, he had to be somewhere else. Although Enzo's mind was drawing a blank. He needed rest first. He'd worry about where he was and getting back to Ravendore later.

Enzo wobbled to the back of the house. He tried to open the latch and push the door open. But the door wouldn't budge. Heaving a heavy sigh, he looked at the door accusatory.

Not knowing what else to do, Enzo slammed his shoulder into the door. He grunted out loud in pain at the contact. But that pain was quickly over-ridden with elation when he saw the door open.

He blinked a couple times trying to adjust his eyes to the darkness within. There wasn't a lamp in sight. And he didn't have any energy within him to create a small portal to use as the light. Enzo huffed as he slammed his feet into the furniture in the darkness.

He gingerly navigated his way around the house, finally stopping when he felt a sofa in front of him. Heaving a heavy relieved sigh, Enzo plopped himself on the sofa. With the darkness and quiet surrounding him, Enzo finally felt at peace. Which was weird considering he had no idea where he was.

The darkness showed him what he'd been missing though. Or rather what he'd forgotten to investigate. He knew he felt Damon's attack sting his back when he was trying to escape. Enzo had completely forgotten about it until now.

... Until he saw the faint yellow glowing thread connected to his back. That couldn't be... could it?

He didn't have the chance to investigate further, however.

Because at that moment, the handle to the front door rattled. Enzo's body stiffened. He stood still, hoping that the darkness gave him enough of a cover for now. He lifted his hands up defensively, ready for any threat that might come in through the door.

But all his worry in that moment turned into confusion when the door opened to reveal a young girl, standing barely to the height of his shoulders, carrying six heavy bags walking into the house.

"Aliya?" Enzo whispered her name. Even though it came out more like a question, Enzo knew that was the girl's name.

And that shocked him. How did he know her name?

Enzo watched as the girl dropped the bags in front of the door before walking into the house. She stopped, standing like a statue. She didn't dare turn or move as if realizing that something was different about the house. Like it was no longer empty like when she left it.

"Don't move." A deep voice said beside Enzo. "Not a step."

No, it wasn't any deep voice. It was his deep voice.

Enzo's worry slowly turned into confusion. *Why am I hearing my own voice? Have I been here before?*

But he was only left with more questions when he saw a faint purple glow, walking closer to the girl.

What's happening? Why am I hearing myself? Enzo looked around.

Everything about this house looked familiar. As if he'd been here before. For a moment, he wondered if he was looking into the future. That couldn't be possible, could it?

No...

No, that couldn't be possible.

Because this was a memory.

Enzo looked again and saw himself stalking up to Aliya. His eyebrows raised when he realized why she was scared.

Memories slowly came rushing back to him. About his meeting with Aliya. How she'd helped him. How the two of them visited her favorite author, Sienna, who happened to be a witch. Not just any witch but one of the last remaining survivors of Pheandra. He remembered Damon's attacks.

All those memories brought him to now. He was attacked again, trying to get Aliya to safety after

He remembered falling unconscious.

Enzo's eyes widened. He'd been unconscious this whole time.

He'd been reliving his memories this whole time. As if his mind realized that he was in a dream, Enzo's mind went blank. Where once Enzo lived in a vibrant false reality, he was now only surrounded by the dark void of his mind. It didn't matter where he turned or which direction he looked. Darkness surrounded him, swallowing his screams of desperation to get out.

He needed to get up now.

No, he had to get up. If not for his sake, for Aliya, at least. He needed to save her. He needed to get Damon away from Aliya.

Enzo didn't know what to do. He didn't know how to get back into the world of the living. He shouted his desperation out into the void. Enzo didn't stop screaming.

Trying his best to break out of the dungeon in his mind.

Something that was easier said than done.

Enzo didn't stop struggling as he felt the darkness of the void swallow him. It wasn't until he felt the light touch of an invisible hand that he was able to calm down.

Enough that he woke up, gasping for air as if he'd been deprived of it all this time - only breathing normally when he saw Aliya's hands brushing his shoulder. Her eyebrow raised as she looked down at him.

Yeah, he was safe. He was no longer in the land of his dreams. He was awake and safe.

And if he was being honest with himself, this was where he wanted to belong.

28

"There's no scarcity for food in this world." –
Damon

D AMON GRUNTED AS HE held onto the shard, still lodged in his
stomach. Sniffing loudly, he counted to three before pulling the
shard out, shouting in pain as the shard dislodged from his wound.

He huffed and panted, laying on the forest floor trying to regain his
strength.

The wound would begin to heal itself in a few minutes. Damon just
needed food to sustain him till then. He needed his energy to heal.

His berserkers looked at him from only a few feet away, quivering with
fear as they stomped in position. Their mewling only seemed to grate on
Damon's nerves.

"Will you two shut it?" Damon grunted, but that only seemed to
agitate the berserkers even more. "I swear, the next time the Dark One
makes more of you, he needs to make sure that you cannot talk."

Damon looked down at his bloodied shirt and the hole where the
shard pierced him.

That was a crafty move. His mind wandered back to the girl.

Damon still didn't understand why the girl was adamant about protecting Enzo. He didn't understand the connection the two of them had.

Yes, he was protective over his Amara as well.

That was only because Amara was like a daughter to him. A daughter he'd adopted when she was almost the same age as the girl. But that still didn't explain the connection between her and Enzo. The connection between those two didn't look like that of a father-daughter bond.

Does she love him? Damon wondered.

It was too short a time for them to meet and fall in love. Especially for a love that meant you'd have to sacrifice your life to save the other person. Damon cursed out loud.

He should have killed the girl when he had the chance. Now, she was just being a menace.

Come to think of it, the girl reminded him of a younger Amara. Maybe that's why he hadn't been able to kill her yet.

It would have been so much easier if he would have gotten rid of the girl and gotten Enzo.

Damn the sentiments. Damon cursed. *Next time, I won't go easy on you.*

Damon sat up slowly. He could feel his wound stitching itself up. But it was much too slow for his pleasure. Groaning, Damon got onto his feet, wobbling and swaying as he tried to maintain his balance.

"Yes, I need sustenance." Damon whispered to himself.

He called on his berserkers, still standing mutely a few feet away. Climbing onto one of them, Damon made his way slowly out of the forest.

A couple hours of walking - painfully, Damon al'Kara might add as his sore muscles had yet to heal completely - and a setting sun giving him and his two berserkers cover, Damon finally stopped.

Damon clutched his chest, heaving at the pain. He'd long torn off the ends of his shirt, turning it into a makeshift bandage for the gash in his stomach. He'd stopped using the berserker for his transportation. Every step the berserker took only seemed to aggravate his wound.

No, it was much better to walk.

But the only problem was that he was losing his energy walking out of the forest.

Damon clutched his chest again, grunting and limping as he walked through the dark alleyway. He was just happy that the sun had set by the time he walked out of the forest with his berserkers. There wasn't any moon to provide them any light either.

The only light that Damon could see once he got out of the forest was from the streetlamps that surprisingly ran without fire and the light from the shop lining the town nearby.

It took Damon painstakingly long to walk into the town, trying not to be startle the people with his berserkers. He'd learnt that lesson on the first night in this world. His berserkers had already killed the first three people they came in contact with.

It took everything within him to stop his berserkers from feasting on every human they came across. It was easier when their only orders were to destroy.

I'm getting too old for this. Damon thought, wincing again as he walked. Even taking a breath in was getting harder. He was sure he'd broken a couple ribs during the fight. Damon stuck to the darkness, away from the people.

His two berserkers growled lowly as they walked behind him. Damon could tell that they were getting antsy. They hadn't had much to eat since their first night in this world.

And Damon was worried that if he let go of what little control he had of his berserkers, they'd turn on him. No, he needed to get them something... or rather someone.

But seeing two berserkers behind him always seemed to scare people, making them scream.

And screaming people brought on more attention that Damon was willing to have at the moment. So, Damon and his berserkers stuck to the alleyways. The darkness provided them a sense of comfort.

Damon scrunched his nose in disgust every time they passed a trash can. The berserkers beside him whimpered and grunted along with him.

"Will you shut it?" He whispered at them harshly. That seemed to shut them up.

Their fight before had done a surprising amount of damage. He was sure he had multiple other bruises along with his broken ribs. The gash on his stomach was the least of his worries now. His muscles on the other hand... That was a different story entirely. He really was getting too old for this.

His berserkers, though, took much of the damage. He could see the blood seeping through the gashes the berserkers had suffered through the fight.

Damon was still hung up on the girl defying him at every turn. She was grating on his nerves, but he had to admit, he liked her bravery. Her bravery was the only thing keeping her alive. Or Damon would have gotten rid of her when he first saw her at the author's house. He just wanted to see how far her bravery would take her.

The courage she showed was not something he'd seen in another person - especially when facing him. Even Amara, the woman he'd come to care for as his daughter, was scared of him when they first met. For the first time in a very long time, Damon was impressed.

The girl had a darkness to her that he hadn't seen in a while.

He still wondered why she was helping Enzo though. That grated on him even more.

All that potential within her and she chose to use it on the one person who'd lose. Oh, the things he would be able to teach her if only she let her darkness consume her.

Damon limped again. He stumbled on a stray rock, sending pain shooting down his spine, sucking the breath out of him. He grunted, holding onto the grimy brick wall beside him for balance as he winced, trying to shut out the pain.

As the pain slowly subsided, Damon took in a deep breath and let out a groan as he leaned against the wall.

His mind raced back to the girl once again. More specifically, his mind raced back to the anger in the girl's eyes. They reminded him of Amara. But more so, the girl's anger reminded him of his.

She'd make a good disciple. He thought.

The way she threatened him, the way she thought of escaping him and his berserkers...

If only he could get her on his side, Damon could only think of how ruthless she would be. Especially as someone who was willing to kill herself to get an upper hand on him at the gas station before.

He definitely had to make her a Disciple. He had to make her join him. She deserved to be by his side. Damon could see it clearly now.

He could see himself present the girl to the Dark One. them using her cunning and brashness to win the war.

The entire Indresal would be at their feet in no time.

When Damon came to a dead-end in the alley, Damon paused to catch his breath. His wounds weren't healing as quickly as before. He needed a little more time before could trace Enzo again. But more importantly, he needed to conserve his energy to try and heal himself. And for that he needed food.

Damon leaned against the wall, ignoring the whimpers of the berserkers beside him and groaned as he crouched down.

He looked around in the darkness. The large trash collector beside him reeked of rotting food. In front of him was a brick wall painted with various graffiti. Trash bags and several equipment that Damon didn't recognize lined the street in front of him.

"Great! How the mighty fall." Damon mumbled to himself as he began to take in his situation.

His berserkers knocked around the bags beside the trash collector making the metallic sound echo in the dark alleyway.

"Keep it down!" Damon hissed at them, not caring who heard. He could only hear the whimpers from the berserkers in response.

Before Damon could say anything else, a voice chimed in. "Who is it?" The voice said, opening the back door to one of the shops.

Light from the shop illuminated the once dark alleyway, making Damon wince at the sudden intrusion of the light. He tried to shield himself, trying not to draw any attention to himself or his berserkers.

But luck was not on his side.

An old man, short and stout, came out of the shop. "Show yourself." He said loudly.

When Damon didn't make any noise, the old man looked around the corner of the trash collector. He placed his hands on his hips as he saw Damon slowly standing up. Giving Damon a once over, the old man shook his head.

"What are you doing here?" The old man asked, as if chastising an unruly teen. When Damon didn't answer, the old man sighed and shook his head. "Are you hungry?" The man asked finally.

Pursing his lips, Damon simply nodded. Hoping that answer was enough.

The old man turned to go back into the shop. From the smell of it, the shop must have been a bakery. Damon could feel his mouth water from the warmth of the baked goods from the bakery. He was just happy at the moment that his beasts didn't make much of a noise.

They'd blended in perfectly with the darkness, not even letting a whine or a howl out. Damon lifted his hand, a silent command to make the berserkers stay in their place. They wouldn't attack until Damon gave them the command.

Damon slowly walked out from beside the trash collector. He'd already been spotted. There was no use hiding now.

The dark alleyway was drenched in light as the door to the bakery opened. The old man stumbled out, carrying a large loaf of bread and a small bottle of water. Holding the bread and bottle in either hand, the old man waddled towards Damon.

"There you go." The man said, satisfied as he handed Damon the bottle. He broke the bread in half before handing each loaf to Damon. "That should cover you for the rest of the day, I hope."

Damon bowed his head in gratitude. "Thank you.' He mumbled. "This is perfect for me."

"That's good to hear." The old man gave him a small, kind smile.

"But my friends here, they cannot eat this bread, I'm afraid." Damon continued.

That seemed to have puzzled the old man. He placed his hands back on his waist. He tilted his head in confusion. "Your friends?"

The man must have noticed Damon staring off to a spot behind him. Following Damon's gaze, the old man turned to see what Damon was looking at.

He didn't have time to even scream.

The two berserkers towered over him as Damon gave them the command to attack. Before the old man could even think of screaming in fear, the berserkers bit at him. At his neck, At his limbs. Anywhere they could grab.

Damon hissed as a spot of blood smeared at the bread he was holding. Scrunching his nose, Damon stepped to the side as he removed the piece of bread stained by blood. He threw it to the ground before taking a big bite out of the remaining loaf of bread he was holding.

By the time he'd finished the bread and drink, there was no sign that the old man was even present in the alleyway.

Damon looked up at the satisfied berserkers, their jaws sprayed red with what was remaining of the old man.

Damon could already feel his body slowly starting to heal itself again. He had already gotten the sustenance he needed, the energy he needed to heal his body. Damon took in a deep breath feeling his muscles relax as each muscle and wound healed itself. He craned his neck, humming in content as he felt his body relax.

Now, it was time for him to track Enzo.

And there was no way Enzo was going to escape from him again. Even with the girl present.

Damon took out a small dial from his pocket. It was a little cracked and sprayed at the edges. All of which were evidence of the battles that the dial had gone through. The glass on the dial was slightly cracked, making Damon 'humph'. This dial was a gift from one of the other disciples. Damon was going to have to find a way to fix it now.

Unlike a normal dial that had numbers, this dial had symbols. Symbols from the ancient tongue that only a few people knew of.

Wiping the dust from the cracked glass, Damon held the dial in both hands. He could see the faint glow of the yellow light that flowed from the dial.

A yellow light that pointed him to where Enzo was.

Damon chuckled. He was surprised Enzo hadn't cut the thread yet. Especially with a witch around. It didn't matter now.

Damon could feel the power of the dark one as he let the dark wisps flow out of him. He directed his wisps, willing them to flow into the dial. Once the wisps consumed the dial, they shot along the yellow light, tracing their way to Enzo. It took Damon less than a second to see where Enzo was.

Damon smirked.

He was going to get Enzo one way or another. And if he had to kill the girl to get to Enzo, that was what he was going to do.

29

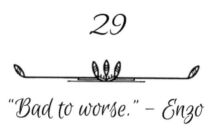

"Bad to worse." – Enzo

ENZO SAT UP, ALARMED. He tried to ignore the world around him spinning, making him want to puke. All the memories came rushing back to him as he woke up.

The battle. Enzo trying to save his soldiers. Him barely escaping the berserkers. Him barely escaping Damon before coming to this world. Enzo honestly didn't know how he was still alive. He was starting to believe Aliya that his life was only fictional and being led by a cruel author. But that couldn't be...

Memories flashed as pictures in his mind as he tried to get a grip on his reality. Enzo remembered entering Aliya's house, finally being able to relax after his battle. But one memory stopped him short.

The faint glowing yellow thread.

Enzo's eyes widened in alarm.

He couldn't see if the yellow thread was still connected to him. Giving them a direct link to Damon. He'd been the loose end to Damon finding them every time. He'd been the reason they'd been getting attacked all this time.

"He sees us." Enzo gasped out. "He knows where we are." Still holding his head between his hands and looking at the ground, Enzo continued. "He'll come for us. He threw a tracker on me before I came here. That's how he's been able to find us wherever we are! We need to get the tracker out!"

Enzo panted out, still trying to get himself under control. When he looked up though, his confusion only increased. Aliya and Sienna hadn't moved from their spot.

Did they not understand how dangerous this was? He wondered.

Enzo could see their gazes trained on him, unimpressed. As if he'd just told them something that they'd already known. They didn't say anything however. Nor did they move from whatever they were doing to remove the tracker from him.

That confused Enzo even more.

"You're a bit late to the camp." Aliya mumbled.

"What?" Enzo asked, not hearing her clearly.

"We already know that." Aliya shrugged. Enzo raised his eyebrow waiting for her to elaborate. Aliya took that as a sign and continued after heaving a heavy sigh. She dropped the metal rods she was holding and turned to Enzo. "We were wondering on our way here about how Damon kept finding us. Sienna thought that Damon might have put a tracker on you. So, once we were a safe distance away, we searched for it and lo and behold, you have the tracker on you."

Aliya got all of that out in one breath. In the end, she gulped the air and gave him a sarcastic smile that didn't reach her eyes.

Now that Enzo looked at her, Aliya did look tired. No, she looked exhausted.

Her curly hair had already turned into a frizzy mane that even her hair band couldn't contain. Her dark circles only seemed to highlight her tired eyes. Enzo wanted to smile when he saw her dimple that only seemed to come out when she gave him a sarcastic smile. Even in the midst of all the running and the chaos, she still looked beautiful.

Aliya hadn't had a good night's rest ever since he'd come into her life. Something that he knew she didn't care about. She thought all of this was an adventure. But for Enzo...

Enzo cared.

He cared that she was helping him. He cared that she never left his side. He cared that she questioned him when he was being overbearing. Even when the danger was right in front of them - and there were many times within the last two days - she didn't let go of him. Sometimes even coming back to help him fight.

She'd make a fine queen. That thought sobered him. Blinking rapidly, Enzo tried to push that thought to the back of his mind.

No, he wasn't going to subjugate Aliya to any more of this danger.

But she's been safe with you. Another thought occurred, bringing with it hope like the light in the dark tunnel. But that hope was squashed when another thought replaced it. *She was in danger because of you in the first place.*

Either way, Enzo couldn't get the thought of Aliya being beside him forever out of his mind.

He shook his head. Maybe changing the topic will get him to stop thinking about Aliya.

"How long was I unconscious?" He asked.

"Almost fifteen hours."

"What?!"

"I'd say from the snore that you had a pretty good rest. Now if you're done resting, I'm going to need your help."

Snore?! That was an accusation that Enzo didn't like. He didn't snore. Although he did have to say that he felt well rested.

Before he could say anything Aliya continued. "Don't worry. We got the tracker out. Although I think we're a bit late."

"Late?"

"The thread was already glowing by the time we got to it. Sienna seems to think it's because Damon had already tracked you down to where we are."

That made Enzo sit up straighter. He still felt dizzy though. Although, he could no longer feel the pain from his wounds. Sienna might have healed him when he was unconscious. And with how long he slept, she had her time to heal him.

"Is that why we're here? Where are we? We need to be somewhere safer. There are trees around us but this is still out in the open." Enzo looked around, quickly trying to analyze their location.

"Don't worry. Sienna found the spell to send you back to Indresal."

It was only then that he paused.

Enzo staggered as he tried to stand up. He held onto the tree trunk, hissing when the scrapes on his hand burned as they came in contact with the rough tree bark. Leaning on the tree trunk, Enzo looked around.

Trees of different sizes surrounded them in every direction. The thick canopy above them barely let much sunlight to the forest floor even though it was early in the evening. Birds sang in the branches above them as the frogs croaked in the creek a little distance away. The forest floor was still wet from the rain that seemed to have poured a while ago.

Even in the serene environment, Enzo's focus was not the calm nature around him.

Instead, Enzo's eyes widened when he saw where Aliya and Sienna were standing.

He took in the thick tree trunk behind Sienna. A thick dead tree with a rough bark with no leaves on its branches. The dead tree's roots clung to the big rock beside it as if the rock was the only thing keeping the tree upright. But that wasn't what caught Enzo's attention, however.

What caught his attention was the scar that spanned the length of the tree and the rock beside it. A scar that looked like a dark hole. Much like the one that he came through from Indresal to this world.

For a moment, Enzo wondered if he was already back in Indresal. That somehow in his sleep, Aliya and Sienna were somehow able to create a portal back to his world. Hope bubbled inside him.

Could it be?

Enzo brought his hand up to test if he got his powers back. He tried to feel the flutter within himself. Something, anything, that told him that he could make his portals again. Before he could start, however, he heard Sienna say out loud.

"We're not in Indresal yet." She bent down to place the big bowl on the ground. "You're not going to get your powers yet. Maybe since your powers are linked to Indresal, once we open the portal, you can get your powers back."

Enzo huffed. He heard a chuckle coming from Aliya in the distance but chose to ignore it.

That was a good theory. One he'd like to test out as quickly as possible because that meant he'd be able to go home.

"I've seen that dark hole before." Enzo mumbled, just loud enough that Sienna and Aliya could hear him. "What is it?"

Sienna stopped what she was doing. She let go of the herbs in her hand into the bowl before standing up straight. Pointing to the dark hole behind her, she said. "This hole?"

"Is there any other dark hole around here?" Enzo countered, earning himself a raised eyebrow from Sienna. An expression that eerily reminded him of his mother. Giving Sienna an apologetic smile, Enzo simply nodded.

"This was where I entered this world from Indresal. From Illadora. It's a tear in the space between our worlds." Sienna said.

A tear was the right word. The air around the dark hole waved like the mirage on a hot road on a warm summer afternoon. Nothing grew around the ground surrounding the dark hole as if the forest itself was afraid of what mysteries the scar held.

"I saw a scar just like that one before in Indresal." Enzo said.

Sienna pointed to the dark hole behind her. "Just like this one. Where did you come from?"

Enzo just shrugged. He was delirious by the time he created a portal to come to this world. It'd be a miracle if he could remember where he was.

But if the scar was similar to the one he'd come from Indresal, could he have come to this world from Illadora? Could he have portaled himself from the battle to Illadora and then come to this world? Questions swirled in Enzo's mind.

Sienna nodded as if trying to understand. "It's probably where I came from." She mumbled before turning back to what she was doing.

Which was...

"What are you doing?" Enzo asked, his brows scrunched together in confusion.

The entire time he'd been awake, Sienna had been mixing the herbs in the bowl. The pendant on her necklace emanated a faint purple glow anytime she used her powers.

"Why does yours glow purple?" Enzo asked. He'd been wanting to ask that ever since he first saw it. "The other mages' pendants glow white. Why is yours purple?"

Sienna didn't react. And for a moment, Enzo wondered if she even heard him. Finally, with a deep sigh, Sienna looked up at him.

"Let's just focus on getting back to Indresal first." Was all she said before turning back to her bowl.

That answer only brought on more questions for Enzo though. But he didn't want to push her just yet. Maybe he'd get an answer out of her once they are back in Indresal. But for now, he'd let it go.

He turned to see where Aliya was.

She'd not said a word the entire time he was talking to Sienna. He remembered her holding his hand as he woke up. Something she was not doing now and that felt... empty. Looking down at his hand, Enzo flexed it, itching to get closer to Aliya but his confusion only grew when he saw what she was doing.

Aliya walked up to the pile of metal rods, picking them up one by one. She placed them in a circle around the dark hole Sienna was working near, creating a fence.

Or at least that was what Enzo thought.

From the looks of it, Aliya had already gotten more than half of the rods in place. There was still a pile of six more rods.

"What are you doing?" Enzo asked.

Aliya huffed, placing her hands on her hips as she stood straight. She panted as she looked at Enzo and said, "Putting my degree to use apparently."

Enzo didn't understand a word. He gave her a small quizzical smile before looking over what she was doing again.

Aliya might have taken his silence as acceptance as she went back to doing whatever she was doing.

"Why are you making a fence?" Enzo asked.

Sweat glistened on her temples as her wet hair clung to her face. Her lips hung barely open as she panted. Heaving, Aliya looked at Enzo again.

"What?" Aliya panted.

"What are you building?" Enzo asked again.

She looked at the rods and then back at Sienna. "A fence?" She said, although it came out more as a question.

"But why?" Enzo asked, still not understanding what the fence was supposed to protect them from.

"So that if Damon and his beasts come by before we can create the portal, we can be safe?" She narrowed her eyes, as if silently asking why he was questioning her.

But her answer only seemed to make him more confused. How was a fence supposed to protect them from the berserkers? It wasn't as if Damon and his berserkers were polite.

It wasn't as if they'd see the fence and stop, letting them create a portal.

Aliya must have sensed his confusion, because she continued. "It's an electric fence."

Those words meant nothing to him.

And electric fence...?

"From what I know about the berserkers, they were once human." Aliya sighed loudly. "And humans and electricity don't mix well together."

Enzo wanted to ask her what electricity was, but that was probably a question for another time.

When she saw that Enzo was still confused, she simply said. "I'm going to fry them from the inside."

That's what those things were supposed to do? Enzo's eyes widened in shock. How was Aliya able to hold them with her bare hands?

But most importantly, had Aliya always been this violent?

Enzo had so many questions and the conversations he had with both Sienna and Aliya only left him with more. But before he could ask any more questions, a low noise in the distance stopped the three of them dead in their tracks.

There were no more birds chirping and singing their songs around them. No more frogs croaking. Even the leaves stilled as the wind swaying them stopped. It was as if the entire forest was waiting with bated breath. Fearful of the beasts that had entered its domain. Unable to protect its inhabitants from the wrath of the beasts.

In the silence of the forest, the low rumble was the loudest sound Enzo had heard. A rumble that could send shivers down anyone unfortunate enough to hear it and low enough that it could paralyze any person in fear.

The low rumble of the berserkers.

30

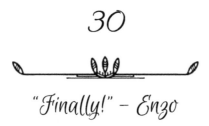

"Finally!" – Enzo

"**W**HERE DO YOU NEED these?" Enzo shouted to Aliya.

The moment he heard the low rumbling, Enzo ran to the pile of metal rods laying a couple feet away from Aliya. He grabbed all the remaining six rods, thankful, once again that he had gotten his strength back.

And even then, the rods were heavy. He glanced back at Aliya, impressed that even with the weight, she'd placed most of the rods in the perimeter surrounding the dark hole and Sienna.

It was only then that he saw Aliya's eyes wide in horror. She hadn't moved since she heard the berserkers. Her strong grip on the metal rod had only tightened.

"Aliya!" Enzo screamed, snapping her out of her daze. "Where do you need these?" He asked... again. He needed her to think of anything else other than the berserkers that would reach them any second.

Looking at the metal rods in his hands seemed to bring her back to reality. Aliya licked her dried and chapped lips. She ran to the perimeter that she was setting up and jammed the rod into the forest floor.

Following her lead, Enzo completed the circle. But for now, they were just rods. How were a bunch of rods supposed to protect them from beasts with claws that could tear them apart just by grazing at them? Before Enzo could say anything, Aliya opened a large bag behind Sienna.

She grunted as she brought out a large box. Or rather something that looked like a box. The way the box was shaped, the ridges and everything else about the box made Enzo question if it was even safe.

Aliya, on the other hand, didn't waste any time. She ran back to the bag. This time taking out long coils of metal wire.

Enzo's heart sped when he heard another growl coming from the distance. A growl much closer than the ones before. If he had to guess, with Damon's tracker leading him to Enzo being cut, they were still searching for Enzo. Enzo only hoped that Sienna would be able to create the portal before Damon found them. They didn't have much time.

Aliya was still struggling with the fence. She held onto the wires, juggling them from hand to hand as she ran around the perimeter, creating a metal wire barrier between the three of them and the beasts that were hunting them. When she was finally done, Enzo looked at the fence incredulously.

It was barely above his height. If the beasts so wanted, they could easily jump over the fence. *This* was her plan?

Another growl.

Enzo could see the faint shapes of the beasts in the distance. He could see Damon riding one of them.

It was as if time slowed when Enzo spotted them. Damon turned his head just in time for Enzo to spot him. The sinister smile that spread across Damon's face sent shivers down Enzo's spine. Damon whistled faintly, making his berserkers change their direction.

As if seeing Enzo, Sienna and Aliya was all the energy they needed, the berserkers charged towards them.

Enzo could feel his heart thud with each stomp of the berserkers. He took a couple steps back, as far as the fence allowed.

"What do you need help with?" Enzo shouted at Aliya who was still focused on the box. Except this time, she was slamming it with her fist, screaming at the box to work.

"Aliya, they're here! What do you need help with?" He screamed at her again.

The berserkers were closer than ever. Their growls grew louder by the second.

"I've got it under control. It'll work!" She screamed back. Although, it sounded more like she was trying to convince herself.

"You might have it under control. But you don't have the time. What do you need -"

Enzo didn't get a chance to finish. Because in that moment, Aliya channeled all her pent up frustration at the box in front of her, screaming as she gave it a hard kick.

Just in time too.

Aliya jumped back as a low hum emanated from the box, pulling Enzo back with her. Her gleeful expression and clapping was the only sign that Enzo had that the fence was successful. Which he found doubtful.

The fence did nothing. There was nothing. It still looked normal with metal rods and wires surrounding it.

Enzo's gaze shifted to the berserkers charging towards them. And then back to the fence. He didn't trust it for one minute. Grabbing Aliya's hand, he pulled her behind him, frowning when she resisted slightly. He didn't care. The closer the berserkers were, the tighter his grip was on her hand. Finally, not caring what she wanted, Enzo pulled Aliya behind him.

He couldn't control the terror building up within him. His face scrunched in horror as he saw the gnashing teeth snapping for them. The beast reached out its clawed appendages as it jumped into the fence.

Enzo shut his eyes, holding onto Aliya behind him. He waited with bated breath for the viscous claws to reach out through the fence to devour them. He waited for the pain when the beasts would snap at them. He waited...

For nothing?

When he didn't feel any mind-numbing pain of being torn to shreds, or hear any of the screams that would have shaken him, Enzo slowly peeked one of his eyes open. Just in time too.

Because he saw the berserker fly into the air, wailing as it fell backwards.

Enzo had imagined many scenarios in his mind. None of them included watching a berserker fly. As if Damon and his other berserker were thinking the same thing, the two of them stopped, watching the scene before them with their jaws wide open.

The berserker fell to the ground with a thud. Enzo could have sworn the earth shook in that moment. The impact of the berserker falling to the ground brought him out of his reverie. Unfortunately for him, Damon and his other berserker seemed to recover from the shock as well.

They continued to charge at Enzo, Aliya and Sienna, not caring for a moment that they might face the same fate as the now delirious berserker.

Enzo had hoped that with how the berserker flew back, it'd have at least been gravely injured or even dead. That would have been one less thing to worry about.

Unfortunately, the fallen berserker only stood up, shook its head for a moment before turning around and charging at the fence along with Damon.

"I was hoping he'd stay down." Aliya murmured, echoing Enzo's thoughts.

Enzo looked at Aliya. Her maniacal smile only widened as she laughed at their fate. But her smile slowly turned into worry when the beast got back up.

It wasn't until the beasts and Damon reached the fence that Enzo began to worry.

The beasts didn't care if the fence singed their skin, burning their flesh. The beasts slammed their hands onto the barbed wires surrounding them, shaking the fence with every punch. The fence surrounding Enzo rattled, making him worry if it would even hold against the onslaught that the berserkers brought on.

Damon, on the other hand, circled the fence, as if searching for a weak spot as his beasts continued their pounding.

The crisp and refreshing smell of the forest that Enzo woke up to was replaced by burning berserker flesh. Enzo couldn't help but gag at the atrocious smell assaulting his nostrils. It didn't matter that the beast's flesh sizzled when it came in contact with the fence. It didn't matter that the beasts whined in pain every time they came in contact with the fence. They didn't step back.

With every pounding, the fence shook. Rattling against itself as the metal poles swayed from where they were stuck on the ground. If Sienna wasn't going to be able to open the portal in the next few minutes, they'd be easy meat for the beasts.

"How long will this fence last?" Enzo asked. Worry began to prickle his heart. He wasn't as anxious a couple minutes ago when the berserker flew across the forest. But now...

Enzo turned to look at Aliya, as if waiting for her to reassure him that her fence would protect them. But when she turned her anxious expression back at him, Enzo's dread only increased.

"I don't know." She mumbled, her face scrunched from the smell. Her eyes conveyed the dread she was refusing to say out loud though.

"What do you mean you don't know? Where did you even get this?" Enzo asked, alarmed. She was the one that made this contraption. Shouldn't she know if the fence could stand a little longer? For now, he was just happy that the fence was tall enough that the berserkers couldn't jump over them.

"None of this equipment was tested for berserkers. I'm making it up as I go. Don't question it."

"What if it fails?" Enzo asked. It was more a rhetorical question. He wasn't expecting an answer from Aliya but he got one blank expression from Aliya anyway. "Do you even know if it's going to work?"

"I'm an engineer. I'll make it work."

"But they're becoming loose!"

"I said don't question it. It'll hold!"

As if the metal rods heard Aliya defending them, they chose the exact moment to disappoint her.

One of the wires connecting the metal fence rods broke from the fence slamming into the box Aliya laid to the side.

And that seemed to have broken whatever power the fence had.

Because the next thing he knew was Aliya jolting to the fence and holding onto the metal rod. Despite its weight, Aliya flipped the rod in her arms and jammed it down onto one of the berserkers.

Enzo's heart thundered in his chest as he saw her struggling.

What is she doing?! He complained to himself before rushing behind her. If they somehow made it out of this alive, he was going to kill her himself.

Enzo grabbed the metal rod. Using all his strength - which now that Sienna had healed him, seemed to have gotten back to his normal self - Enzo stabbed the berserkers. Their pained howls and screeches didn't stop them from pushing forward though.

Enzo strained to look at Sienna behind him. Ever since Damon and his berserkers began the ambush, she hadn't spoken one word.

Sienna, for her part, didn't let the berserkers deter her from creating the portal. Although, she seemed to rush through the ritual. She crushed the leaves in the palm of her hands and grinded the nuts before tossing them into the bowl. Her pendant glowed purple the entire time she mixed the ingredients.

It was as if she sensed that Enzo was about to ask her how long it would take.

Sienna stood up. She held onto the bowl, so tightly that Enzo could see that her knuckles had turned white. She quickly turned towards the dark hole, not daring to even peek at the berserkers behind her. Although her small flinches at the beasts' snarls told Enzo that she wasn't completely zoned out.

Grabbing the potion she'd just created, Sienna slathered a symbol - one that Enzo didn't recognize - in the air near the dark hole. As if by command, the symbol hovered in the air. It seemed that Sienna didn't have to voice out any spell - at least not that Enzo heard her with the beasts growling in his face.

The minute Sienna connected the two ends of the symbol, it glowed a blinding yellow.

Bright enough to startle not only Enzo, but also the berserkers and Damon in the distance.

Enzo didn't know what to think of the light. He didn't have much time to ponder anyway.

He felt the ground beneath him shake and tremble. As if the ground itself was preparing itself to split open.

Enzo felt Aliya fall onto him as the ground continued to shake. Holding onto her arms, he steadied her. Enzo looked at Sienna again, incredulously. Sienna's serenity was the only reason Enzo wasn't worried any longer. He wondered if this was the side effects of the spell working.

He didn't have to voice that question to Sienna, however.

Enzo felt it before he could even see the portal open.

He felt the flutter in his chest.

He felt the tingle in his chest - a sensation that traveled down from his chest to his hands. It was like he could breathe again. Enzo rolled his shoulders and rolled his neck, letting his power wash over him. A small smile graced his face. He was never going to take his powers for granted again.

The power was a part of him and losing it...

Oh, Enzo couldn't even describe that feeling. It felt like a gaping hole in his chest which has only now been filled. To Enzo, it felt like home.

Enzo only turned around one last time to confirm that the portal was open. He didn't need the confirmation. But in the two days that he'd been in this world, he'd come to miss Indresal and Ravendore.

Between the trembling ground, the glowing sigil, and the dark hole, Enzo saw a fissure open. Tearing open the dark hole as the air around the sigil sizzled.The yellow glow enveloped the dark hole, the tree, and the rocks surrounding it. The fissure slowly crept open, like little tendrils reaching out tearing the fabric of this world to open it to Indresal.

And just like that, Enzo could see the forests of Indresal come into view. It didn't take Enzo long to realize that the portal opened to the same area he left Indresal from. He'd recognize the serene woods anywhere.

Smiling, Enzo pushed Aliya back. Not caring that he'd used his full strength to get her as far away from the berserkers as possible. He knew she'd be angry at him for that. But that was ok. He'd apologize later.

He turned to look at her with a smirk. Enjoying the shock on her face. Her eyes wide and mouth agape.

Because he knew what he looked like at the moment.

Encircled in purple glowing light, this was Enzo in his full power. A sight that he was sure that Aliya had read about until now.

And she was getting to see how powerful he truly was.

31

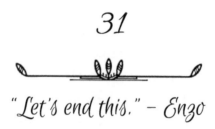

"Let's end this." - Enzo

NOT SPARING ANOTHER GLANCE at Sienna or Aliya, Enzo created a portal on the ground.

Before the berserkers could claw at him, Enzo jumped into the portal. When he finally portalled himself behind the beasts, outside the fence, Enzo began to chuckle at Aliya's confusion.

With Enzo out of the way, the berserkers charged into the fence at their new target - Aliya and Sienna. Aliya's eyes widened as she brought her hands up to her face, shielding herself from the oncoming beasts.

Oh, no you don't. Enzo thought as he watched the beasts.

He created a portal in front of the beasts only to release them behind him. Keeping them as far away from Aliya as possible. The beasts stumbled around for a moment, confused that the meal in front of them just a moment ago was no longer there.

Enzo chuckled when he noticed the shocked yet relieved expression on Aliya's face. That was slowly starting to become his favorite expression on her. Enzo began to wonder what else would make her shocked.

He didn't have time to ponder though. When the beasts realized he was closer, Enzo became the new target.

Maybe now he could show her his true power. Maybe he could show her that she made the right choice in picking him as her favorite fictional character.

Second favorite fictional character. He scoffed when his mind added unhelpfully.

It didn't matter that her first favorite character was Sienna's brother. It didn't matter to Enzo that Sienna's brother was actually dead.

No.

Enzo was determined to take that first spot. Maybe after seeing him fight the berserkers with his true power, he could take that place.

The berserkers almost became an afterthought. At this moment, he just wanted to show off his powers to Aliya, enjoying her shocked glee with every attack he aimed at the beasts.

Every time the berserkers lunged at him, Enzo created a portal making them punch the other beast, almost making them fight each other.

Much to his delight, the berserkers actually did hit themselves. Injuring themselves to the point that they were beginning to slow their attacks. Enzo knew he shouldn't waste precious time. He didn't know how long the portal would last. But he was having too much fun to stop now.

He continued to play with the berserkers, making them attack each other, thrashing them around the forest. The trees around them didn't stand a chance as the berserkers crashed into them. Stray bark and branches flew around them. But Enzo didn't care.

It was almost becoming a game with the three of them.

The berserkers lunged.

Enzo created a portal.

He chuckled when the beast's fist hit the other knocking it out of the path. He'd then turn to look at Aliya and smile widely when he saw her chuckling. Enzo could feel his heart flutter every time he saw Aliya chuckle.

Although he didn't know if it was from her laugh or from his power. He was enjoying this though.

That was until he noticed Damon creeping up to Aliya and Sienna. Enzo's eyes widened only a fraction.

In his little game that he was playing with the berserkers, he'd completely forgotten about Damon so far. And considering how close Damon got to Sienna and Aliya, he'd already figured out that the electric fence was no longer protecting the two women.

Enzo didn't stop making the beasts attack each other. But his focus was now on Damon. Enzo quickly created a portal beneath Damon - just as Damon was about to step behind Aliya. Damon didn't seem to anticipate it.

He stepped into the portal, losing his balance. He tried to grab onto something but with the trees a couple feet away from him, Damon lost his balance. He fell through the portal. Not wanting to give Damon time to recover, Enzo opened the portal high above in the sky making Damon fall through.

Enzo hoped for a moment that the impact would knock the wind out of Damon or even better, kill him.

But it did none of that. Instead, given how high Enzo opened the portal, it seemed to have given Damon time to recover from his shock. So, instead of Damon falling on his back as Enzo had hoped, Damon created a small cushion of air for himself to land on.

Damn it. I shouldn't have made it that high. Enzo scowled. Now, he had to deal with the two berserkers and Damon at the same time. *That's not ideal.*

He no longer felt like playing anymore. Enzo shook his head, trying to clear his thoughts of Aliya and any chance of him showing off his powers. No, he needed to settle this with Damon once and for all.

Just as he turned to Damon, the older man charged at him. Damon no longer had the smug grin that he'd been sporting ever since Enzo encountered him in the forests of Illadora. Instead, he looked angry. Hatred for Enzo seemed to pour through every single pore.

Not missing a beat, Damon bolted to Enzo. He raised his hands, his dark power concentrating in his palms. Enzo's eyes widened.

Not bothering about the berserkers for a moment, Enzo leapt out of the way. He barely missed the sizzling ball of black fire that Damon threw near him. The dark flames hit the tree where Enzo was standing only a moment before. Shattered tree bark burst in all directions at the impact.

Enzo couldn't take a second to recover, however. He felt another ball of black flame whizzing past him. He rolled and tumbled as he crawled away from Damon's attacks, hiding behind the thick trees and trunks or boulders. But Damon's dark flames seemed to shatter anything Enzo used to shield himself.

He could hear Aliya's screams in the distance. Even though it'd only been a couple days since he'd known her, he knew that she was trying her best to be beside him and help him. And the fact that she wasn't currently standing beside him meant that Sienna was successful at keeping Aliya at bay.

He needed to thank that witch once all of this was over.

For now, Enzo was just happy that Damon and his berserkers were focused on him rather than the two women. He'd been the reason for them being in danger in the first place. And he'd be damned if either of them got hurt because of him.

He looked around the forest for something sharp. Sharp enough that he could use to pierce flesh.

Preferably Damon's.

As if to help him in his quandary, Damon threw another ball of dark flame. This one connected to the tree Enzo was hiding behind. Shattered bark flew in every direction making Enzo bring his arms to his face to shield himself. It was when one sharp bark almost grazed him that he realized he could sharpen the bark.

He didn't waste a moment. Not bothering to move from his position even after repeated attacks from Damon. He didn't have to worry about Damon's beasts at the moment.

The beasts were still busy pummeling each other thanks to Enzo's magic creating a portal every time they tried to charge at him. Damon, on the other hand, seemed to be content with throwing blow after blow trying to bring Enzo out from his hiding.

Enzo chose this moment of distraction to quickly grab the nearby shattered bark. He rubbed the thick bark against the tree behind him, trying to make it as sharp as he could. When he finally deemed it perfect, he let out a sharp breath, readying himself.

Enzo created a portal right behind Damon. But it seemed that Damon might have anticipated his attack. Because the moment Enzo stepped through his portal, raising his hand to Damon's back, Damon swiveled on his feet. He turned to face Enzo, blocking Enzo's attack. Damon held onto both of Enzo's arms, slowly bringing them down.

It didn't matter how much Enzo struggled in the older man's grasp. Damon seemed to be able to control Enzo's limbs easily.

It was only then that Enzo realized how strong Damon truly was.

Damon might have looked old but his strength surpassed Enzo's.

Holding both of Enzo's hands in one of his, Damon snatched the sharpened bark. He brought it up to his face, chuckling as he examined it.

"You thought to kill me with this?" Damon scoffed, not containing his mirth any longer. His chuckle grated on Enzo's nerves, making him scowl. "You need much more than this to kill me, boy. This is child's play. Nothing more."

Enzo tried his best to get out of Damon's grip. He trashed in Damon's arms, trying anything to get out of the vice grip Damon had him in. But the more he struggled, the more Damon tightened his grip on him.

"Stop struggling boy." Damon hissed, bringing Enzo closer to him. "You'll only make this worse on yourself."

Damon brought up the sharpened bark to Enzo's face, dragging out the sharp end down Enzo's cheeks. For the first time since this fight started, Enzo hoped Sienna had a good grip on Aliya. Because if the past two days had taught him anything it was that she would do her best to be by his side. Her faint screams in the distance attested to that.

Normally, that would have been admirable. Especially coming from her. But if Damon's attention shifted from Enzo to Aliya, Enzo didn't know how he would respond. He'd lost enough people on his side. He couldn't have Aliya's on his consciousness as well. Not when all she'd done was help him ever since he'd met her.

The last thing he needed to worry about was Damon using Aliya to get to him.

He tried to tune out her screams. He needed to get out of this predicament first.

"You'll not get what you want from me." Enzo gritted out. But that only seemed to make Damon chuckle.

"I already have you. I don't need anything else."

"And what will you do with just me? I can tell the witch, right here, right now, to close the portal and she will. You'll be trapped in this world." Enzo scoffed, hoping this might rattle Damon. "What use are your powers and your ambition to take over the world if you can't even get to Indresal?"

Enzo smirk widened when Damon was quiet. But that smirk only lasted a moment, until he saw Damon smile.

"You see, boy. Your powers come from Indresal itself. Lose contact with Indresal and you lose your powers. Weren't you having trouble getting back to Indresal these past few days?" Enzo didn't want to give him the satisfaction of saying yes. But his expression seemed to be enough.

Instead, Enzo looked over at the berserkers still fighting each other in the distance - courtesy of Enzo and his portals, of course. Slowly, very slowly, with only his wrists, Enzo created a portal under the guide of him still struggling against Damon's grip.

Damon chuckled again. "Unlike you, I am the Disciple of the Dark One." The pride in his voice was undeniable. Enzo scowled. "My powers come from the Dark One himself. For me to get back to Indresal, all I need is you. Now tell me my boy, who's at a greater disadvantage here?"

A small portal formed behind Damon - one that Enzo hoped Damon wouldn't see. Through the portal, he could see the berserkers' claws on the other side. He waited for the right time when one of the berserkers' claws came through the portal.

The sharp claw was close.

So close to tearing Damon's flesh. So close.

But it was as if Damon had anticipated Enzo's attack. He threw Enzo in the distance, discarding Enzo as if he was just a rag doll. In one swift move, before the berserker claw could even reach him, Damon threw the black flames at the berserkers through the portal that Enzo created.

The minute Damon's black flames touched the berserkers, they shrieked. Letting out loud howls that Enzo was sure could be heard through the entirety of the forest. Sounds that would give nightmares to anyone unfortunate enough to listen to them. Black flames engulfed the two beasts, searing their bodies. The smell of burnt flesh permeated through the forest, gagging Enzo.

Enzo hadn't expected this reaction from Damon. He didn't expect the extent to which Damon didn't care for the beasts. Because why would he? If he needed more berserkers, Damon or one of the disciples could easily raid one of the villages for more people.

Enzo didn't have much time to react.

Because just as Damon shot the black flame through the portal to the beasts, he turned around to face Enzo. He threw the sharpened bark at Enzo with enough force that Enzo knew would pierce his heart.

It was purely instinct really.

Enzo closed his eyes and brought his hands up protecting himself. But with the little motion with his wrists, Enzo created a small portal, this time redirecting the sharpened bark right above Damon's heart. Enzo could feel his chest heave with anticipation as he waited for the pain.

And waited...

But when he didn't feel any pain, Enzo dared to open one of his eyes, only for them to widen in surprise at the sight in front of him.

Damon gasped, blinking hard as the pain from the shard piercing him seemed to knock him off his balance. He brought his hand up to touch the bark protruding from his chest, as if he was confused how it got there.

Damon stumbled, wailing his hands as he fell to the ground. He grunted in pain, gasping for breath. But the more he tried to breathe, the more blood seemed to pool in his mouth.

Not wanting for him to recover, Enzo quickly got up from his position. He'd be happy with his luck later. But now...

Enzo quickly crawled up to Damon. He wanted to make sure Damon was done for. This was his revenge. For all the men he'd lost in the battle. For putting him, Aliya, and Sienna in danger.

Enzo looked at the old man.

The once powerful Disciple who brought fear into the hearts of the people of Indresal just by his name. Now reduced to a whining, gasping, mess on the ground at Enzo's feet. Dying by a simple stab wound to his chest. Blood began to pool down on the forest floor beside Damon.

Enzo knelt down beside the old man.

"Huh, apparently, I didn't need that much to kill you." Enzo said. His lips lifted into a small smirk.

Enzo brought his hand up to the shard protruding from Damon's chest. But instead of pulling it out, he slowly, very slowly, pushed it more into Damon's chest.

"That's for the people of Indresal." Enzo said. Damon struggled against Enzo's hands, screaming in pain as the shard destroyed his heart. Enzo could see Damon's eyes clouding over as his life slowly left body. "Your reign of terror is coming to an end."

32

"I should, shouldn't I?" – Aliya

ALIYA STOPPED STRUGGLING THE moment she saw the bark pierce Damon. She could still feel Sienna's arms around her. She'd held Aliya the entire time Enzo fought the berserkers and Damon.

Aliya wanted to run to him. She wanted to help him. She even grabbed the metal rod, charging it up and was about to run to Enzo. That was until Sienna got ahold of her.

How is she so strong? Aliya had thought multiple times that she struggled to get out of Sienna's grip.

But no matter how much Aliya struggled or screamed for Enzo, Sienna didn't let her go. She continued to hug Aliya from behind, refusing to let her go.

But the moment Aliya saw the shard pierce Damon's heart, Sienna's grip on her loosened. She didn't turn back to look at Sienna. Nor did she try to run to Enzo. If she had to guess, Sienna was just as surprised as Aliya.

Damon was dead. Or was close to death.

Aliya saw Enzo creep up to Damon, pushing the shard deeper. Damon thrashed in pain. He howled and screamed. But the screams and howls only grew weaker as the seconds passed. And only a few moments later, what was once the most dreaded person Aliya had ever met was no longer alive.

Damon's body laid limp on the ground with no sign of life in him.

Aliya was surprised that she didn't feel sad at seeing a person die in front of her. Instead she felt relieved. Unlike any she'd ever felt before. It felt like a weight was lifted off her shoulders. She didn't have to look over her shoulder any longer. There were no berserkers she had to run from. There was no Damon to terrorize her. They didn't have to run any longer. She could finally breathe.

Enzo looked at Damon's dead body for a moment longer before turning back to face Aliya and Sienna. Although, Aliya couldn't understand his expression. He slowly walked up to them, shoulders slumped as if he'd lost all energy. But the smile on his face only grew the closer he walked to them.

His gaze didn't waver from Aliya though.

Aliya looked him over as he walked to her, trying to see if he'd been hurt badly. But the little scars and gashes that he'd received had already started to stitch themselves.

Right. The portal to Indresal is open. She thought.

He could access the power of Indresal again.

The portal was open and he could go back home. That was a reminder that she didn't need.

Enzo stood in front of her, gazing into her eyes with an expression she couldn't place. He brought his hands, cupping her face. His thumb caressed her cheeks as he looked deep into her eyes.

Aliya's eyes fluttered when he bent down, pressing a long and deep kiss on her forehead. Her eyes widened and breath hitched when she felt his lips on her forehead. She held her breath, not daring to breathe, lest all of this was just a dream.

When Enzo looked down at her again, his smile only widened seeing her expression. "Thank you." He said. "I don't know how to thank you for all your help." Aliya felt her heart crush. Was this just his way of thanking her? Enzo caressed her cheek again with his thumb. "I don't know how I could have done any of this or been able to go back to Indresal without you."

That brought Aliya out of her reverie. What was she expecting? That he was going to fall in love with her and ask her to come to Indresal with him.

No, this was where her journey ended.

You're not even from their world. What are you going to do? She questioned herself.

Yes, she was looking at her favorite character right in front of her. He'd even kissed her on her forehead. How many people could say that? She shouldn't be expecting more.

Aliya nodded, giving Enzo a tight smile. She tried not to show how hurt she was - not that she thought had any right to be hurt.

She held onto his hands and gently removed it from her face. Aliya took a step back trying to put a little distance between the two of them. She needed that distance to think clearly.

Her actions seemed to confuse Enzo. His brow furrowed and his hands flexed as if he'd already missed holding. As much as Aliya wished, she wondered if that was even true.

Aliya gave him a small smile and nodded. That was all she could do. If she opened her mouth, she didn't know if she could stop herself from asking him to stay. But he was real. He was the Crown Prince. He needed his people. Her, on the other hand, he didn't need.

"It's time to go, Enzo." Sienna's soft voice chimed in from behind them.

Enzo gazed into her eyes. He waited, a hopeful expression passed his eyes as if he was debating something. But in the end, Enzo simply shook his head. He returned Aliya's smile, stealing himself before walking past her.

He would have gone through the portal that was still open - albeit much smaller than when it was first created. It'd been open for so long that Aliya began to wonder how long it'd truly last. But just as Enzo walked to the portal, Sienna placed her hand on Enzo's arm, stopping him.

The two of them looked at each other, having a silent conversation that Aliya wasn't privy to. He could see the concern grow in Enzo's eyes. The reassuring nod that Sienna gave him only made him question it for a second. He turned to look at Aliya. His eyes wide with hope and an unspoken question.

"Will you join me?" He asked. Hope and fear seemed to battle in his eyes.

That question left Aliya agape. She hoped for it to happen. She wished for it to happen. But never, not even in her dreams, did she think he'd actually ask her to accompany him.

Enzo must have taken her lack of reaction or response as her saying no. So, he quickly continued. "Only if you want, of course. I'm not going to force you. We can bring you back just as quickly as you say you want to come home. I just wanted to know if you wanted to explore Indresal because you love my world so much."

Enzo continued to blabber, not once looking at her as if he was afraid of her reaction if he were to look at her.

The small smile Aliya sported turned into a full blown giggle. It was only when Enzo heard Aliya laugh that he stopped speaking. His relief was evident in his expression as he let out a heavy sigh. Enzo laughed along with her. He held out his hand, waiting for her to come to him.

When Aliya did, he gave her a soft smile that turned into a smirk.

"Watch me go through and then you can follow." He said. Enzo bent down to her height, to look into her eyes. "Don't be afraid. I'll be there to catch you on the other side."

Poking Aliya's cheek, making her giggle again, Enzo walked through the portal. There was only a moment where Aliya couldn't see Enzo. But only a second later, she was able to see Enzo in the forests of Illadora waving to her with a giddy smile. He held his arm out for her.

Aliya rubbed her hands together. But no matter how much she encouraged herself, she couldn't feel her feet move.

"Just walk through, Aliya. I'm right here." Enzo shouted from the other side.

"What's stopping you?" Sienna asked from beside her.

"I've never done this before." Aliya bit her lip. She looked up at Sienna beside her only to see the older woman giving her an incredulous expression.

Sienna blinked a couple times, before letting out a breath.

"Would you like to see me do it? That way you could just follow behind me?"

Aliya didn't even wait until Sienna finished her sentence to nod her head. Sienna chuckled before walking up to the portal.

"It's simple, really." She said. "Just step in and you'll be on the other side."

With that, Sienna stepped through the portal. Just like Enzo, Sienna stepped on the other side, in the Illadoran forest, just a second later.

Why are you afraid? Aliya asked herself. *Why are you being a coward? It's just like the teleporter in Star Trek. Not that different at all. You'll be here one second and there the next. It's fine. Completely fine.*

Aliya bit her lip and looked at the portal again. Was it always this small? She would bet on it that the portal was much bigger when they first created it.

What would happen if I step through and the portal collapses? Aliya's eyes widened. The thought itself horrified her.

"Aliya," Enzo called out softly. Aliya shifted her wide doe eyes to him. "I'm right here. I'll be right here. I'll catch you if you fall."

Biting her lip, Aliya nodded. Her gaze didn't waver from Enzo's.

Giving him a small smile, Aliya stepped through.

What's the worst that can happen?

33

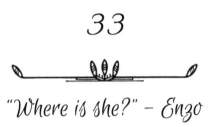

"Where is she?" - Enzo

ENZO WAITED PATIENTLY, HIS hands outstretched. He watched Aliya's hopeful expression as she bit her lip and nodded.

He promised her he'd be there to catch her when she came out of the portal. And he would. He'd be there for her. Whether she needed him or not, he'd be there.

Aliya clasped her hands. She let out a harsh breath before walking through the portal. Enzo waited with bated breath.

But the moment Aliya stepped through, the portal dissipated.

What once was a fizzling portal in the space in front of him was no longer there. In its place was the quiet Illadoran forest.

Enzo looked at the empty space dumbfounded for a second. Not believing what happened.

His brows furrowed. When his mind finally grasped the fact that the portal closed when ALiya stepped through, his eyes widened in fear. He quickly turned to Sienna who looked just as dumbfounded as he was just a moment ago.

"Where did she go?" He shouted. His fear getting the best of him. "How did the portal close?"

His shouting seemed to bring Sienna out of her reverie. Instead of answering him, Sienna rushed to mix the ingredients for the potion again. Enzo could see his chest heaving. But Sienna didn't answer him.

It didn't matter how many questions Enzo fired out. Sienna remained silent. Enzo could see that she was worried too. But that didn't stop him from asking her what happened? She was the one that created the portal. She should know what happened to the portal, right?

...Right?

But Sienna didn't know. No matter how many times Enzo asked her. Finally, getting tired of his questioning, Sienna answered back forcefully. "I don't know!" That shut him up. Sienna calmed herself down before answering him again. "I don't know." She said again, this time much softly. "This is only my third time creating a portal between worlds and I've never seen it happen like this before. So, please be quiet. I'm trying to open another one. I need to see if she's still on Earth."

That seemed to quiet Enzo down. The worry was still evident on his face, but he didn't speak the rest of the time Sienna did the ritual to open the portal.

The most they heard the sizzling, creating the portal to forests they'd just come from, Sienna and Enzo peaked around the portal to see if there was any sign of Aliya.

But they had none.

The only sign that Aliya had been standing in that spot were her shoe prints on the forest floor. It was as if she'd disappeared into thin air.

"Where is she?" Enzo gasped out. He looked around the portal. Everywhere. In every direction.

But no matter where he looked, Aliya was nowhere to be found.

"Could she have changed her mind?" Sienna asked. Just like Enzo she was trying to look for some explanation for Aliya's disappearance. No one could disappear into the air like this.

Enzo shook his head. "No. She loves Indresal. She'd never lose an opportunity like this."

The two of them still looked through the portal.

But the only thing Sienna and Enzo could see on the other side of the portal was the dead bodies of Damon and his berserkers.

But look as they might, there wasn't any sight of Aliya anywhere.

"Could she have ended up somewhere else in Indresal?" Enzo asked.

Sienna didn't need to answer. But the horror on her face was enough.

Enzo's eyes widened as fear gripped his heart.

Where are you, Aliya?

Epilogue

ALIYA SCREAMED AS SHE fell through the portal. The sensation was not at all like what she'd expected. The minute she stepped foot into the portal, it was as if she was being pulled into the portal as if she was near a black hole and pushed onto the other side.

She wanted to land gracefully as she stepped out of the portal. Very much like she'd seen Enzo and Sienna had done. Aliya wanted to replicate how Sienna described Enzo in all her books.

But alas...

The minute Aliya stepped foot on the other side, Aliya lost her footing. Her eyes widened as she fell onto the ground. She only brought her hands up to protect her face at the very last minute.

Aliya grunted at the impact, groaning as she turned around, laying on her back. She gingerly rubbed her arms, breathing heavily.

"You could have helped!" She muttered, her eyes still closed as she reeled from the impact.

When neither Enzo nor Sienna came to her to help her stand, much less answer her, Aliya turned around. Her brows furrowed when she didn't find either of them anywhere near here. In fact, the place she fell into looked nothing like the place Enzo and Sienna went.

Instead, Aliya saw a figure standing in the darkness just a few feet away from her. Aliya squinted, trying to get a better view. She expected to see Enzo and Sienna. She expected to see them cackling, or at least silently chuckling to spare her the embarrassment, at her attempt to look cool as she entered Indresal.

She expected to see the lush, tranquil forests that they entered. She expected to feel the forest ground at her feet - or rather, now on her back. She expected chirping birds, majestic animals Sienna had described in the books.

That was not what surrounded her, however.

Instead of the lush forests she saw Enzo and Sienna enter, Aliya saw charred walls that looked as if they'd been demolished.

Rubble from the walls was strewn across the floor making Aliya wonder if it was the rubble that made her stumble. She was beginning to wonder when the building was destroyed as nature was beginning to take over.

This is not where they entered... Aliya thought. Her eyes narrowed suspiciously as she looked at the building around her. *Is it?*

"There's only one person I know that can create portals." Aliya heard a voice say. The person's deep, silky voice echoed through the empty room. "If you are from him, this is a terrible spot for you to end up though."

A man with silvery white locks and dark eyebrows smirked at her as she began to sit up. The deep scar on his cheek made Aliya wince even though it looked like it had healed a long time ago. She could see exactly how big he was as he stepped closer to her.

His long sleeved black tunic did nothing to hide his broad shoulders and muscular arms. A silver sigil was engraved on the man's tunic. A sigil that Aliya had never seen before. The man was easily three times Aliya's size. Size that was evident the closer he walked towards her.

The man looked past Aliya at the fizzling portal behind her. The portal closed, sputtering the last embers. His hooded eyes narrowed slightly as he tilted his head, as if he was remembering something.

"Hm, interesting." He thought out loud as he brought his hand up to stroke his chin.

His hands bereft of any jewelry, save for the ring on his left index finger. Aliya couldn't get a clear look at it though. Before she could say anything, the man continued. "I'm sure he didn't intend to send you here of all places." The man scoffed.

"Who are you?" Aliya asked.

She hadn't read about his character in any of Sienna's books. Aliya's mind ran through all the books Sienna had published thus far.

When she couldn't remember reading about him, she began to wonder if he was even a character in the stories. She was starting to wonder how much of this world she truly knew. *Maybe he was in the other books that Sienna had yet to publish? Is he another side character?*

But all thoughts seemed to flee her mind when the man turned to look back at her. His gaze darkened as his sweet smile turned into a wicked grin.

Aliya's throat became dry at the sinister smile he gave her as he approached her. A smile that didn't reach his eyes. His sneer made her scuttle back on all fours, trying to put as much distance between the two of them as possible.

But it seemed that the man was faster.

In three long strides, the man reached Aliya. He bent down reaching out his hand for her. The sneer on his face only made Aliya's heart race.

Aliya didn't have any time to react. She wanted to bring her hands up. She wanted to smack his hand away from her. She wanted to...

Aliya yelped when she felt his hand grasp her hair, lifting her from the ground. Her hand clasped around his, trying her best to release herself from his grasp. But the more she pulled the more she only hurt herself. His grip on her scalp didn't loosen.

"Let me go!" Aliya grunted out.

But instead, the man brought her closer to him, roughly, making Aliya whimper. She shuddered at how close they stood. Seeing his cold gaze land on hers. His iron grip didn't let her look anywhere else but at his dark brown eyes that only conveyed a level of hatred Aliya had yet to encounter.

His gaze flitted around her face, as if examining her for something. Her eyes searched his as she urged him to let her go.

Aliya could feel herself shake. A cold shudder traveled down her spine, the longer he looked at her. Silence seemed to engulf them. And Aliya was too scared to want to disturb that silence. She had a feeling he wouldn't appreciate it if she did disturb it either.

The man bent down closer to Aliya, enough that she could feel his breath fan across her face. She tried to claw herself away from him. She really did. But her strength was no match for him.

"Oh, this is going to be fun." Was all he said before dragging her off as Aliya screamed for him to let her go.

Irina held onto the golden tray as if her life depended on it as she walked through the corridor of the Melorne Residence.

Although with how big the residence was, it could have easily been called the Melorne Palace. The tray shook along with her hands as she tried her best to contain her nerves.

The golden tray Irina was holding onto had a single letter on it. Irina didn't know what was in the letter. She didn't dare open it. Didn't even dare to ask either.

But the expression from one of the spies giving her the letter didn't exactly give her the confidence that it was any good news.

Normally, Irina wouldn't have cared much for spies. Their information and their politics only brought her trouble in the past. And here at the Melorne Palace, she didn't have to.

Irina would normally keep her head down, working in the kitchen for the day. She only ventured out into the gardens for a break, sitting under the large banyan tree in the corner of the courtyard and taking a nap. The shade gave her the perfect temperature from the warm afternoons and the rustling leaves providing her the perfect lullaby to lull her into a deep slumber.

When she was done with her rest, Irina would venture back into the kitchens, helping the others with the preparation of a feast for the evening. She didn't care who the food went to. She didn't care if they liked it or not either. She'd done her job for the day... meaning, she got to go home when the head cook gave her the say so.

Others had told her that this was the most boring way to spend her time. But Irina didn't bother. After escaping the atrocity that had been her childhood, this quiet, boring, mundane routine was most welcome.

Irina looked at the tray she was holding again. But this...

This was new.

Irina had been walking in the garden to get to her banyan tree for her daily afternoon nap when she was stopped. She turned around to see a young boy, barely fifteen, walk towards her in tattered brown clothes.

He held a golden tray with a single closed enveloped letter on it - something that contrasted distinctly from the tattered clothes he was wearing. She wanted to scowl and tell him off for disturbing her routine. But the sigil on the golden tray made her stop.

The symbol of a snake eating its tail.

The sigil of the lady who owned this palace.

"Please deliver this to the Lady." The boy said, shoving the tray into her hands. Before Irina could protest, the boy ran away.

So, now, here she was. Gulping and shaking in fear at the thought of even visiting the Lady of Melorne Palace.

Irina could feel her nerves raise with every step she took. Her heart pounded in rhythm with her footsteps and with every ornately carved column she passed, Irina could feel the dread pool up in her gut.

Her grip on the tray tightened so much that she doubted there was any circulation to her fingers at this point. She gulped, biting her lips as she entered the main hall of the residence.

Her eyes immediately searched for the person the letter was addressed to. Not that it was hard to find her.

The Lady was sitting on a lone sofa - almost built like a throne, sitting atop a couple steps in the far end of the room. She lazily lounged on the chair as another group of women helped to dry her wet, long dark brown locks. Her brown skin glistened with the sunlight that streamed in from the windows making her look divine.

Maybe she actually was. No one knew exactly how old the Lady was. She was here when the eldest servant in the castle died of old age and Irina was sure that the Lady would be here even after she was gone.

Looking at the woman chatting and laughing now, no one would have assumed that the woman sitting on the throne was one of the Disciples of the Dark One.

Amara el'Damyrys

As Irina got closer, she could hear the soft laughter from Amara. Her steps faltered as she got closer to the sofa. Irina had heard of Amara's wrath.

Amara's wrath.

That thought alone made Irina shudder.

Amara's anger was not one to be trifled with. Because Amara's anger was silent and deadly. She never raised her voice. But all her attacks on her enemies made sure that they suffered before dying - whether it be emotionally, physically, or mentally. She didn't care. Amara just loved to watch them crumble.

And now, Irina was bringing Amara news that wasn't very good. She'd much rather prefer to not be in Amara's presence when Amara read the letter.

"Do you have something for me, little one?" Amara asked, her voice chiming like bells on a warm, windy, summer afternoon. Amara's lips curved into a smile as Irina nodded, inviting Irina to come closer to her.

When Irina hesitated, Amara continued. "I'm not going to harm you, little one." She said, making Irina wonder if Amara read her mind.

Maybe she did. No one knew exactly how powerful or what powers the Disciples truly held. "Come closer. Give me the letter." Amara said, lifting her hand up to receive the letter.

Amara was smiling. But that was a command. One that Irina was going to follow whether she liked it or not.

Irina could see the golden tray shake as she held it up to Amara so she could take the letter. She bowed her head, not daring to lift it to see Amara's expression. The chuckles that had filled the hall just moments before had faded. In its place was silence.

A deadly quiet.

The hall that was once filled with chatters and giggles of the women was now replaced with the sounds of birds chirping and the leaves rustling from the gentle breeze in the garden outside.

Seconds turned into minutes but the silence stayed the same. Biting her lip, Irina dared to lift her head.

Amara's gaze hadn't lifted from the letter. Her eyes moved from side to side as she read to its contents. Her jovial expression just moments before had transformed into one of rage. Pure unbridled fury.

An expression that Irina was told Amara never expressed.

What's in the letter that she can get that angry? Irina wondered.

But more importantly, Irina wanted to get out of the hall before Amara's anger burst. She'd heard the stories of Amara's silent rage before. But Irina didn't trust the stories.

Quiet rage was not the kind of rage that Irina was used to. No.

She was much more used to the kind of rage that turned people irrational and impulsive. She was used to the kind of rage where people lashed out, not caring about the people who they hurt.

Irina had always feared that kind of rage.

But this was different. The stories was correct. Amara's rage was silent. Deadly.

When Amara finally finished reading the letter, she ordered quietly. "Everyone out."

Letting out the breath she didn't know she was holding, Irina turned around. Although she stopped when she heard Amara again. She cursed herself for not moving faster when Amara ordered them out. Maybe she'd have avoided being alone with the Lady now.

Irina almost scoffed out loud at the thought.

This was Amara el'Damyrys. If she wanted something - whether it was information, an object, or a person - she'd get it one way or another.

"Not you, little one." Amara said.

Irina gulped when she saw that Amara was speaking to her. She nodded and bowed as she waited for everyone to leave. She could feel the pensive stares the women left her as they left the room. That didn't help her thundering heart.

"Who gave you this letter, little one?" Amara asked as sweetly as possible. Although Irina could still detect the seething anger barely contained behind every word.

What could agitate her so much that she actually shows her anger? Irina wondered before answering Amara.

"I was only told to deliver this letter to you. I don't know where it's from." Irina answered truthfully.

Irina simply nodded, turning the letter in her hands as if she was inspecting it.

"Do you know what's written in it?" Amara asked again. Irina didn't know if Amara wanted her to answer. It was almost as if Amara was talking out loud to herself. So, Irina simply chose to shake her head no. Words had failed her every time Amara looked at her anyway.

"Hm." Came Amara's only response.

It was another moment of uncomfortable silence that Irina wondered why she was the only one in the room with Amara.

"It would seem that Damon al'Kara is dead." Amara sighed.

Irina's eyes widened at the admission. Everyone knew how important Damon al'Kara was to Amara. Everyone knew what he meant to her. If he was dead...

Irina dreaded what was to come next.

Amara, however, simply arched her eyebrow as she pursed her lips, giving Irina a tight smile. "It would seem that the next few months would be... interesting."

A Note to the Reader from Sienna el'Manaeryn

PHEANDRA HAS FALLEN.

    Pheandra. Has. Fallen.

That was what they all said. Stories passed down from mouth to mouth. From person to person. But all it took was one generation for the story to change enough that no one knew, or even remember, where the history ended and the myth started.

But all the stories had one saying in common.

Pheandra has fallen.

That was what the myths and legends said. For more than fifty years.

That saying was uttered from the lips of every parent wishing their child would not fall into the hands of the Dark One. A parent's desperate attempt to keep their young ones safe. To keep their children as far away from the dark tendrils of influence from the Dark One that slowly crept onto their lands every single day.

The fall of a mighty and noble kingdom was rendered to nothing more than a fairy tale to tell the children of the dangers of the darkness.

It'd been so long since anyone uttered the true travesty that happened at Pheandra that I don't believe anyone living now would actually be able to remember it.

Not one person in Indresal spoke of the brave people that fought the Dark One, or how - even when scattered - the last few remaining people wish to rebuild their kingdom to its former glory. From the misty mountains that greeted the sun's rays in the morn to the cold, calm rivers that wished the star a safe passage till the next day.

Pheandra has become a myth.

Relegated to the histories and the books that only the nobles seemed to be interested in studying. Not to remember the people of Pheandra. Not to keep their memory alive.

But rather to study their strategies of where the Kingdom had gone wrong in fighting the Dark One.

Pheandra has fallen.

To the surviving people of Pheandra scattered along what remained of Indresal, this saying was not a reminder of what they'd lost. No. Rather it was a war cry. A cry and a promise that they'd be back. They'd have their kingdom back.

But just as the kingdom of Pheandra had been relegated to a myth as time gone by, so did the quote that all the people of Indresal muttered. Not many know of the real saying. Spoken in the language of the Pheandrans - a language that had become a rarity after all these years - and roughly translated.

As the memory of Pheandra slowly dwindles, I give you, dear reader, the burden to remember.

To remember the quote of the Pheandrans' grit, of their defiance. Because I know you carry the same grit and defiance in you.

Pheandra has fallen before,

But come darkness or light, Pheandra has risen again.

Like a phoenix from the glowing embers of a blazing fire,

Through the blood and sweat of its people.
And so, if Pheandra were to fall again,
May the gods above save you all,
For this time, the ashes that Pheandra will rise upon again shall
be yours

So, my dear reader, I give you this curse to remember.

But fret not. You do not have to carry this burden for long. Because in the end, come what may...

Pheandra will rise again.

Acknowledgements

First and foremost, thank you to all my dear arc readers and my readers for taking a chance in this story. I hope you enjoyed it as much as I loved writing it. I'd be remiss if I didn't mention Lexie – my book cover artist – who always goes along with my crazy ideas and somehow makes them not only work but also make them phenomenal, somehow?! My beta reader Lyndsey, thank you so much for reading the story when it was just a jumbled word mess of a book and being patient enough to give me feedback and answer every question I had! You are a god sent! Kalista Neith, John Wesley, and Anne, thank you for all your help in getting this book out! I love you guys!

About Akira

Akira is a Fantasy, Sci-Fi, and Romance enthusiast who would rather live in the world of mythical creatures than only dream about them. She began writing when Supernatural, Marvel, and Doctor Who – all the movies and shows she'll gladly discuss with anyone who asks her – started killing off her favorite characters. And although she wants to write more in this section to sound interesting, she's too much of an introvert to go outside and do anything else. When not writing or reading, you'll find her sitting in her sofa, crying over the new show or the new fictional character that might have broken her heart, you could find her somewhere out in the art museums or by any water body – whether it be a lake, pond, river, or the ocean.

Also by

The Codex of Indresal (Quadrilogy)
Only a Portal Away (July 2nd, 2024)
Book 2 (2025)

Thread of Fate Series (Trilogy)
The Forgotten Prince (April 4th, 2023)
Book 2 (2024)

A New Dawn Duology
A New Dawn (June 2nd, 2023)
Book 2 (2024)

Of Love and Redemption Series (Quadrilogy)
The Curse of Immortality (May 2023)
Book 2 (2024)

Milton Keynes UK
Ingram Content Group UK Ltd.
UKHW051329260524
443099UK00004B/233

9 798218 409913